SAPPHIRE
BATTERSEA

www.**kidsatrandomhouse**.co.uk

ALSO AVAILABLE BY JACQUELINE WILSON

Join the official Jacqueline Wilson fan club at
www.jacquelinewilson.co.uk

Jacqueline Wilson

SAPPHIRE BATTERSEA

ILLUSTRATED BY NICK SHARRATT

A new name
A new life for
HETTY
FEATHER

CORGI YEARLING

SAPPHIRE BATTERSEA
A CORGI YEARLING BOOK 978 0 440 86927 6

First published in Great Britain by Doubleday,
an imprint of Random House Children's Publishers UK
A Random House Group Company

Doubleday edition published 2011
This edition published 2012

3 5 7 9 10 8 6 4

Set in New Century Schoolbook

Corgi Yearling Books are published by Random House Children's Publishers UK,
61–63 Uxbridge Road, London W5 5SA

www.**kids**at**randomhouse**.co.uk
www.**totallyrandombooks**.co.uk
www.**randomhouse**.co.uk

Addresses for companies within The Random House Group Limited
can be found at: www.**randomhouse**.co.uk/offices.htm

THE RANDOM HOUSE GROUP Limited Reg. No. 954009

A CIP catalogue record for this book is available from the British Library.

Printed and bound in the CPI Group (UK) Ltd, Croydon, CR0 4YY

For my two best girls

1

My name is Sapphire Battersea. Doesn't that sound beautiful? I write it over and over again on the covers of this private notebook. I stitch a secret S.B. inside the neck of my uniform. I stir a swirly S.B. into the soup when I am helping the cook. I scrub a soapy S.B. when I am cleaning the floor. I whisper my own name in bed at night in the freezing dormitory, and my breath rises and forms the letters in the dark.

I am Sapphire Battersea, but nobody calls me by my real name, not even my dear mother. Mama chose to call me Sapphire because my eyes were so blue when I was born. But even she calls me Hetty now.

'I'm *not* Hetty. It's such a stupid name. It's just a hateful foundling label. I *hate* the way they change all our names, making them up randomly. They don't sound like real names. Hetty Feather! It's ridiculous.'

'You could have had worse,' said Mama. 'Just

think, you could have been *Grizel Grump*.'

Poor Grizel is a girl in little Eliza's year at the Foundling Hospital. Everyone calls her Gristle, and consequently she is always a grump, like her name.

'Sapphire is so elegant, so romantic. It's a perfect name for a writer,' I said, signing it in the air with a flourish.

'Let us hope you become one, then,' said Mama, a little tartly.

'You wait and see. I will publish my memoirs and make our fortune. Miss Smith will help me. My story will be turned into a proper book with gold lettering and a fancy picture on the front, just like all her own Sarah Smith stories published by the Religious Tract.'

'I'm not sure *your* stories would be suitable for a religious press, Hetty,' said Mama, laughing.

'*Sapphire!* Why won't you call me by my true name – the one you chose for me?"

'I suppose Hetty has become a habit, dearie,' said Mama, tweaking my red plait.

'I always call you Mama when we're alone,' I said, a little hurt.

'Yes, but I wish you wouldn't. It's tempting fate. One slip in front of the others and we're done for,' said Mama, and she pulled me close.

'I will never slip, Mama,' I swore fervently. 'No one will ever find out that you are my real mother.'

I hadn't known myself for the first ten long years of my life. Poor Mama had been forced to give me to the Foundling Hospital when I was a little baby because she had no means of supporting me. I was soon fostered out to the country. I lived with a kind family. I loved my foster mother and father and all my foster siblings. I especially adored my foster brother Jem.

I had hero-worshipped him. I treasured the silver sixpence he'd given me when I was taken off to the Foundling Hospital at five. He promised he'd wait for me and marry me one day. I was so little and stupid I actually believed him – until young Eliza arrived at the hospital from the same foster home five years later. She prattled away about *her* dear Jem. I found out that he'd made exactly the same empty promises to her. I couldn't forgive him. I decided to put him out of my mind for ever.

I had found the rigid life of the hospital horribly hard. Some of the nurses were kind, but the two matrons were excessively cruel. I suffered from the attentions of Matron Pigface Peters when I was small, and of Matron Stinking Bottomly when I went into the Seniors. They each went out of their way to punish and humiliate me. I hated them both.

I found it difficult to make friends with the other girls too. I made downright enemies of Sheila and Monica. When Polly came to the hospital, we were like soul mates, but she was adopted by rich folk and we never saw each other again.

My only true friend was Ida, the kitchen maid. I ran away from the hospital on Queen Victoria's Golden Jubilee – and when I came back, Ida was so overwhelmed that she called me her own child when she hugged me. I could scarcely believe it! Ida was my true birth mother. She had skivvied and slaved at the Foundling Hospital for years just so that she could get a glimpse of me every day. She'd slip me an extra potato at dinner, or sprinkle secret sugar on my breakfast porridge. She'd always had a smile or a kind word, and helped me to blossom in that bleak institutional world.

When I became aware of the wondrous truth of our relationship, my whole life changed. I cannot say I became an exemplary foundling. Whether I am Sapphire or Hetty, I still have a temper that lives up to my flaming red hair. But whenever Matron Stinking Bottomly slapped me for impertinence and forced me to scrub the whole length of the hall, I knew Mama was nearby, watching and waiting, burning with sympathy. She'd catch my eye across the crowded dining room at mealtimes, and I'd feel calmed.

Sometimes, when everyone slept in the dormitories, I dared creep right out of the door, along the shadowy landing, down, down, down the great stairs, through kitchens that still smelled of stewed mutton and rice pudding, along the winding corridor to Mama's own tiny bedroom. I'd push open the door and she'd leap up from her bed and hug me hard. We'd sit together and whisper well into the night. Sometimes we'd lie close together on Mama's narrow bed, clasping each other close. I'd trace her dear face in the dark and she'd wind my long plaits around her own neck. We'd feel utterly united, making up for all those many years we'd lived apart.

But then – oh, I can hardly bear to write it. It was all because of Sheila. She was always a light sleeper. She must have woken when I crept through the long dormitory. She didn't call out. She lay there, waiting, and then slid stealthily out of her bed, intent on following me, the sly cat. She was so furtive and silent on her bare feet that I didn't hear her padding behind me. I didn't notice the creak of the stairs as she followed me down to the ground floor.

She stole along behind me all the way to Mama's room. I wonder how long she waited outside, her ear to the door? She suddenly burst in upon us, as Mama and I cuddled close in a fond embrace, clearly visible in the flickering candlelight.

'Whatever are you *doing*, Hetty Feather!' she exclaimed. 'Why are you lying there with *Ida*?'

'Go away! Get out! Get out of Mama's room!' I cried in furious passion.

'*Mama's* room?' said Sheila.

'It is just Hetty's little game,' Mama said quickly, giving me a shake.

But Sheila was no fool. 'You are Hetty's *mother*?' she said.

'No! Like Ida said, it's just my silly game,' I declared, springing off the bed.

Sheila was still staring, open-mouthed. 'Yes, now I see it!' She darted between us, staring rudely. 'You two *are* alike. You're both so small and slight – and you both have blue eyes. Oh my goodness, how extraordinary! Have you known all this time, Hetty? I'd never have thought you could keep such a secret so long,' she said.

It was no use denying it further.

'It's the most private, precious secret! If you dare breathe a word of this to anyone, I'll tear out your tattle-tale tongue and feed it to the pigs,' I said.

'Temper temper!' said Sheila, eyes gleaming. 'So, what will you do for me to keep me sweet and silent?'

'This isn't a schoolgirl game, Sheila,' said Mama, getting out of bed and gripping her by the shoulders. 'I haven't lived this life year after year to have it carelessly destroyed by a spiteful girl. You *mustn't* tell a soul. If those matrons find out, then we're done for. Swear that you'll keep silent!'

'I won't say a word to anyone, I promise,' said Sheila, but her eyes were still bright. I feared she'd tell Monica the moment she was back in the dormitory.

I'll never know how much she'd have told and whether she'd have deliberately betrayed Mama and me. We were discovered anyway. Mama and I were used to whispering, but Sheila had a high clear voice that travelled far. By terrible chance Matron Pigface Peters had shuffled down to the kitchen, seeking out a midnight snack from the pantry. She heard Sheila repeating, 'Just fancy Ida being your real mother, Hetty!'

Matron Pigface barged her way into Mama's crowded bedroom, a hideous sight in her nightcap and ruffled gown, her greasy hair coiling in true pig's tails about her cheeks. She stared at Mama, at Sheila, at me.

'Repeat what you said just now, Sheila Mayhew!' she commanded.

'I – I don't remember what I said,' Sheila stammered.

'The girls were playing a silly game, Matron. I was about to scold them and send them back to their dormitory,' said Mama.

'Don't lie to me, Ida Battersea!' She was

squinting at her now, then peering at me. 'Can this really be *true*? Are you Hetty Feather's mother?'

'How could I be?' said Ida. 'It's a game, I told you, an idle fancy, because the girls all long for their mothers.'

Matron Pigface Peters dragged me over to the candle, clutching my chin, turning my face this way and that. Then she went to grab hold of Mama.

'Don't you dare touch me! And take your hands off that child too – look, you're hurting her!'

'It's the truth that hurts, Ida Battersea! I see the likeness now! How could you have been so devious? You've been deceiving us for years and years! You were supposed to give up your ill-gotten child for ever – not work here with her glorying in your disgraceful situation. Have you two been secretly communing all this time? It beggars belief! How *dare* you both deceive us like this!'

'It wasn't Hetty's fault, Matron. She didn't know – not for ever so long. I meant no harm. I just wanted a glimpse of her every day – that was enough,' said Mama, starting to sob. 'When she disappeared on the day of the Jubilee, I could hardly contain myself. I worried fit to burst. When she came back at last, I was so relieved I fainted dead away.'

'Oh yes, I remember that!' said Sheila. 'We all

thought you'd died on the spot! So did you tell Hetty then?'

'Hold your tongue, Sheila Mayhew! This is nothing to do with you. Go back to the dormitory this instant. You are to keep utterly silent on this shameful matter,' said Matron Pigface.

'It's not shameful to love your own child!' I said furiously. 'Mama's done nothing wrong.'

'We'll see if the Board of Governors agrees with you! It's my opinion they'll take a very grave view of this deception. I would prepare yourself for instant dismissal, Ida Battersea – with no character reference, so don't expect to get another job in any decent God-fearing establishment. You're morally corrupt and an evil influence on all our girls.'

'How dare you threaten Mama like that!' I cried. 'You wait, Matron Peters! My friend and benefactress Miss Sarah Smith is on the Board of Governors. She will never send my own mama away. *You* will be the one who's sent away, because you're cruel and wicked, and you have no heart at all inside your big fat chest!'

She dragged me away, shouting and screaming. I did not even have time to kiss Mama and say goodbye. I struggled hard, but Matron Pigface slapped me about the head and picked me up bodily. Half the girls from the dormitory were clustered on the stairs, gawping at me.

'Go back to your beds this instant!' Matron Pigface shrieked, and they scuttled away.

She carried on dragging me up another flight of stairs.

'No! No, please don't put me in the punishment room!' I screamed. 'I can't stand it there, you know I can't!'

'You deserve to stay locked up in there for ever!' said Matron Pigface, thrusting me into the terrifying dark cupboard.

'No, please, I beg you! Don't lock me in! Please, I haven't done anything *wrong*!'

'You're the most evil child I've ever come across. You have no shame, show no respect! You act as if you're as good as anyone else. Just remember you're a common foundling, born in sin, without a father. I wouldn't be surprised if you were the spawn of the Devil himself,' she panted, and she locked the door on me.

It was the longest, most agonizing night of my life. I hit the door and walls until my knuckles were bloody – and then I cast myself down on the floor and wept. I called again and again for Mama, but she didn't come. I was frightened they'd locked her up too.

When one of the nurses let me out in the morning, I pushed right past her and ran all the way downstairs to Mama's room . . . but she wasn't there! Her cap and apron and print dresses were gone from the pegs on her wall, her brush and comb and her cake of soap and her flannel were gone from her chest. The very pillowcase and sheets had been stripped from her bed, leaving a bare black-and-white striped mattress. There was no trace left of Mama. It was as if she had never existed.

2

I sobbed myself into a stupor. I could not eat. I could not sleep. I became so fuddled I could barely stagger out of bed. Matron Bottomly and Matron Peters both declared I was faking illness, but I was burning with such a fever that the nurses were frightened and summoned the doctor.

'There is nothing wrong with the child, Dr March,' said Matron Bottomly. 'She simply screamed herself into a passion. I have never known such a wilful child as Hetty Feather. She deserves a good whipping – though of course we would never lay a finger on any of our foundlings,' she added hastily.

Dr March laid the back of his hand on my forehead, then listened to my chest. 'The child is clearly ill, Matron, wilful or not,' he said. 'She's a frail little creature and I fear her chest is weak. She must be kept here in bed, wrapped in wet sheets to lower her fever, and be fed an invalid diet of bread and milk.'

'I think it is criminal to cosset such a wicked girl,' Matron Bottomly murmured to the nurse, but she did not dare disobey the doctor's orders. I was kept isolated in the infirmary. My fever left me after several days but I was still strangely ailing. I could barely sit up in bed. I ate nothing, took just a few sips of water, and lay with my eyes closed, not talking to anyone.

'Come along, Hetty Feather,' said Matron Stinking Bottomly. 'Get up at once.'

'Stir yourself, you lazy girl. We know you're faking,' said Matron Pigface Peters.

They pulled back the sheets but I didn't move, though it was freezing cold.

'Get on your *feet*!' they screamed, and dragged me out of bed.

I stood shivering in my nightgown, while the room whirled violently round and round. The two shouting matrons whirled too, playing a crazy game of ring-a-roses before my eyes. I fainted clean away, cracking my head on the stone floor.

I came round to find blood trickling down my cheek and into the neck of my nightgown. The two matrons were the colour of the infirmary sheets, thinking I had died there and then. Dr March was hastily sent for again. He dabbed at the great gash on my temple, sighing, and told both matrons that it was dangerous to try and rouse me in such a manner.

'But her fever is gone, I am sure. There is nothing wrong with her physically,' said Matron Bottomly.

'Ah, physically, maybe, though she'll be groggy for a couple of days after that bang on the head. No, it's what's going on *inside* her head that concerns me.'

'I'm all too aware of what's going on in that red head of hers. Mischief, lies and total insubordination!' Matron Peters murmured to Matron Bottomly.

Dr March sat beside me, taking my hand in his and patting it gently. I was so overcome by this unexpected kindness I started weeping.

'There now, child. What is troubling you so? What is it you want?'

I swallowed, licked my dry lips and croaked, 'I want *Mama*!'

'Ah, I thought that might be the reason for this bizarre performance,' said Matron Peters. 'Well, want away, Hetty Feather. Your mother has been sent packing and she's never coming back.'

I wept as the word *never* tolled in my head like a mourning bell. I lay in my bed. My head throbbed but I didn't care. I didn't care about anything, only Mama.

Then one morning I had a new visitor. I smelled lemon verbena soap and freshly ironed linen. I opened my eyes and saw the plain neat form of Miss Sarah Smith. She looked at me gravely.

'Oh dear, Hetty,' she said, shaking her head. 'You look like a little ghost!'

'Miss Smith!' I forced my head up off the pillow. The room lurched and tilted but I made a fierce effort to steady myself. 'Oh, Miss Smith, you have to help me!'

'What can I do for you, child?'

'What can you *do*?' I was so desperate I forgot to be polite and deferential. 'You can get Mama back, that's what you can do!'

'I'm afraid I can't do that, my dear,' she said.

'Yes you can! You're on the Board of Governors! You do all that charity work and publish all those books. They will listen to you. Listen to *me*! Mama didn't do anything *wrong–*'

'She had a child out of wedlock, Hetty,' Miss Smith said quietly.

'So did the mother of every foundling in this whole hateful institution!'

'They all gave up their babies to the hospital. They didn't sneak back here under false pretences.'

'Surely that proves just how much Mama loves me. And I love *her*, and I cannot bear it that she's been cast out like a common criminal and denied a character reference.'

Miss Smith tried to interrupt, but I went on

16

talking, sitting bolt upright and shouting now. The infirmary nurse came rushing to restrain me, but Miss Smith stopped her.

'What will poor Mama do? She can't get a new position without a character reference. She's only ever worked here – and three terrible years in the workhouse. What if *they* won't take her back? Then she will be left to fend for herself on the streets. You dare ask me what the matter is! How do you think I feel, knowing my own dear mother is sitting in some mire-filled, squalid gutter, weeping–'

Oh, Hetty, you have such a majestic imagination! Don't get too carried away now! I assure you, your mother is *not* weeping in any mire-filled, squalid gutter. I like that phrase! I might well borrow it for one of my books.'

'Are you *mocking* me?'

'Only a little. I understand your anguish, but it's unfounded. Your mother, Ida, is well provided for. She has a new position already.'

'You're lying!'

The nurse gasped. 'Hetty Feather, how dare you address the lady like that!'

'It's quite all right, Nurse. It's good to see Hetty in a passion. It tells me that she's on the mend already,' said Miss Smith. 'I suggest you go and attend to your other patients, while Hetty and I continue our little chat.'

When the nurse left, with obvious reluctance, Miss Smith put her pale plain face close to mine, looking me straight in the eye. 'Do you really think I'm a liar, Hetty?'

I took a deep breath and then shook my head.

'I will always tell you the truth. Your mother is safe and well, and has a good position. You must trust me.'

'I do trust you, Miss Smith – but I don't trust anyone else. *They* could be lying to you,' I said.

'Hetty, I took it upon myself to raise your mother's case with the Board of Governors. We agreed that we could not possibly create a precedent by keeping Ida in our employ. Many other mothers would start seeking work at the hospital, and that would never do. We've always taken great care that no foundling should be singled out in any way, for treats or praise or special coddling–'

'Hmph! *I* am *constantly* singled out for scoldings and slappings.'

'Yes, and perhaps you deserve them, Miss Hetty Feather! Now listen to me, please. The matrons pressed for instant dismissal, and that was understandable – but it seemed to me singularly unfair to turn Ida away without giving her a good character. She's been an exemplary worker in all her years here, even if it was for a particular reason. She's been hard-working and cheerful, willing to lend a hand with anything. I wrote exactly that in her letter of reference.'

'*You* gave her a character reference! Oh, Miss Smith, thank you, thank you!'

'And I found her a new position too, as a general housekeeper to an elderly lady at Bignor-on-Sea on the south coast. She's an acquaintance of an aunt of mine, an invalid who I'm sure will treat Ida fairly.'

'But the south coast – that's miles and miles away! I shall never see her! Couldn't you have found her a *closer* position, Miss Smith?'

'Sometimes I think you can never be satisfied, Hetty!'

'Can we visit at all?'

'I'm afraid the Board of Governors do not think that a wise idea. But I dare say you will be able to write to each other.'

'Truly? I will get letters from Mama?'

'Yes, I'm sure she will write to you every now and then.'

I'd never had letters before, apart from one from Polly. I'd written my weekly letter home to my foster family. I wasn't sure Mother knew how to write, but Jem certainly did. He had taught me my own lettering when I was barely toddling. I had written for years, but they never once wrote back. Very few of the foundlings received letters, and yet in the junior school we all wrote once a week without fail.

My heart beat harder in my chest. 'Will they give me Mama's letters?' I asked fearfully. 'They don't always give us our letters, I am sure of it.'

I *wasn't* sure – but the expression on Miss Smith's face told me that I'd hit on the truth.

'I do believe there *is* a little censoring. I certainly don't approve, but it's done for well-meaning reasons. Apparently, letters from foster homes are frequently inappropriate or upsetting and would not help the children to settle down at the hospital . . .' Miss Smith's voice wavered.

I seized her hands. 'That's outrageous, Miss Smith, and you know it!'

'Hetty, Hetty, calm down! I do agree with you, it is in most circumstances outrageous, but I do not think there is anything I can do to change matters. It is the custom.'

'Then it's cruel and pointless telling me Mama will write if I can't receive her letters!' I protested.

'Hush now!' She held my hands tightly and put her face close to mine. 'I have given Ida my own address. I will tell her to send all letters to me. I will bring them to you on a regular basis and I will post your replies. That way you will *know* that the letters are being sent – if, of course, you trust me?'

'Oh, Miss Smith, of course I trust you!' I said, and I threw my arms around her.

'Now, now, Hetty, compose yourself. Still, I am pleased to see you are almost back to your old self – in a furious rage one moment and in a fever of excitement the next,' she said, laughing at me. 'If you're truly grateful–'

'I am, I am!'

'Then you must get better quickly and be a good, polite, hard-working girl for your entire future stay at the hospital.'

'I'm not sure I can quite manage that,' I said truthfully.

Miss Smith laughed again. 'Well, do your best, dear,' she said. She called to the nurse. 'I think you'll find that Hetty is on the mend. I have a feeling she'll be able to get up tomorrow. I'm sure she'll definitely be her old self by the end of the week. Isn't that right, Hetty?'

I nodded emphatically. My head ached, and I still felt weak and dizzy when I tried to get up, but I persevered. I ate as much gruel as I could to get stronger, although it didn't taste the same without Mama's loving sprinkles of brown sugar and spoonfuls of cream.

I was still punished when I returned to the schoolroom and my own dormitory, but I didn't care. I listened to the scoldings of Matron Stinking

Bottomly with my head held high. What did I care if she thought me deceitful and dishonest and a disgrace to the whole hospital? I even held my tongue when she said bad things about Mama. I knew she was simply trying to goad me into flying at her, and then she could legitimately fling me in the punishment room. I knew now that Mama was well provided for and would be writing to me, and that special secret knowledge kept me silent and seemingly obedient.

I performed all the extra housework tasks the matron set me. I did not even murmur when she had me scrubbing out the privies.

Sheila came across me performing this unpleasant task. She would normally have laughed delightedly to see me scrubbing with one hand and holding my nose with the other, but this time she hovered anxiously. Then, to my astonishment, she took up another brush and started scrubbing too.

'Whatever are you doing, Sheila?' I asked.

'What does it look like?' said Sheila. 'Ugh! This is disgusting!'

'But why are you helping me? You, of all people?'

'Because I feel badly about you and Ida. I think it was all my fault that Matron Peters came downstairs, poking her nose in. I tripped on the stairs

22

when I was following you. I think she must have woken then.'

'Oh! But even so, you didn't tell on me.'

'I wouldn't tell on my worst enemy,' said Sheila, scrubbing.

'I thought *I* was your worst enemy,' I said.

'Well, there you are, then, I still didn't tell,' said Sheila proudly.

'You're definitely not *my* worst enemy any more. If you carry on helping me perform this disgusting task, I shall have to recategorize you. You will be a dear friend,' I said.

Sheila went a little pink. 'I'm not sure about that, Hetty! But I do feel especially sad that you've lost your mother all over again. And Ida would be a *lovely* mother–'

'She is, she is!'

'You must be so worried about her now.'

'I am. But Mama is strong-willed and very determined. I have a feeling she is safe and in good hands now,' I said.

I did not want to tell her about Miss Smith's reassurances. Sheila might be almost my friend now, but I wasn't sure I trusted her totally.

'I wish I could discover *my* mother,' said Sheila sadly. 'Do you think you will ever see Ida again, Hetty?'

'Of course! When I am fourteen I will leave this hateful hospital, and I will search the length and breadth of England until I find her again!' I said fervently.

Miss Smith came to the hospital a few days later, supposedly to check on the state of my health and mark the progress of my memoirs. (She had bought me my beautiful red Italian notebook and encouraged me to start my life story on its smooth creamy paper.) We usually sat in the corner of the schoolroom when Miss Smith visited, under the watchful eye of my teacher, Miss Morley – but this time Miss Smith said I still looked very pale. She fancied a turn in the gardens would do me a power of good.

Miss Morley did not dare protest, because Miss Smith was on the Board of Governors and a well-known, powerful lady to boot.

We went down the stairs and out through the back door, a forbidden joy in itself. We girls went outdoors to 'play' every day, but we had to cluster in the front courtyard, where the big girls strolled and the little ones skipped. All our school-work and training happened indoors: reading, writing, counting, sewing, serving, scrubbing – so that we would be competent servants by the age of fourteen.

The boys were going to be soldiers so they were

encouraged outdoors. They did Physical Education every day. They marched up and down, they swung their arms, they ran on the spot. They did not have to perform a single household task. Instead they were marshalled out into the gardens, where they dug and hoed and watered our potatoes and turnips and carrots, our cabbages and kale, our peas and beans, our blackberries and gooseberries.

There were all the senior boys now, digging away in their shirtsleeves. Although they were under the supervision of Old Joe the gardener, they were calling to each other and whistling merry tunes as they worked – while *we* had to work in total silence. If we so much as whispered, we were punished.

'Oh, lucky, lucky boys!' I said to Miss Smith.

'I agree with you, Hetty. Boys seem far more free and fortunate than girls, no matter what their station in life.' She stared over at a tall thin boy standing by himself. Two sturdier fellows were slyly pelting him with potatoes whenever the gardener's back was turned. The boy did not shout or swear or try to retaliate. He simply stood there like some anguished martyred saint, accepting this punishment.

'Poor lad,' said Miss Smith. 'It doesn't seem much fun for him.'

I watched with a heavy heart, biting my lip to stop myself crying out. I knew the boy. He was my dear foster brother, Gideon. I wanted to rush to protect him. I still loved my strange, shy, solitary brother so much, though we scarcely saw each other now that we were at the hospital.

If only I could give the two tormentors a taste of their own medicine. I looked down at the freshly turned earth beside the path. I bent down and grabbed a handful, squeezing it into a muddy lump.

'No, Hetty, no!' said Miss Smith.

'I have to,' I said, and hurled my clod.

It landed most satisfactorily right in the face of the biggest boy. He gave a muffled shriek – unable to cry out loudly with a mouthful of earth. I hoped there were big juicy worms wriggling right down his throat. He bent over, coughing and gagging, while his friend whirled round and round in comical anxiety, wondering from whence the attack had come. All he could see was a stern lady and a small female foundling demurely taking the air in the gardens.

Gideon looked over too, and saw me. I was dressed in our hideous brown uniform, but my cap could not contain all my flaming red hair. I hoped he would wave and smile when he recognized me, but he hung his head and looked more miserable than ever. I had meant to help, but I had only shamed him.

'Oh dear, perhaps I shouldn't have done that,' I murmured.

'Yes, you should be ashamed of yourself, Hetty. Such behaviour!'

'Pointless, stupid behaviour,' I agreed, sighing.

'I am sure Matron Bottomly or Matron Peters would feel you should be severely punished in some particularly painful way. They might think that depriving you of all post is a suitable punishment,' said Miss Smith.

I put my hand in hers. 'But you are not a matron, you are my own dear Miss Smith, and you are going to give me my post, are you not? Oh, do I truly have a letter from Mama?'

Miss Smith patted the pocket of her skirt and smiled at me. We went round the corner to the greenhouses, out of sight of the gardener and all the boys. She reached into her pocket and offered me a small white envelope.

I carefully wiped my muddy hands on the back of my uniform and took it. I was shaking now, my fingers clumsy. I unpeeled the flap, trying not to tear it at all, because it was so very precious – and then pulled out the letter.

18 Saltdean Lane
Bignor-on-Sea
Sussex

My deer little Hetty – no, my brite bloo-eyed Sapphire!

I miss you so my darling child, but if it wernt for the ake in my hart I wuld be happy for I am now working for a lovly old lady Miss Roberts and she is a deer to me, much sweeter than those meen old matrons.

It is a butiful place here. The see is such a site. How I wish you wer with me to take the air and run on the sands. But be of good cheer, you will be out of the hospital befor too long, and then when I have savd enuf muny we will be togever forever deerest child.

With all my love

Your mama Ida

P.S. Please furgiv the look of this letter. I am not used to putting pen to paper and I canot figure out how to spel all the wurds.

I read my letter again and again, though the dear words blurred because my eyes filled with tears.

'Is Ida well?' Miss Smith asked quietly.

'Oh, she sounds very well and likes her position, but she is missing me and, oh my goodness, I am missing her,' I said, holding Mama's letter to my chest.

I did not want to show it to Miss Smith because it was so precious and private, and I could not bear her to see that Mama had a little difficulty with her spelling. Miss Smith seemed to understand. She brought out another envelope from her pocket with a blank piece of paper inside, and a sharpened cedar pencil.

'I thought you might care to reply straight away,' she said.

'Oh, Miss Smith, you are *such* a dear friend!' I said.

We sat down together on the old brick wall. Miss Smith started jotting things down in a small note-book, intent on writing another of her stories, while I scribbled hastily to Mama.

The Foundling Hospital

Oh, Mama, dearest, most special Mama in the entire world,

I am missing you so enormously much. I cannot believe fate has been so unkind to us, tearing us apart again in this way – though if I had been more cautious and Sheila less nosy (though she is sorry now), we would still be together. How lovely of you to write to me. It is such a relief to know you're in a good house with a kind lady – though heavens, Satan himself would seem kind compared with those wicked matrons.

I was taken poorly when you had to leave the hospital, but the doctor was gentle, and Miss Smith was wonderfully reassuring, and I am totally better now, though my heart aches too and I long to have your dear arms around me.

With all my love,

From your own daughter Sapphire (the most beautiful name in the world because you chose it specially for me).

Mama and I have been writing to each other ever since. I have all her precious letters in little bundles tied with silk. Nurse Winnie gave me a yard of narrow green silk ribbon as a secret present when I helped her with her sewing classes for the little ones.

'Remember *your* first darning lesson when you were five, Hetty?' she said, smiling at me. 'You were all fingers and thumbs, you poor little mite, and sewed the toe of your stocking tight to the heel!'

'I was a very stupid little girl, Nurse Winterson,' I said.

'No, no, you were bright as a button. There was always something distinctive about you, Hetty. I knew you would go far.'

'How far is that?' I said, sighing. 'So far that I will scrub people's floors and dust their mantelpieces for the rest of my working life?'

'I have a feeling you won't be a servant for ever,' said Nurse Winnie. 'And even if you are, you will still lead a very different life from here. Servants have days off, you know. You will be able to do as you please. And pretty servant girls have followers.'

'I dare say – but I'm not the slightest bit pretty,' I said. 'I am the smallest, skinniest girl in my whole year and I have bright red hair.'

'I think your hair is a beautiful colour, dear,' she said – and the next time I helped her she gave me the green ribbon. *'To tie up your bonny red hair,'* she sang, pulling one of my plaits.

Dear Nurse Winnie! She was the only person in the whole hospital I cared for now, apart from Eliza, my little sister. Eliza was brought to my old foster home in the country when she was a babe. I was sent off to the hospital before I turned six – and five years later Eliza followed me.

I had greeted my little foster sister joyfully,

desperate for news of home. It was a hard blow when she spoke of our brother Jem so fondly. I had adored Jem passionately when I was a tiny girl. He had cared for me tenderly and played with me patiently. He had even taught me to read and write . . . He had been like a mother and father to me as well as a foster brother. I'd hoped that one day, far in the future, he'd be my dear husband too. When I played dressing up as a bride, Jem had kissed my finger and promised that he'd put a ring on it one day.

I had believed him utterly. I had thought of him as *my* Jem, but when little Eliza chatted away innocently enough, I realized that he was *her* Jem too. He had played all the same games with her. I could not bear it. I felt he had betrayed me. I stopped writing loving little messages to him in my weekly letters home. There seemed little point in writing anyway, as he never bothered to reply. Though perhaps he *had* written? Miss Smith had actually admitted that many of our letters were confiscated.

Tears sprang to my eyes when I thought of Matron Pigface's trotter-fingers fumbling with my precious letters, tearing them to shreds and tossing them into the fire. I wondered what Jem would have written . . .

No, what did I care? I had been a silly little

child and he had been a kindly lad, that was all. It was ridiculous to believe that our love had been real. I would not be wearing my green ribbon for Jem, or for any other young lad, come to that. I did not want foolish followers. I only cared for Mama.

3

I woke very early and sat up in my narrow bed. I looked down the long dormitory of sleeping girls in the silvery dawn light. This was the very last time I would ever see them!

I clasped my hands around my knees, hugging myself. It was not unduly cold but I shivered in my nightgown. Today I was leaving the hospital for ever. Hetty Feather was no more. I would leave her behind, along with my brown gown and apron and cuffs and stupid great floppy bonnet.

I peeped down at the basket at the end of my bed. My new clothes were neatly folded, waiting for me. I felt a thrill of excitement at the thought of putting them on, though they were ordinary work clothes – a plain grey dress and coarse cream apron. I knew nothing of fashion after all my years of incarceration in the hospital, but I could always dream of a real silk dress to match my green ribbon, long frilled skirts, fine lace, white silk stockings, and shoes as elegant as Cinderella's glass slippers.

I had no new shoes at all – my hideous brown clumpers still fitted me, so they were deemed suitable for my new position.

I was going as an under-housemaid to a gentleman who lived in the suburbs of London.

'Not just *any* gentleman, Hetty,' Miss Smith had told me excitedly. 'He's a writer! Mr Charles Buchanan.'

'Do you know him, Miss Smith?'

'I know *of* him, dear. He writes children's stories for the Religious Tract, as I do. Very moral tales. He is apparently a very moral *man*. He applied to the hospital because he thought it an act of charity to take a foundling child into his employ – and I did my best to persuade the Board of Governors that you would be an ideal candidate, Hetty. It was a hard task. Matron Bottomly seems to feel that you are quite unsuited to such a worthy gentleman's establishment, but I argued your case, stressing that Mr Buchanan might be a very good influence on you. Why are you staring at me like that? Surely you're pleased?'

'I'm pleased you stood up for me, Miss Smith, of course I am, but if I'm completely truthful I do not really *want* to be this very moral gentleman's servant,' I said.

'Well, whose servant *do* you wish to be?' said Miss Smith, looking aggrieved.

'I don't want to be *anyone*'s servant,' I said, folding my arms obstinately.

Miss Smith sighed. 'So how do you propose to earn your living, Hetty?' she asked tartly.

I swallowed hard. Wasn't it obvious? I clung to my own elbows to give me strength to come out with it. 'I – I hoped my memoirs would be published, and I would earn money that way,' I said.

'Oh good Lord, Hetty, how could you possibly think such a thing!'

'Well, you said as much – in a roundabout fashion. You said I had a vivid turn of phrase and excellent powers of description, and a powerful imagination.'

'That's all too true.'

'Well?'

'But that doesn't mean that your memoirs are fit for publication!'

'But why have you praised them so?'

'I wanted to encourage you, my dear. I never dreamed you thought you could publish such a work!'

'I know it's a little childish in parts because I wrote most of it years ago – but I can polish it a lot, maybe rewrite sections. Oh, Miss Smith, *surely* it stands some chance of publication?'

'It's a wonderful piece of work, Hetty, but only as a private journal. It is not *fit* for publication. Be reasonable! Only recollect the things you've written about Matron Peters and Matron Bottomly!'

'But they're true, every last word – I swear it!'

'I dare say, but there would be the most terrible scandal if such a fiercely condemnatory document about such a well-respected charity were published!'

'Well, surely a scandal would be good. It might sell more copies!'

'Hetty, you're incorrigible! You can never publish your memoirs – they're much too bold, too personal, too passionate, too violent, too bitter, too unlady-like, too ungrateful, too every single thing!'

'Then why didn't you tell me this years ago?'

'Because I felt it was very good for you to have a private outlet for your pent-up feelings. I know how hard it's been at the hospital. It's been exception-ally good for you to develop a writing discipline. You have remarkable literary skills, far beyond your age and station, but you must channel them carefully if you ever hope to write for publication. Oh, please don't upset yourself so, dear!'

I had started crying bitterly, utterly cast down. I had so believed my memoirs would be published and make my fortune so that Mama and I could live together without serving a soul.

Miss Smith lent me her lacy handkerchief. When

I continued to cry, she put her arm round me and mopped my face herself. Her kindness softened me, and I tried hard to stop sobbing.

'There now, perhaps you really *will* be a writer some time in the future. But not yet a while, my dear. You can accept this perfect position with Mr Buchanan and be patient. I am sure you will observe good writerly habits if you work in his establishment.'

'I'd sooner work for you, Miss Smith,' I said.

'If you were my servant, I'd expect you to go "Yes, missus," and nod obediently every time I spoke to you,' said Miss Smith.

'Yes, missus,' I said, bobbing her a curtsy – and she burst out laughing.

'I scarcely recognize this new persona, Hetty! Carry on in a similar vein at Mr Buchanan's like a good sensible girl. You really must try to act humbly and do as you're told. I'm starting to feel a little worried about Mr Buchanan. There he is, thinking he's taken on a meek little foundling girl who will be very grateful for her good position. You are a *little* grateful, aren't you, Hetty?'

'Yes, Miss Smith,' I said, because I supposed I was grateful to *her*. I did not see why I should be grateful to anyone else. Even after nine years' hard training at the hospital, I still did not see *why* I had to be content to be a servant.

Every Sunday in the chapel we sang:

'The rich man in his castle
The poor man at his gate,
God made them, high or lowly,
And ordered their estate.'

Why did I have to be stuck being lowly? Why couldn't Mama and I be rich women in our castle?

'You wait, dearest Mama,' I whispered as I sat in bed my last morning. 'I will earn our fortune with my writing one day, no matter what Miss Smith says. Then we *will* have our castle. Well, maybe not a *castle* exactly, but a grand villa with our own pretty bedrooms, where we will live very happily and harmoniously together, just the two of us. We will be rich enough to have a whole troop of servants, but we won't employ a single one. We will not want any poor girls working for us. We will look after ourselves splendidly. I will clean for you, Mama, and you will cook for me, and we will be private and cosy and comfortable.'

I slid out of bed and walked down the long dormitory, past all the sleeping girls. I tiptoed out onto the landing, and then down the long wooden staircase, the grand portraits staring at me sternly.

'Frown all you like. I'm not afraid of you. I shall

never have to stare up at you ever again,' I declared.

I crept right downstairs, across the girls' dining room, the table already set for our meagre breakfast. There was no clattering from the kitchen. The cook must still be sleeping. I moved as silently as a shadow through the great room, which still reeked of yesterday's mutton, and proceeded along the servants' corridor.

I halted outside Mama's room. I could not go in. There was another maid living there now, a large, clumsy girl called Maud. She was harmless enough, but I hated her simply because she had taken Mama's place. I could not stand the thought of her gimcrack possessions littering Mama's chest, her dirty brush and comb on Mama's washstand, her fat, ungainly body sprawled all over Mama's bed.

I stood outside the door, leaning my head against the varnished wood, remembering all the precious times I had spent with Mama within those four walls.

I wrote on the door with my finger: *I love you, Mama*, and then crept away. I returned to my bed undetected. If only I had been so lucky before! We would have had some chance of regular meetings if Mama were still employed at the hospital in London and I were not too far away in the suburbs. A simple bus ride, perhaps.

41

My heart started beating faster at the thought of my journey today. I had Mr Charles Buchanan's address written inside my journal: *8 Lady's Ride, Kingtown*. I had no idea how I would reach this destination. I had only been outside the hospital grounds once, when I was ten – the day of Queen Victoria's Golden Jubilee. We had been escorted all the way to the great children's celebration in Hyde Park. I had seen the circus there, and had run away to try to find my childhood idol, Madame Adeline, the magical spangled woman who had let me sit on one of her rosin-backed horses and had won my heart for ever. I had taken an omnibus ride that day, as bold as brass. I tried hard to remember how I had hailed it and how much money I had paid. What happened when you wanted to get off? Did you ring some kind of bell? How would I know where 8 Lady's Ride was? How would I know anything at all in the outside world?

I remembered how the children in Hyde Park had pointed and jeered at me. Would people still point me out and ridicule me? I clenched my fists. I would make them sorry if they did. I was Sapphire Battersea, and I would show everyone. I was not content to be a common servant. One day my name would be famous, recognized all over London.

I shut my eyes and saw *Sapphire Battersea* in big fancy lettering on advertising posters, *Sapphire*

Battersea in bold print in newspapers. I heard the name *Sapphire Battersea* shouted through loudhailers, *Sapphire Battersea* acclaimed by thousands of mouths.

Then a handbell clanged along the corridor – and I was Hetty Feather again, back in my dismal dormitory. All the girls groaned and yawned and struggled out of their beds, hopping from one bare foot to another on the cold linoleum. They tugged on their brown frocks and fumbled with their aprons and cuffs.

I stood too, pulling on my new grey dress. It smelled so different, fresh and clean. Although the material was brand new, it felt remarkably soft after my thick, itchy uniform. The other girls circled me enviously, stroking the folds, holding out my skirts admiringly, while I brushed and plaited my hair.

'Will you put your hair up now, Hetty?' Emma Baxter asked. She was a kindly, helpful girl who slept in the bed next to mine.

'Of course,' I said, but I had no hairpins, and my flimsy new cap could not easily accommodate all my hair. I tried for two minutes, and then had to give up and keep my schoolgirl plaits hanging down my back.

'Oh dear, you don't look very grown up,' said Emma.

I knew she was speaking the truth. I was no

bigger than the ten-year-olds at the hospital and I didn't look much older either. Emma herself had grown curves, whereas I was as straight up and down as any of the boys.

I drew myself up as tall as I could, my head held high. 'I shall just have to *act* grown up,' I said.

The other girls gathered round to wish me luck. Some sighed enviously, but the timid ones clutched each other, glad that it wasn't their turn just yet.

'Aren't you scared, Hetty? I'd be all of a tremble, going off to the outside and being with all those strangers.'

'I'm not the slightest bit scared,' I lied.

I tried to eat a hearty breakfast in the dining room just to show them. I remembered that Monica had been in such a state she'd had to rush outside to the privies to be sick after a few spoonfuls of porridge. Even fierce Sheila had been very pale, her high forehead wrinkled with anxious frown lines. She had given me a sudden hug after breakfast and murmured, 'Don't ask me why, but I shall miss you, Hetty Feather.'

I did not feel the same way for any of these girls I had grown up with, but I felt a terrible squeezing of my insides when I looked down the long, long table and saw Eliza, craning her neck to peer at me forlornly.

We were not allowed to get up from the breakfast

table till the bell went, but it was dear Nurse Winterson on meal duties, and she was never strict. I clambered off my bench and shot along the room to Eliza. I threw my arms around her and hugged her hard.

'Oh, Hetty!' she wailed, pressing her face against my flat chest. 'I shall not be able to bear it here without you!'

'Of course you will, Eliza. You have many, many friends,' I said, which was true enough. Eliza was a sunny, cheery little creature with curly hair and dimples. Everyone wanted to be her friend. Even the fierce matrons softened when they saw her. No wonder my Jem had found it easy to forget me and lose his heart to Eliza.

Nurse Winnie came over to us. She was shaking her head, but smiling too. 'Now, now, Hetty dear, I know it's your last day, but you know the rules well enough. Go back to your bench, dear.'

Eliza burst into floods of tears.

'Oh, please may I kiss Eliza one more time?' I begged.

'Of course,' said Nurse Winnie. Her own eyes were brimming. 'Do not worry about Eliza, Hetty. I promise I will look out for her.'

I kissed Eliza five or six times on her rosy cheeks, wiping away her tears with the soft cuffs of my new dress. 'There now, darling. Don't take on so. You will be fine,' I promised.

Nurse Winnie put her arm round me as she walked me back to my bench.

'I will miss her so,' I said, struggling not to weep myself. 'But I will not worry about her. It's poor Gideon who breaks my heart. Oh, Nurse Winterson, please, please, please may I go and find him and say goodbye?'

'Oh, come now, Hetty! You know perfectly well that I can't let you go to the boys' quarters!'

'No, but you could perhaps turn your back and not notice if I slip out. I promise I'll be ten minutes at the most. Oh *please*, dear Nurse Winterson. I shall miss *you* so much. You've always been my very favourite nurse.'

'And you've always been the most artful of my girls,' said Nurse Winnie – but she turned her back.

I rushed right out of the room before she could change her mind. I thought I would still have difficulty in getting to the boys' dining room. I passed several nurses, but none of them stopped me. Then I caught sight of myself reflected in a window. I didn't look like Hetty Feather the foundling any more. I looked like a maid in my grey dress, albeit a very miniature version. I stood staring at myself for a full minute, turning this way and that. It was exciting being this new person, but very odd, as if my own head had been stuck on an entirely different body.

The bell rang for the end of breakfast, and I came to my senses and scurried off to the boys' wing. They were swarming out of their dining room, along the hall, up to their classrooms. They were mostly silent, but they still made much more noise than us girls. They stomped harder with their boots and thumped about bizarrely. I looked all about me, jostled as I threaded my way through them. It was so hard to distinguish one particular boy amongst this vast crowd of brown figures. But then I saw him, sloping along by himself, his head bent.

'Gideon! Oh, Gideon!'

He looked over in my direction, his eyes still blank.

'Gideon, it's *me*, Hetty.'

He came rushing towards me and stood over me, a full foot taller than me now, though as little babes we had once fitted together in a basket.

'Oh my goodness, Hetty! You look so different out of uniform. So, are you going today?'

'Yes, I am to be a maid to a gentleman called Mr Buchanan. He writes children's books.'

'You might like it there, then.'

'No I shan't.'

'Well, *I* would like it. I'm leaving at the end of the month, to go to Renshaw Barracks.'

'Oh, Gid, I would give anything to change with

you. It will be such an adventure for you. Just think how fine you will look in a soldier's uniform. You might even get to travel abroad!'

'Yes, what splendid fun – to be shot at and blown to smithereens,' said Gideon bitterly. 'It's all right for you, Hetty. It's so all *wrong* for me. I am a coward.'

'No you're not! You can be ever so strong and brave and stoical. My goodness, you couldn't survive *here* if you weren't.'

'All the other lads mock me. I don't blame them – I'm so very different. It will be worse at the barracks. I've heard such tales.'

I could not bear to see my dear foster brother in such torment. 'Then do not go!' I said. 'You could just walk right out of the hospital! You've got the whole of London to hide in. You're tall and smart. You will be able to bluff your way, find some kind of work and get lodgings. It's so much easier for a boy.'

'I have thought of it often. Perhaps I will find the courage to do that – but I rather think not. I told you, Hetty, I am a coward. We should have swapped places with each other when we were in that baby basket. I should have been the girl and you the boy.'

'Come along there, Smeed! Stop dallying with the servants and get to your lessons, boy,' someone shouted.

Gideon flinched.

I held his hand fast. 'Remember, Gideon, I am your dear sister and I love you very much. I will always care for you. Maybe one day when you are on leave, you can come and take me out. I should love to be escorted by a fine soldier in a splendid uniform,' I said earnestly.

'*Gideon Smeed!* Are you listening? Head in the clouds as always! *Move*, or I'll prod you!'

'I have to go, Hetty,' said Gideon desperately.

'Goodbye, dearest Gid. Good luck!' I said, and I reached right up and kissed him on the cheek.

The boys surrounding us jeered and whistled, and Gideon went as red as his waistcoat, but he blew me a very quick kiss in return. Then he went on his way and I wondered if we would ever see each other again.

I felt so cast down that I nearly lost my courage. I almost wished I were staying at the hospital. It was a cold, cheerless place, especially without dear Mama, but it had been my home for nine full years. I tried to have faith in Miss Smith and her writing gentleman, but I wasn't at all sure that this was a good move. Maybe I should take my own advice to Gideon, and make a run for it the moment I stepped outside the hospital gates.

I had survived my two or three days of freedom when I was ten. In many respects I had had splendid adventures – and even earned enough to feed myself too. I was much better equipped now to find myself some desirable employment. Perhaps I should take this one and only chance! I felt badly about Miss Smith, but perhaps she would understand.

I gathered my few possessions in my small brown travelling box, ready to go. But Matron Bottomly called me to her room first. Matron Peters was there too, both of them shaking their heads at me.

'Well, Hetty Feather, you are leaving us at last,' said Matron Stinking Bottomly.

'We will always remember *you*,' said Matron Pigface Peters. 'You are undoubtedly the wildest and most wilful girl we have ever had in our care.'

'You will come down to earth with a bump once you've had a taste of the working world outside,' said Matron Bottomly. 'Beware, Hetty Feather! If you stick to your sulky ways, you will be dismissed for insolence, without a character, and *then* where will you be?'

'Following in the footsteps of your mother, I dare say,' said Matron Peters, and they both sniggered.

'I'll thank you not to bad-mouth my mother,' I said. 'I don't have to listen to either of you ever again. I shall be off now. Goodbye.'

'Goodbye and good riddance!' they said in

unison, like Tweedledum and Tweedledee. Nurse Winnie had read us the two *Alice* books in her sewing class when I was little.

They accompanied me along the landing and down the stairs. Nurse Winnie came running up. She took no notice of either matron and threw her arms around me.

'Good luck, little Hetty! I can't believe it's fourteen whole years since I held you in my arms and tried to comfort you. I've never known a babe scream so much! But I knew even then that you were a very special child, and would go far.'

'Oh, dear Nurse Winnie! Thank you so much for being so very kind to me over the years. I will never forget you,' I said, suddenly close to tears.

'Come *along*, Nurse Winterson. There's no need to single the girl out. She has a high enough opinion of herself already,' Matron Pigface snapped.

'It seems to me you thoroughly spoiled her and ruined her character when she was in the junior school,' said Matron Bottomly. 'It was very hard for me to make a serious impression on such an imp of Satan. You must heed the warnings of the Good Book, Nurse Winterson – spare the rod and spoil the child.'

'That's nonsense!' I cried. 'Nurse Winterson is the only nurse here who shows us real love and care. That's the only way any of us have thrived in this grim prison!'

'Hush your mouth, Hetty Feather! How dare you talk to us like that!'

'I dare say anything I wish, because neither of you have any power over me any more,' I declared.

'Don't be so sure of that! We will be checking up on you vigorously. If you fail to please your new employer, we have the power to call you back to the hospital to retrain you,' Matron Bottomly threatened.

That certainly unnerved me! I didn't want to risk going to Mr Buchanan's now. I'd start afresh, where no one could keep track of me. I wasn't going to be Hetty Feather any more. I was Sapphire Battersea, only child of dear Ida. I would show these pig-faced stinking matrons. I would make my own way in the world, no matter what. I had to make a bolt for it now.

But my spirited plans were instantly thwarted. There was a strange woman lurking in the entrance hall – strange to me, and certainly strange in appearance. She was a very *large* woman. She made even Matron Pigface Peters appear sylph-like. She was dressed in a bizarre dark-red costume that made her resemble an immense slab of bloody meat. She wore a bonnet to match, trimmed with white, like mutton chops with paper frills. I stared at her in astonishment. She seemed equally bewildered by me.

'This scrawny little creature cannot possibly be Hetty Feather!' she said, hands on her hips. 'I thought you said she was fourteen and a good strong girl? This child is barely ten – and her arms and legs look as if they should be in a box of Bryant and May.'

'This is Hetty Feather, ma'am, and her fourteenth birthday was three full months ago – isn't that correct, Hetty?'

I hesitated. I didn't know what to say. I didn't like the look of this great meaty woman at all. I felt a further few weeks in the hospital might even be preferable. What was she doing here? Why had *she* come to fetch me? Where was Mr Buchanan?

'I thought I was going to be Mr Buchanan's servant,' I mumbled.

'Indeed you are, child. *If* you are of age.'

'Speak up, Hetty, and reassure the lady. You've never held your tongue for long previously,' said Matron Bottomly.

'I'm fourteen. I've always been very small.'

'With carrot-coloured hair too! I hope you don't have a temper to match. Lord knows why we've been lumbered with you,' said the meaty one, giving me a prod in the chest. 'Come along then, child. We've got quite a journey ahead of us.'

'Goodbye, Hetty Feather. Try your hardest to be

dutiful and diligent. Might I suggest, ma'am, that you treat her severely right from the start. She has wild ways,' said Matron Bottomly.

'Frankly speaking, she could do with a good whipping every now and then,' said Matron Peters.

I glared at them. My lips were pressed tight together. I wouldn't even say goodbye. I clutched my box in both hands. My heart was beating fast. I decided to run for it the moment the great door was opened, but the large woman seized me by the shoulders, her fat fingers digging into my flesh, kneading me like bread. She marched me down the long pathway to the outside gate. I twisted my neck to look one last time at the hospital where I had been locked up for so long. I stared at the barred attic window and saw a ghost of myself looking down.

I shivered in the cold air because I didn't have any kind of mantle or shawl.

'Ah, you're not quite so bold now!' said Mistress Meat. 'You're quivering like a jelly in a mould.'

'I am simply a little cold, ma'am,' I answered, my chin up – but she only laughed at me.

She called to the porter at the gate. 'Is that hansom cab still waiting? Come along, Hetty Feather – he'll be charging us a fortune as it is.'

She hustled me through the gate towards a horse and cab. I couldn't help feeling a little thrill of excitement at the thought of such a journey. She pushed me up inside the cab and followed me close, spreading her dark-red skirts all around me. I had a glimpse of her legs in pink silk stockings, like vast pork sausages. I wriggled away as far as possible in such an enclosed space, while the driver above us clicked to his horse. As it started trotting I heard shouting. I couldn't make out the words clearly, but I was almost sure that someone was calling my name.

I struggled round, half hanging out of the cab window, and saw a young man in brown corduroy running after us, waving his arms and shouting.

'Sit *down,* miss! You don't want to tumble out and break your head,' said the meaty one.

'But that man is calling me! He's waving as if he knows me,' I said, bewildered. 'Please let's stop the cab and see what he wants.'

'Don't be so silly, child. We're not stopping the cab for you to chatter with any Tom, Dick or Harry. We have work to do! I came to fetch you out of kindness, in case you were confused on the journey – but I shall be terribly behind all day long now.'

She commanded the driver to get a move on. We soon rounded the corner of the street, going at such a pace that there was no way the young man could catch us.

Whoever could it have been?

4

I looked long and hard at the meaty woman as we rode along together, squashed up like two pigs in a poke.

'Why are you staring at me? Have I got a smut on my face?' she asked.

'No, ma'am. I was just wondering who you are,' I said truthfully. 'What is your name?'

'I am Mrs Briskett,' she said, announcing her name as proudly as if she were the Queen of England.

Mrs Briskett? Wasn't brisket a type of beef? Oh, what a glorious name for this great bovine woman! I felt the most insistent giggles tickling my inside. I had to clench my teeth and suck my cheeks to stop myself erupting. I set myself to thinking why she was a Mrs Briskett. If she was Mr Buchanan's wife, why did she not bear his name? Was she perhaps a neighbour of his, come to fetch me as a favour?

'Excuse me, ma'am, but do you live at Mr Buchanan's house?'

'Of course I do, you silly girl.'

'And – and *Mr* Briskett?'

'There is no Mr Briskett. It is a courtesy title,' she said.

I thought on. I remembered all the cook's *Police Gazettes* I had secretly read at the hospital.

'Then are you – are you under Mr Buchanan's protection?' I asked.

I thought I'd asked the question delicately, but she coughed and spluttered, her face flushing darker than her bonnet.

'How *dare* you suggest such a thing! I can't believe my own ears!'

'I'm sorry! I didn't mean to cause offence. I didn't understand. I simply thought—'

'I am Mr Buchanan's cook-housekeeper,' said Mrs Briskett. 'I cannot *imagine* how you could possibly have dreamed otherwise. However, you are a poor ignorant orphan, Hetty Feather, so I suppose you simply do not know any better.'

'Oh no, I'm not an orphan, ma'am. I have a very dear mother, Ida Battersea. In fact, I'm not really called Hetty Feather at all – that was just the name the Foundling Hospital inflicted on me. My name is Sapphire Battersea. Please may I be called by that name? It could be my courtesy title.'

'*Sapphire?* What kind of ungodly, fanciful name is that for a little servant girl? Don't be ridiculous, child. Were you christened when you arrived at the Foundling Hospital as a babe?'

'Yes, ma'am.'

'And what name did they christen you?'

I took a deep breath. 'Hetty Feather, but—'

'No buts! That is your name, and you will not be known by any other. Sapphire indeed!'

Yes, Sapphire, Sapphire, Sapphire, I said silently inside my head. *It is a beautiful name and it is my name, and you can 'Hetty Feather' me a thousand times a day, but I know my real name now and you cannot take it away from me.*

'I don't care for that expression on your face, Hetty. I hope you are not a sullen girl. Do you realize how lucky you are to be given this opportunity?'

I felt like the least lucky girl in all the world, but I rearranged my face into an ingratiating smile and nodded vigorously. It was clear that Mrs Briskett had a quick temper and her fingers seemed as sharp as meat hooks. I was sure my shoulders were all covered over with bruises.

The horse slowed down and stopped, and Mrs Briskett nudged me to climb out of the cab. We were in front of a vast, imposing building, practically as big as a palace. It seemed dimly familiar.

'Is this Mr Buchanan's house?' I asked doubtfully.

'Dear goodness, how can you be so stupid, child? This is Waterloo Station! We are continuing our journey by train.' She paused, then said slowly, as if speaking to a simpleton, 'A train is a huge carriage with a massive engine at the front, powered by steam.'

'I know what a train is, Mrs Briskett,' I said with some satisfaction. 'I travelled in one when I left my foster home in the country.'

She snorted. 'You must have been only five or so at the time. I doubt you can remember anything about it.'

'Indeed I can! I remember it all very vividly,' I said. 'Mother took Gideon and me, and we were so sad. My dearest brother Jem came with us to the station, and he told me to be a good brave girl, and he promised he would come and fetch me home one day–' And then I stopped and moaned as if in pain.

'What is it? Did you bite your tongue?'

'Oh, Mrs Briskett, we have to go back!' I said, trying to clamber back into the hansom cab.

'What are you doing? Don't be so tiresome, child. We've finished with the cab. We have to go and catch the train.'

'No! No! I've only just realized – that young man waiting at the gate! It might have been Jem.'

I couldn't be sure. He had been very tall, a good six foot, with the strong shoulders of a man – but of

60

course my Jem would be nineteen now, no longer a boy. I had had no contact with him – he hadn't bothered to answer a single one of my letters – though Miss Smith had indicated that some at least of my letters had been confiscated. He had played fast and loose with me, filling little Eliza's head with daydreams that he was going to marry her – but I had been his first love. Perhaps he had calculated when I was due to leave the hospital, and had come all the way from the country to meet up with me? And I had walked straight past him, not giving him a second glance!

How could I have been so cruelly ignorant? I had been boasting this very minute to Mrs Briskett about my powers of recollection, yet I had failed to recognize my dearest Jem.

'Please, please, *please* let me return,' I cried. 'It is a matter of life and death. I *have* to see that young man, the one waiting for me at the hospital gates.'

'I beg your pardon, missy? You surely cannot have followers already – you're only a little girl!'

'No, Jem is my *brother* – my foster brother. Oh, it was him, I am sure of it now. Please, Mrs Briskett, I will be a good girl for ever – I swear it – if you'll just let me go back and tell him I haven't really forgotten him.' I seized hold of her meat-red sleeve imploringly.

She shook my hand off straight away. 'You're being ridiculous, Hetty Feather. Control yourself, otherwise I shall feel obliged to have a word with the master about your impulsive behaviour. Then you will have the unusual distinction of being dismissed before you have even taken up your position,' she said. She wagged her fat finger in my face. 'This is your last chance!'

I *knew* it was my last chance. I should have dodged away from her and run like the wind all the way back to the hospital – but I hesitated fatally. I did not know my way through the bewilderingly busy streets of London, but that was no excuse. I struggled, but not determinedly enough.

Mrs Briskett marched me into the great noisy station, pushing me so hard in the small of my back that I stumbled in my clumsy boots and nearly fell to the floor. She jerked me up and hauled me up the steps into a carriage. She seemed so powerful I feared she was going to hang me by my feet from the coat-rack like a skinned rabbit – but she thrust me into a corner seat instead, sitting down so close beside me I could not budge.

'There now. Sit quiet and no more nonsense,' she said firmly.

I sat with my eyes closed, thinking back to that moment outside the hospital gates. I tried hard to bring that tall brown figure into focus. Had it *really* been my Jem? I could not be quite so sure now.

I thought back to my early childhood. I remembered Jem lifting me up in his arms, carrying me everywhere. I remembered our times in the tree-house, when he patiently played my childish pretend games. I remembered him teaching me my letters and reading to me night after night. I remembered the way he'd held me tight on that long trip in the wagon, when I was leaving home for ever. I kept my eyes shut, but I could not stop the tears seeping out from beneath my lids and rolling down my cheeks.

'There now, child,' said Mrs Briskett, her voice surprisingly soft. 'Don't you cry now. I can't abide tears. No doubt this is all queer and strange to you. You'll be feeling homesick for the hospital, but that's only natural.'

It would have been exceedingly *un*natural for me to be homesick for the hospital, but it seemed simplest to let her think that. I was amazed by her sudden change of tone. She'd been so tart and testy previously.

She patted my shoulder in a comforting way. 'I remember *my* first position, as a kitchen maid in a huge great house in the country. It was very grand, but it felt so dark and strange and gloomy compared to our cottage at home. I cried myself to sleep for weeks – and I cried in the daytime too because the cook in that kitchen was a truly terrifying creature. That temper! If you chopped the carrots unevenly or curdled the custards, my goodness, she'd start throwing the saucepans at you. The copper ones, mind, so if you didn't duck sharpish you'd be knocked unconscious.'

I blinked at Mrs Briskett in alarm.

'Don't look so fearful, Hetty Feather. That was in the bad old days. Little servant girls are treated with kid gloves now. I won't be throwing any saucepans, so long as you try hard, keep quiet and mind your p's and q's.'

I nodded, though I wasn't at all sure what my p's and q's might be. Problems and queries? I seemed to have a lot of both.

I stared out of the sooty train window as the train chuntered its way out of London. At first I saw ugly great factories spouting thick smoke, then mile after mile of terraced rows of dark little dwellings – but soon these started to thin out. Now I saw green fields and trees all about us.

'Is this the country?' I asked, wondering if I might possibly be near my dear foster home.

'No, no, we're only in Wimbleton – it's a while yet. We've a few stations to go through before we get to Kingtown. That's where Mr Buchanan has his establishment. It's a big fine house too, though not *quite* as large as Waterloo Station.' Mrs Briskett chuckled at my foolishness.

'Is Mr Buchanan a kind man?' I asked timidly, wondering if I might somehow cause offence again by my mild enquiry.

Mrs Briskett remained relaxed, undoing her bonnet strings and giving her grey hair a good scratch. 'Excuse me, dear. My best bonnet's very fine but it certainly sets me itching. Mr Buchanan? Oh, he's kind enough, though he has his little ways, of course. He's a very important writer, you know. You'll often see his articles on education in the newspapers, and there's a whole shelf full of his books in the best bookcase.'

'Might I be able to read one?' I asked.

Mrs Briskett looked at me, her head on one side. 'Can you read then, missy? Proper reading, great long sentences? I've worked with several little girls from the workhouse and they couldn't read to save their lives.'

'I've been reading fluently since I was four years old,' I said proudly. 'My brother Jem taught me.'

I shouldn't have mentioned his name. I felt my lip quivering.

'Well, I'm not sure it's suitable for you to be reading Mr Buchanan's books, though they are all written for children, I believe. It will tickle him to know you've asked – but I don't think there'll be

65

any time for book-reading, Hetty Feather. You'll be helping Sarah and me from six in the morning till ten at night.'

I didn't like the sound of this work regime at all!

'I do so love to read. Could I not read when I go to bed?' I said.

'I'm not having you ruining your eyes and wasting candles,' said Mrs Briskett. 'And if you're doing your job properly, you'll be fast asleep the moment you clamber into your bed.'

'Perhaps I could read during my recess?' I said.

'*Recess?*' said Mrs Briskett, as if she didn't understand the word.

'My playtime,' I said.

The hospital had divided our days rigidly – mostly work and very little play, so it was always particularly important.

'Playtime!' Mrs Briskett chortled. 'Oh, Hetty Feather, you're going to be the death of me! You're not a schoolgirl now. There won't be any playtime for you, my girl. It will be work work work, seven days a week, with Sunday afternoons off *if* you've been a good girl.'

I listened, chastened. It was upsetting to to discover how little I knew about everyday life. The matrons had told me they were preparing me for work, but they had only taught me to darn and scrub floors. These did not seem very useful accomplishments. An hour's darning or scrubbing had seemed interminable. How was I going to keep going all day long? I so wished I could ask Mama's advice. She had tried to prepare me. She had even taken to sending me her best recipes in her weekly letters, just in case they came in useful.

'Do you happen to know if Mr Buchanan likes game pie or beef pudding?' I asked hopefully.

'I dare say,' said Mrs Briskett. 'The master's partial to all kinds of pies and puddings.'

'Then perhaps I could make him one specially?' I suggested. 'I have a very fine recipe.'

But Mrs Briskett was laughing again. 'You – cook? Whatever will you come out with next? *I'm* the cook, missy – you're just the little maid of all work.'

I stared out of the train window again, dispirited. I didn't *want* to be the maid of all work. There were bigger houses built right up close to the railway track now, so I could spy straight into their back gardens. I saw a girl about my own age in a bright blue dress swinging in her garden. Why couldn't I be that girl, kicking up her heels without a care in the world? Why did *I* have to be the maid – and Mama too. Oh, if only we could live in a little house together – *our* home.

I gritted my teeth. I vowed there and then that I would make it come true some day. I knew I could never achieve such a thing on a meagre maid's wage. Even Mrs Brisket could not afford her own establishment. Was Miss Smith really right when she said my memoirs were unpublishable?

'Don't frown, child, it makes you look disagreeable,' said Mrs Briskett, tapping me on the forehead. 'Gather your things up now. We alight at the next station.'

I had hoped that Kingtown would look a little like the country village of my early childhood, but when we emerged from the station I saw we were in a smart town of big emporiums, very much like London itself.

I stared around curiously, startled anew by the noise and bustle, the rattle of the carriages and cabs, the clatter of the folk in the street, the blinding colour of everyone's clothes, when I was so used to the drab brown of our foundling uniform. Even Mrs Briskett's extraordinary dress seemed muted and ordinary amongst the purple and peacock-blue and emerald-green gowns and bonnets.

I whirled round, staring after this lady and that, with their great long skirts swirling about their boots, rows of flounces cascading down their behinds at the back. I had thought my own new dress bright enough, but now it seemed drab in the extreme. I caught a glimpse of myself in a shop window and saw what a scarecrow I looked, my sleeves so long they hid my hands, my skirts skimped and unadorned, my cap bizarre.

'I'm not dressed at all fashionably, am I, Mrs Briskett?' I said forlornly.

'Of course you're not, Hetty Feather. Servants don't follow fashion! You just have to look neat and serviceable,' said Mrs Briskett, but she couldn't help glancing admiringly at her own reflection.

A horse-drawn omnibus went past quickly, the wheels sending a mound of horse dung spraying up in the air, perilously near us on the pavement. Mrs Briskett jumped nimbly aside, mindful of her red skirts.

'That's a *bus*, Hetty Feather,' she announced, as if I were a toddling child.

'I know, Mrs Briskett. I journeyed in one once,' I said. 'Will we be catching a bus now?'

'No, it's only a shortish walk to the master's house. This way!'

I trotted along beside her, looking all around me. I passed several buildings with comical names: the Dog and Fox; the Wheelwright's Arms; the Three Fishes. They all had the same strange, pungent smell. I hung back, peering curiously through the coloured-glass windows.

'Come along, child. You don't want to go peeking into those dens of iniquity,' said Mrs Briskett, giving me a firm tug.

'Dens of iniquity?' I repeated.

'They are public houses. Gin palaces. Wicked places where foolish men waste their money on strong drink and weak women lose their self-respect,' she told me, twitching up her long red skirts, as if she could not bear to share the same pavement with such people.

These horrific dens looked rather cosy places to me, but I knew better than to argue. I was conscious of another even more pungent smell emanating from a huge brick building. I wrinkled my nose. It smelled worse than the hospital privies. Could it possibly be a huge public convenience? I buried my nose in the cuff of my sleeve.

'It's just the tannery, Hetty. Step lively and we'll soon be past,' said Mrs Briskett.

A tannery? When Matron Pigface Peters had been really angry, she'd say, 'I'll tan your hide for you, you cheeky varmint.' Was the tannery a grim place of correction? I shivered.

'You don't know what a tannery is, do you, Hetty Feather?'

'I know it's something dreadful,' I said.

'What? It's where they tan the cow hides to make your boot leather, silly child.'

I peered down at my stout boots. I had had no idea they were made out of dead animals. I felt my toes wiggling in disgust. There was so much I didn't know about the outside world. The hospital had always boasted that they were giving us an excellent education, but now I realized I was as ignorant as a newborn babe where most things were concerned.

I trudged along in my strips of withered cow, breathing more freely as we left the tannery and crossed a large green field. The grass felt soft and springy, so different from the hard pavement. I remembered stamping across fields barefoot when I lived in the country. I felt a pang again, thinking of Jem.

I was distracted by a beautiful grey building with a tall spire and lots of little archways and a grand gothic door. It looked very much like a palace I'd seen pictured in my precious fairy-tale book, a gift from Mama. It had a curious garden, planted with weathered grey slabs of stones instead of flowers and fruit and vegetables.

Mrs Brisckett saw me staring, and this time seemed pleased by my interest. 'Yes, Hetty, you will be attending St John's on Sunday afternoon. There's a splendid vicar there. Sarah and I find his sermons very uplifting.'

It wasn't a palace at all. It was a *church*. I had attended chapel every Sunday of my hospital life, but it had looked very different to this.

'Why does the vicar have such a strange stone garden?' I asked

'What?' Mrs Briskett stopped in her tracks. 'Are you being disrespectful, child?'

'No, ma'am.'

'Oh dear Lord, have you never heard of a grave-yard? Those stones mark the graves of all the dead people in this parish.'

'*Dead* people?' I echoed, shocked.

'Don't you know *anything*, Hetty Feather? When you die, you're put in a coffin and buried in a graveyard.'

This was the answer to a long-time puzzle of mine. From time to time children at the hospital had died. My own foster brother Saul had died from influenza. He had simply disappeared overnight. Nurse Winnie told me he'd gone up to Heaven, but I wasn't so sure. Saul had a poorly leg and couldn't walk properly. How could he have journeyed all the way up to Heaven? I'd seen his bony little back enough times when we were bathed together as small children. I knew there were no wings folded away for future use. Besides, I wasn't so sure they'd let Saul into Heaven. He'd certainly never behaved remotely like a little angel.

So *this* is what happened to dead people! They were planted in the garden like potatoes. I stared over the churchyard fearfully. I did not care for this new world at all, with dead animals on my feet and dead people lying all around me. I hoped they stayed safely underground. We had frightened each other at the hospital, telling ghost stories when we went to bed at night. In fact I had done most of the frightening – recycling tales of murder and mayhem from the *Police Gazette*. I'd thoroughly enjoyed myself whispering about poor Minnie who stalked the corridors, a knife stuck in her heart, leaving bloody footprints across the linoleum. What if the dead didn't *stay* dead? They might start growing in the night, heads bursting through the earth, then shoulders, arms, till they were free of earthly clay and could walk the world again.

'Is Mr Buchanan's house near the churchyard?' I asked fearfully.

'We have several streets to go. So come along, child, step out briskly.'

I was happy to do that, even though my arms were aching from holding my box and I was longing to set it down. A boy ran up to us, whistling loudly, carrying an immense laden basket with seeming ease. He was very small, barely my own height, but there was a knowing glint in his brown eyes, and I guessed he was about my age.

'Watcha, Mrs B!' he cried out, walking along with us.

'Mrs Briskett to you, lad,' said Mrs Briskett.

'Who's this, then?' he said, ogling me.

'Don't you be so nosy,' said Mrs Briskett.

'Is she your long-lost daughter, then?' the boy said, chuckling.

'Stop that nonsense! She's Hetty Feather, our new maid. Master thought it time Sarah and I had a little help, seeing as we're getting older and creakier. We were hoping for a big strapping lass – but look at the size of this one!'

'She's little all right,' said the boy. 'I hope you got her half price because she's only half size!'

'Talk about the pot calling the kettle black!' I said, sticking out my chin. 'You're a little runt yourself.'

'Oooh, she speaks – and with a temper to match her flaming hair!' he said, grinning at me.

I pulled a hideous face at him. He stuck out his tongue at me, waggling it vigorously.

'I'll tell Jarvis about your cheek!' Mrs Briskett threatened, but he just laughed and ran off with his huge basket, the muscles in his skinny arms popping.

'Who's that boy, Mrs Briskett?'

'Oh, take no notice, that's just Bertie, the butcher's boy,' she said. 'He delivers all the meat to our neighbourhood. He's not a bad lad, but you have to be firm with him.'

I decided I would be *very* firm. I did not care for

silly lads cheeking me. All the same, I could not help marvelling at his strength. I wondered if my own muscles would get stronger now I was out at work. I ached all over and my boots were rubbing my feet sore. I wasn't used to such long walks.

We started trudging up a hill, which made matters worse. I had to lean against a gas lamp to steady my box and get my breath back. But at last, at the summit, Mrs Briskett pointed.

'See the big white house with the stained-glass set in the door? That's your new home, Hetty Feather.'

5

It was a new, large, three-storeyed house, very grand and imposing.

'It's very fine,' I said.

'Yes, indeed it is,' said Mrs Briskett proudly.

She opened the painted iron gate and we walked up the red-tiled path. I put one foot on the snowy white steps, but Mrs Briskett tugged me back by the hem of my skirt.

'Not the *front* steps, girl! We never, ever go in the front door!'

I stared at her. How were we supposed to get into the house – climb through the windows?

'We go down the area steps at the side!' She grabbed me and steered me towards them. I glimpsed a garden at the back with a great green lawn and an ornate white iron sofa padded with cushions – but I knew enough now to realize I'd never be reclining there.

Mrs Briskett whisked me through the basement door. Suddenly I felt almost at home. The corridor was dark, painted cream and brown. I smelled familiar scents of soda and black lead. I walked into a large kitchen very similar to Mama's old domain at the hospital. I stood there, quivering, because it was so very like, with its scrubbed table and shining pans, and yet not like at all, because Mama wasn't there. There was just Mrs Briskett and a strange pale woman in a print frock, who was sitting at the table eating an enormous hunk of bread and cheese.

'Ah, here you are at last!' she said, springing up. 'Let's have a look at her!'

She seized hold of me, dragging me downwards towards the window so she could get a proper look at me. She pulled a comical face, as if she did not like what she saw. I was tempted to pull a face back, but decided I had better be cautious. She didn't look as cheery as the butcher's boy. If Mrs Briskett reminded me of meat, then this new woman was definitely potatoes. She had a pale, lumpy face with little warts here and there, like eyes in a potato. Her figure resembled a whole sackful of them. Mrs Briskett's whalebone stays kept her figure solid, but if this creature wore corsets, they had long given up attempting to contain her.

'This can't be the new maid!' she said, prodding my face with a finger, turning me left and right.

'She's just a child. She can't be old enough, Mrs B.'

'She's fourteen, believe it or not. I know she's a skinny little thing, but we'll just have to fatten her up. Her name's Hetty Feather, though she tries to call herself something outrageous. What was it again, child?'

'My name is Sapphire Battersea,' I announced firmly.

The two women started chuckling as if I'd cracked a joke.

'Oh yes, and I'm the Queen of Sheba,' said Potato Woman, bobbing a mock curtsy. 'Sapphire Battersea indeed!'

'It isn't a comical name at all. I don't know why you're laughing,' I said indignantly.

This made them laugh even more.

'Hoity-toity! Still, what can you expect with that hair? Well, we've been lumbered with a right dud, but I suppose we'll have to make the best of it. Now, listen to me, missy. I'm Sarah, the parlourmaid. Mrs Brissett rules the kitchen, and I rule the rest of the house. You're to do as we say – do you understand? Now, come and have a bite to eat and then I'll take you to meet the master.'

I sat down at the table between the two great women. I stared in astonishment at the food. It was simple enough – cold meat and cheese and bread – but the portions were huge. Mrs Brissett cut me a huge slab of meat that would have fed five foundlings for a week, and buttered me a slice of bread so thickly that my teeth made dents in the yellow when I took a bite. There was strange lumpy brown jam too. I tried a spoonful and spluttered, my eyes streaming.

'What's up, girl?'

'This jam tastes very sharp, ma'am,' I said.

'Jam? It's pickles, you ninny!'

'Don't she know what *pickles* are?' said Sarah.

'This one don't know *anything*. She's so quaint in her ways I'm starting to wonder if she's simple.'

I was too dispirited to argue with her. I had always been the cleverest in my year – well, perhaps first equal when Polly was at the hospital. I was used to thinking myself bright and sharp-witted. Even Matron Pigface Peters and Matron Stinking Bottomly remarked on my intelligence, saying I was as sharp and sly as a cartload of monkeys. But now that I was out in this new topsy-turvy world, I realized I had to start learning all over again. I did not know the simplest things. As a child I had longed to visit the pink and yellow and green foreign lands on the geography map hanging on the classroom wall, but now I realized that my own country was a totally foreign land to me. I did not know the language, the terrain, or any of the customs.

'What's the matter with you now, child?' said Mrs Briskett. 'You're not about to cry again, are you? I told you, I can't abide tears.'

'She's just wanting attention, so take no notice,' said Sarah.

Their talking about me as if I wasn't even there made the tears roll down my face. I could not be Sapphire Battersea here. I wasn't even Hetty Feather. I was simply 'child' or 'girl' or 'missy'. It made me feel very small.

'Come now, no tears,' said Mrs Briskett. 'Have a spoonful of syrup – that'll sweeten you up.'

I still hadn't eaten more than a mouthful of meat and strange pickles, but I took the proffered sticky spoonful and sucked hard. The sweetness soothed me. I licked my lips, remembering the spoonfuls of sugar Mama had once pressed upon me as secret treats.

'Aha, she likes that all right!' said Mrs Briskett. 'That's a good girl. Stop that silly crying now. You don't want to go and see the master all over tearstains – it won't give the right impression at all.'

They fussed over me considerably for this meeting with the master. Sarah took me out through the back door to the privy, and waited for me to relieve myself. The privy was very dark, and as I squatted there, something terrifying ran over my foot.

'Lord save us, stop that squealing! Whatever is it, Hetty Feather?'

'I don't know! Something touched me!'

'Don't be silly, child. It will just have been a spider – or maybe a mouse.'

'Oh! Help!' I screamed louder, and hurtled out of the privy.

The hospital's facilities had been dark and depressing, but they were in their own special building, free of wildlife. I resolved to severely limit my visits to the privy. Maybe I could commandeer a chamber pot and use it privately?

Sarah caught hold of me, dragged me into the scullery, and held a cloth under the tap. She then proceeded to wipe my face fiercely while I wriggled and squirmed.

'Hold still, child – you're covered in soot and smuts from the train!'

'I'm not a baby. I can do my own face!' I protested indignantly.

'You certainly *act* like a baby,' said Sarah. 'And whatever's happened to your hair? You're a right little mophead. Come here!'

She whipped off my cap, combed my hair with her hard fingers, and then pulled it up into a knot, securing it with a couple of pins from her own head. Then she jammed my cap back on, pulling it down to my eyebrows, and twitched at my apron to straighten it.

'There! You still look a funny little creature, but at least you're clean and tidy,' she said. She turned my shoulders to show me off to Mrs Briskett. 'Will she do, Mrs B?'

'She'll have to,' said Mrs Briskett. 'Though I still think she's going to give the master a bit of a surprise.'

Sarah led me out of the kitchen and up the stairs. I was very nervous now, but I took comfort in the fact that I had something in common with this mysterious master. We were both writers. Miss Smith had told him all about me. Maybe he wouldn't treat me like a servant at all. I wouldn't be a maid of all work – of *any* work. Maybe he would let me sit in his study and write beside him. We could have interesting conversations about the joys of composition. Then, at the end of the day, he'd read my stories and give me gentle advice and encouragement.

This idea was so beguiling that I almost believed it. I skipped up the stairs eagerly, scarcely taking in the green embossed wallpaper and the many painted portraits staring down at me, eyebrows raised.

'That's it, look lively,' said Sarah. She led me along a crimson-carpeted landing and gave my face another polish with the hem of her apron. Then she knocked on a door. We stood waiting.

'Yes, yes, yes?' muttered a male voice.

Sarah opened the door and pushed me inside. I thought she would come in with me, but there I was, all alone with this strange new master. For a few seconds I was so dazzled by his room I could scarcely take him in. I felt as if I'd stepped into fairyland. There were books everywhere: books arranged upright on shelves; books piled sideways on the floor; books balanced on desks, tables, even chairs; books lining the floor like a leather carpet. I looked around, mesmerized by beautiful big brown volumes, little crimson pocket books, fancy white vellum, gilt-embossed gift books.

The master sat at the biggest desk behind two huge piles of books. He was a surprisingly small, light man, half the size of Mrs Briskett and Sarah. He wore an odd orange fez with a tassel on his head, and a quilted crimson jacket with gold cord fastenings. I blinked at him, bewildered. He didn't *look* like a gentleman at all. He was dressed like an organ-grinder's monkey. His features were disturbingly simian too, with dark circles under his eyes and wrinkles puckering his face. I had to fight the urge to peer behind his desk to look for a long tail.

I bobbed him a curtsy instead, and arranged my face in a subservient smile. He had rescued me from the hospital, after all. I needed to show true gratitude.

He didn't smile back. He frowned at me, increasing his wrinkles alarmingly. 'Ah! You must be the new maid from the Foundling Hospital. But, oh dear, oh dear, surely you're not old enough for service, child!' he said, in a reedy voice.

I sighed a little. 'I'm fourteen, sir.'

'Good heavens! But you look so poor and puny!'

I felt he was being rather rude, but I realized it wasn't my place to take offence.

'I *am* small, sir, but I am sure I will grow a little,' I said.

'I wanted a good strong girl to help my two servants. They are maturing in years and starting to need assistance.'

'I am very good and very strong,' I said, lying on both counts.

'And you have bright red hair! No wonder Miss Smith was so determined that I take you under my roof. She wouldn't take no for an answer, and I can see why now. No one else would take on a redhead like you – it's asking for trouble. I'm not having any temper tantrums, do you hear me?'

'Certainly not, sir. I never ever give way to temper tantrums,' I declared, telling three lies in less than a minute.

'I should have asked to see you before acceding

to Miss Smith's suggestions. I only agreed because I felt obliged to support a literary colleague.'

'If you please, sir, *I* am a kind of literary colleague too,' I said. 'I have been writing my memoirs. Perhaps Miss Smith spoke of this. I've been showing her my work for years.'

'Ssh, now!' said Mr Buchanan, a finger to his thin lips. 'I am surprised. I thought the hospital would have taught you to speak only when you are spoken to! Yes, Miss Smith did indicate that you have a penchant for romancing. If you work diligently, I might be willing to give you a little guidance in the future. But we will have to see how hard you work, missy, and whether you learn our ways quickly enough. I am taking a grave risk in employing you, but I am a charitable man and keen to do my Christian duty.'

He bobbed his monkey head at me and I nodded back, though I felt my face flaming the colour of my unfortunate hair. I hadn't realized Miss Smith had had to work so hard to get him to employ me. I wasn't specially chosen as a promising candidate for his household. I seemed to be practically unemployable, judging from Mr Buchanan's blunt words. Doubtless he'd prefer any other girl from the hospital – stuttering Mary, slow Freda, even poor mad Jenny.

I did not feel like Sapphire Battersea any more.

I was Hetty Feather, despised by everyone – except my dear mama. I thought of her, longing to pour out my heart to her in a letter. But how was I to send a letter to her now? I had always given my letters to Miss Smith. Would she come and visit me here, in my strange new home? Perhaps not as regularly, if at all.

I thought hard about the vital penny stamps I needed. Mr Buchanan seemed to have run out of things to say to me, and was making dismissive waves at me with his monkey paws.

'Off you go, then, child. Be a good girl and mind Mrs Briskett and Sarah. I'm sure they will instruct you admirably.'

'If you please, sir,' I said. 'I – I will be earning a wage, will I not?'

He peered at me as if I'd said something impertinent. 'Yes, fourteen pounds a year. I negotiated with the Board of Governors at the Foundling Hospital. It's a very generous sum for an untrained child.'

'Yes, sir, certainly, sir – but will I be receiving the generous sum at the end of the week, or the month, or the quarter?' I asked anxiously.

'I cannot see that that is of any consequence to you, Hetty Feather. You do not require any money while you are under my roof. You will receive all your meals free of charge, and I believe Sarah will give you a length of material so you can sew more clothes as you require them.'

'Yes, sir, but I also require several postage stamps,' I said, desperation making me bold.

'Why do you need to correspond with anyone?' he asked.

'I need to write to my mother, sir.' I thought hard. 'I wish to tell her how lucky I am to have been taken on in your household. I want to tell her how kind you have been,' I added artfully.

He looked surprised. 'I wasn't aware that there was any contact between foundling children and their maternal parents,' he said.

'There isn't usually, sir – but my mama is especially concerned,' I said, bobbing a curtsy to seem deferential. 'I would very much like to reassure her that I have an extra special position in a lovely place.'

'I can understand your desire, child. You will be paid quarterly, like Mrs Briskett and Sarah, but I shall take it upon myself to provide you with postage stamps. Here you are, child . . .' He opened his desk drawer and gave me one.

I swallowed again. 'Please, sir – might I have some more?'

I thought this a risk. I did not want to make him angry with me.

To my great relief he chuckled. 'You're a

veritable Oliver Twist, Hetty Feather,' he declared.

I wasn't sure who Oliver Twist was, but if he encouraged Mr Buchanan to be generous, then he seemed a fine friend. Mr Buchanan counted me out six stamps, which I seized eagerly, tucking them into my apron pocket.

'Now run along and try not to take any more liberties, child,' he said, though he did not look annoyed.

So I did indeed run. Sarah was waiting for me outside the door.

'I hope you weren't giving the master any cheek, my girl,' she said.

'No indeed. We were getting along like a house on fire,' I said.

Sarah looked at me sideways. 'Don't you get above yourself, missy,' she said. 'Come along. I'll show you all over the house and give you some idea of your duties.'

She took me into the drawing room and dining room, rattling off detailed dusting and polishing and sweeping instructions. I tried to pay attention, but was constantly distracted by the splendour of the house. Every room was crowded with furniture and ornaments and assorted knick-knacks. There were two sofas, four easy chairs, and six uprights in the living room alone. Mr Buchanan only had one behind, and a puny one at that. Why would he need such an immense variety of seats? It would surely take an entire regiment of maids to dust every single item adequately. I'd no idea this was how proper folk lived their lives. I imagined what it would be like to lounge on the purple-velvet chaise longue, to dine at that polished table, to prop my feet on that intricately stitched footstool.

It grew ever more fascinating upstairs, peeping into Mr Buchanan's best bedroom, picturing him in his nightgown and cap tucked up beneath those sheets. I could not help also picturing him getting up in the night and making use of the chamber pot under the bed – though it was disconcerting to be told that it was my job to empty it.

Mr Buchanan's lavatory arrangements were a matter of total astonishment to me, because he also had his very own bathroom with a water closet. Sarah demonstrated how you pulled the chain so that everything was neatly flushed away.

'This is splendid! So why do we use that awful, scary, spidery privy in the garden when we could use this water closet?' I asked.

Sarah looked horrified. 'This is the master's private room! We could not possibly use the same facilities!'

I resolved then and there that when I was set to scrubbing the bathroom, I would quite definitely use the facilities. I pulled the chain again myself, experimenting.

'Stop messing about, Hetty. This isn't a game. Come along now.'

She showed me the best guest bedroom and then the second-best guest bedroom – both seemed incredibly grand to me, especially the beds themselves. I was used to the narrow beds in the hospital. These ones were enormous. I stroked the counterpanes. They felt incredibly soft and silky. Perhaps I could occasionally sneak into one of these guest bedrooms and have a little lie-down?

'Does Mr Buchanan often have guests sleeping in these rooms?' I asked.

'Rarely. The master isn't one for entertaining. He's too engrossed in his work,' said Sarah, leading me up yet another flight of stairs. These had brown linoleum instead of carpet, and there were no paintings looking down at me from the walls.

'These are the attic rooms,' said Sarah. 'You will dust and sweep and polish here too, but you don't need to be quite so particular, because they are only *our* rooms.'

Sarah's room was very small compared to Mr Buchanan's, and the ceiling sloped sharply overhead. Her bed was narrow, her washstand basic, her chest small, with only three drawers. There was no fireplace there so it must be icy cold in winter. She had no ornaments whatsoever – just a brush and comb on her washstand, a Bible by her bed, and one small painting hanging on the wall. It was a portrait of a large lady, not very well executed. She looked like a stiff puppet, not a real woman at all. But Sarah looked up at her and gently touched her cheek, as if she were a real and lovely lady. I knew that gesture, that feeling.

'She is your mother!' I said.

'Yes, dear Mother. My cousin Luke painted her likeness. It's very good, isn't it?'

I thought it very *bad* but for once I knew how to behave. 'Yes, it is. Your mother looks a very fine lady,' I said. 'Does she live far away? Do you get to see her often?'

Sarah's potato face flushed. She shook her head sadly. 'Dear Mother passed away many years ago,' she said, shaking her head. 'I still miss her so much.'

'Oh, Sarah, I'm so sorry,' I whispered.

A sudden new fear clutched at my chest. How would I ever stand it if *my* mama died? I had only known she was my mother for such a cruelly brief time. I could not bear it if she were snatched away from me.

It was the one terrible disadvantage of loving

someone. You couldn't bear the idea of being without them. I reckoned up the people I had loved during my fourteen years. I loved Mama most of all, of course. She shone like the sun in my life – but there were stars too. I had loved Nurse Winnie a little, and my dearest friend Polly a great deal. I had cared for young Eliza, and thought wistfully about my whole foster family. I loved them all – though of course Jem was the one I'd truly worshipped and adored.

I thought again about the man waiting outside the hospital. I'd read about the magical method of photography. I wished I had a photograph of that young man so that I could pore over his image and see if he could really be my own dear Jem. I fingered the stamps inside my apron pocket . . .

'Hetty Feather! Don't daydream, girl. Come, I will show you Mrs B's bedroom.'

Mrs Briskett's bedroom was twice the size, with a large bed. A vast pair of bloomers sprawled on the covers, legs akimbo. I felt my mouth twitching, and Sarah herself sniggered, but then straightened her face, looking guilty. Mrs Briskett did not have a portrait of her mama. She had several coloured lithographs of great pink pigs, black-and-white cows, huge woolly sheep and assorted hens and ducks. She seemed to have deliberately surrounded herself with the raw materials of her trade. I wondered if she lay on her big bed looking at these animals by candlelight, plotting massive roasts and stews.

There was only one more room upstairs – a little inconsequential garret with the ceiling sloping severely. I thought it would be *my* room, but it was overly occupied already, stuffed full to bursting with trunks and old chairs and pictures in frames, and box after box of old ornaments and curtains and cushions and whatnots.

'This is the box room, the only room in the house you don't have to bother with,' said Sarah.

'Am I to sleep here?' I asked, in a small voice.

'Of course not, you ninny. I know you're tiny, but I think we'd have difficulty bedding down even a little mouse in here,' said Sarah.

'So where *am* I to sleep?' I said, bewildered, because we'd inspected every single room in the house.

Sarah put her head on one side, looking at me. 'Well . . . perhaps if you curled up very small, you could sleep on the privy floor?'

'*What?*'

Her eyes were twinkling, and as I exclaimed in abject horror, she burst out laughing. 'Oh, Hetty, your face! Dear Lord, you thought I was serious!'

she chortled, clutching her sides and heaving with laughter.

I did not feel inclined to join in. And when she told me where I was in fact to sleep, it didn't seem an especially superior alternative. I was to go to bed in the scullery! This was a little dark room off the kitchen. It had a big lead sink, a wooden draining board, a mangle, hooks for all the assorted dusters, mops, brooms and brushes, and several dark depressing cupboards full of matches and candles and cakes of coal-tar soap, Nixey's Black Lead and Japan lustre shoe-blacking. Sadly, there was no food. Mrs Briskett kept all her edible supplies in the larder, and she locked it up each night with the key she kept round her neck.

There was a small fold-up bed in the last cupboard, and Sarah pulled this out with a flourish. 'There we are, Hetty. Don't look such a sour-puss. See, you have a proper bed, and you can use the sink to wash in.'

I hoped she was joking again, but she was serious this time. I felt my eyes filling with tears.

'Lord help us, what's the matter now?' said Mrs Briskett, coming to inspect my 'bedchamber'.

'I don't want to sleep in the scullery! It's like the punishment room!' I sobbed. 'I haven't done anything wrong yet!'

'Hey, hey, don't be so dramatic. I jolly well hope you *don't* do anything wrong. Little maids have to be as good as gold or else they get dismissed! Sleeping in the scullery isn't a punishment, silly. I slept in the scullery when I had my first job as a kitchen maid,' she said. 'It was practically the self-same bed.'

I looked at her. 'But – but you wouldn't fit it,' I said, between sobs.

Sarah burst out laughing again. I realized I had not been tactful.

'I was a slip of a girl then, missy, not much bigger than you,' said Mrs Briskett, looking offended.

'I am sorry – I didn't mean . . .' I stammered. It was impossible to imagine Mrs Briskett as a slip of a girl. I was sure that she was vast even as a babe in arms. I pictured her in meat-red swaddling clothes, at least half the size of her poor mama . . . I found I was laughing too, but I pretended my snorts were still sobs.

'Now, now, calm down, child, do. I'm going to start baking or we'll have no tea – and Mr Buchanan will start complaining bitterly if he has to do without his cake. You come and sift the flour for me, Hetty, while I change out of my good clothes,' said Mrs Briskett. 'Cheer up, dearie – you know I can't abide tears.'

I did cheer up considerably that afternoon. I had worked with dear Mama in the hospital kitchens, and was quick and capable. I sifted flour, I cut up butter, I cracked open eggs and whisked them to a froth. I measured currants and cherries and walnuts, taking a sly nibble every now and then, while Mrs Briskett was staring at the stove and Sarah's head was bent over her mending.

She set me to darning an old torn nightshirt when I had finished helping with the baking. It seemed strange to hold the nightshirt in my lap, knowing that it had covered Mr Buchanan's bony body, but I darned the worn patch obediently. I had spent nine years darning at the hospital, so it was second nature to me now.

'My, Hetty Feather, that's even neater than I can manage!' said Sarah, peering at the patch. 'Look, Mrs B, you can hardly see the stitches.'

'Well done, dearie,' said Mrs Briskett, patting me on the back with a floury hand.

I felt like bursting into tears again. No one had ever praised me at the hospital.

When Mrs Briskett had made her currant cake and her walnut cake, she laid neat slabs out on a fancy plate, and set a tea tray with a pot of tea, a little jug of milk, a dainty sugar bowl, a pretty cup and saucer. Sarah picked up the tray – and then handed it over to me.

'Why don't you save my legs? You go and serve the master, Hetty,' she said.

She lent me her best cap and fancy white apron with frills, though the cap came down past my eyebrows and the apron hem swept the floor. Sarah and Mrs Briskett laughed heartily at this spectacle, but in a kindly fashion.

I wasn't sure *how* to serve the tea and cake, so Mrs Briskett sat at the kitchen table, frowning and scribbling with her hand, pretending to be the master, while Sarah mimed serving 'him' with his tea and cake, while I watched carefully.

Then Sarah gave me the real tray and sent me on my way. The tray was wooden, covered with a lacy cloth, and heavy. It was a struggle for me to carry it steadily, and as I started up the stairs the teacup rattled on its saucer and the milk slopped out of its jug, but I managed to get all the way up to Mr Buchanan's study without serious incident.

I knew I had to knock on the door before entering, but didn't see how I could do so without growing a third useful hand straight out of my chest. I tried putting my leg right up under the tray to balance it for a second, but it tipped precariously. I was determined to do this properly. I set the tray down on the floor, tapped twice on the door, and when the master eventually murmured something, I opened the door a crack, bent down, hauled the tray upright, edged my bottom through the door, and ended up successfully inside the study.

'I've got your tea and cake, Master,' I said.

'Mm,' he replied absent-mindedly, still writing. He made vague waving gestures with his other hand, indicating that I should set down the tray and serve him. I peered around the room but could not spot a single bare surface for my tray. In the end I had to balance it across two piles of books, but it seemed steady enough.

I served his tea on a tiny corner of his desk and offered him the plate of sliced cake. His hand hovered, first over the walnut, then the currant.

'Which is best, Hetty Feather?' he asked.

'They're both delicious, sir – and I should know because I helped make them,' I said proudly. 'Why don't you take a slice of each?'

He took two slabs – the biggest – and proceeded to eat them, taking alternate bites of each. He made the waving gesture again, this time dismissively.

'Will that be all, sir?' I asked, and he nodded, his mouth full of cake.

I was a little disappointed. I wanted him to say,

'Well done, Hetty. Here's two more postage stamps as a reward – and take this book of fairy stories to read tonight – and here's a blank manuscript book and a fresh quill pen for your memoirs.' But maybe this was overly optimistic. I made do with his grunt, and bobbed out of the room.

When I got down to the kitchen, Sarah patted me on the back and Mrs Briskett cut me my own slice of cake. They were starting to act more like mothers than matrons.

When I trundled my meagre bed out of its cupboard that night, I sat up and wrote a letter to Mama by candlelight. I had helped myself to a good supply of paper and envelopes from the hospital.

Do not worry about me, dearest Mama. I will be a good, obedient little servant girl for a while. My new master, Mr Buchanan, is a strange man rather like a monkey, but he has been quite kind to me, I suppose. Mrs Briskett and Sarah have sharp tongues and mock me at times, but they mostly mean well. I am as happy as I can be WITHOUT YOU.

I signed my name with many kisses, and then tucked my letter into an envelope and stuck on my stamp. Then I started a new letter.

Dearest Gideon,

I can't say I LIKE being a servant, but I suppose it's not as bad as I feared. I do so hope that you will find being a soldier is not so bad either. At least you will wear a splendid uniform. Mine is very plain – but then so am I.

Keep well, dearest brother. Remember I am always

Your loving sister,
Hetty

Mrs Briskett had only given me a stub of candle, and it was already flickering – but I reached for another sheet of my precious paper. Because I knew I only had a few minutes before total darkness, I wrote hastily, without time to compose my words.

Dear Jem,

Was it you at the hospital gates???

I am so sorry we did not get time to speak.

But you can write to me at this address. I am a maid here, and it is quite a good house and the people are tolerably kind but I do not think I am cut out to be a servant.

With affection,

Your one-time sister,

Hetty Feather

P.S. Eliza is doing well at the hospital. She is a

good kind child and rarely gets into trouble –
unlike me. She says you are going to marry her
one day. I hope you will be very happy.

I remembered the address accurately enough, and applied another postage stamp to the envelope. My candle guttered, and then extinguished itself. I lay down on my hard little bed. There was a dank smell of soapsuds and stale cooking, so I had to cover my nose with my sheets. It was so dark I could not see my hand before my face, and alarmingly quiet too. I was used to sleeping in a large room with scores of other girls. I was accustomed to snores and sighs all night long. I lay tensely, feeling terribly alone. I tried to picture Mrs Briskett and Sarah up at the top of the house, and Mr Buchanan somewhere in the middle, but they seemed very far away.

I thought of the young man in brown and wondered if he really was Jem. If so, had he gone all the way home to the cottage now? I thought enviously of my foster family, all crammed together under that thatched roof.

Then, as always, I thought of dear Mama, tucked up in her faraway home by the sea. I whispered to her in the night . . . and after a while she seemed to whisper back to me:

Night-night, Hetty, my love. You've been a good

girl and tried hard, and I'm proud of you. I miss you so much, my darling, but don't worry. We'll be together again some day.

'Some day *soon*,' I murmured, and at last I fell asleep.

6

'**G**et up, get up, you lazy little girl!'

It was Mrs Briskett, shaking me so hard I had to cling to the sides of my bed, in danger of tumbling to the floor.

'I said you had to be up at six to light the kitchen fire. It's nearly half past now, and I can't start cooking till the stove heats up. We're going to be all behind like a sheep's tail, and I can't bear that! Get up, Hetty Feather!'

I got up and barely sat down again the whole day long. I didn't have time to wash myself properly – just a quick dab. I didn't even brush my hair, I just crammed my cap on top. I scarcely had time to rush to the terrible outside privy.

I was put in a corner to clean Mr Buchanan's boots while Mrs Briskett genuflected in front of the kitchen range. She tried to show me what to do, but it was so complicated and temperamental I couldn't get the hang of it at all. I was sent off in disgrace to sweep and clean the downstairs grates. Then I was given a brush and cloth and polish, to clean the doorstep and brasses. I scrubbed my fingers raw trying to impress, but Sarah was in a bad mood too and sniffed at my efforts. Next I had to haul a huge jug of hot water up the stairs to set on Mr Buchanan's washstand. He was sitting up in his bed, wearing a nightcap instead of a fez, but looking more monkey-like than ever. The sleeves of his nightgown rumpled up, showing excessively hairy thin arms. Maybe that long tail was lurking under the bedcovers after all.

I had to serve him a cup of tea, and then scurry back downstairs to down a cup myself. The kitchen was warm now, and something smelling delicious was sizzling in the pan. I sniffed at it hopefully, suddenly remembering the pigs we kept long ago in my country foster home.

'Don't you go making big eyes at me, Hetty Feather,' Mrs Briskett snapped. 'Lazy girls go without their breakfast.' But she gave me a rasher of wondrous bacon, and a sausage too. I wished I had time to savour them properly, but I had to run to the dining room to serve Mr Buchanan *his* breakfast.

I would have thought a tray would suffice for one gentleman, but oh dear, no. We had to lay a white damask cloth over the table, with the fold exactly in the middle. Sarah fussed over a centrepiece of flowers and ferns, and then set me laying two small knives, two small forks, a dessertspoon, a dish, a plate, and an intricately folded table napkin before Mr Buchanan's chair. I had to refold the wretched napkin three times, and even rearrange the cutlery, because I didn't have the bowls of the spoon on the table and the prongs of the fork upwards. As if it mattered!

Then there was fuss fuss fuss with the salt cellar and pepper box and mustard pot, and the loaf of bread had to be precise upon its platter, and the butter – oh dear goodness, the butter had to be fashioned into a little rose shape with a pair of pats.

We set it all up, with covered hot-water dishes containing enough rashers, sausages, tomatoes and mushrooms to feed an army, plus two boiled eggs in a napkin and a rack of toast. I saw Mr Buchanan left his toast, two rashers, a sausage and several mushrooms when I went to clear the table, and I crammed them all into my mouth quick to keep me going.

I was sent upstairs to clean Mrs Briskett's and Sarah's rooms, and then I did the master's bedroom. He'd used his chamber pot even though he had his splendid water closet a few steps across the landing. I tried out the water closet for myself while I was stuck inside cleaning it. I clung hard to the edge of the seat just in case I was sucked down the hole by a sudden spurt of water – it still seemed eerily mysterious to me.

He'd left his bed for me to strip and make up. Thank goodness the beds in the guest rooms were still pristine, though I had to dust and sweep these rooms too. I was ready to crawl into bed myself, but Mrs Briskett was calling for me, needing me down in the kitchen to peel the potatoes and carrots and chop the cabbage. I chopped my finger too and had to suck it hard to stop it bleeding.

Then I had to see to the fires in the dining room and living room while Sarah flapped around with a duster. While Mr Buchanan was having his lunch, Sarah let me into his study to stoke his own fire, but I wasn't allowed to touch anything else. Sarah dusted here with elaborate care, picking up books and papers reverently and replacing them precisely.

I hoped I might get time to breathe after *my* lunch, and maybe do a bit more fancy darning so that Sarah and Mrs Briskett would marvel at me again – but any chance of that vanished when I spilled a whole pitcher of milk trying to carry it out of the larder with greasy hands. Mrs Briskett smacked me hard about the head and set me to scrubbing the entire floor.

'But my hands are all sore already, Mrs B, and my finger's actually bleeding – look!' I said, thrusting it at her.

'And my heart's bleeding listening to your endless excuses. And don't you go calling me Mrs B: it's
Mrs *Briskett*. Let's have a little respect around
here. Get going with that scrubbing brush. Milk's
the very devil when it spills. I'm not having my
kitchen reeking like a dairy. Go to it!'

I started scrubbing, squatting down and wiping
the floor cautiously, because my hands were really
throbbing.

'Not like that! Get down on your knees and put
some elbow grease into it, or you'll go without any
supper!' she commanded.

How could I have ever thought she was like a
mother! She was even worse than Matron Pigface
Peters and Matron Stinking Bottomly. I scrubbed
viciously, cursing Mrs Briskett under my breath at
every stroke, imagining the flagstones were her big
meaty face. I put such effort into it that my behind
waggled in the air.

'My, that's a very tempting sight!' said a loud
Cockney voice. It was Bertie the butcher's boy,
bringing us a basket of meat.

'Less of your cheek, you,' said Mrs Briskett.
'Now, let's have a look at that minced beef. I hope
it's not all gristle and bone – I asked for prime
mince.'

'It's the finest chopped-up backside of bovine,

109

Mrs B,' said Bertie. 'Here, have a sniff, it's lovely and fresh.' He offered her a paper of meat as if it were a bunch of roses. She laughed and swatted his hand away, not seeming to mind at all when *he* called her Mrs B.

I muttered miserably to myself that it wasn't fair.

'What's that you're saying, Beautiful?' said the boy.

He squatted down beside me. 'Oh dear, what a face! You must have been a bad girl to be set to scrubbing at this hour! Remember, cleanliness is next to Godliness – so you and the kitchen floor will be wafting around the heavenly clouds one day.'

'One day *soon*, I expect,' I said. 'When I faint from loss of blood, seeing as I have an open wound.' I sucked my poor hacked finger.

'Let's have a look.' Bertie held my grubby hand surprisingly gently and squinted at my finger. 'Call that a cut! Look at mine!'

He spread his left hand out in front of my eyes, fanning his fingers – and I saw that the tops of three of them were entirely missing, not even a vestige of a nail left. He laughed when I gasped.

'Now they really *did* bleed when I chopped the tips off. Old Jarvis minced them up lovely and everyone's cottage pie tasted *real* good that day, with all my prime boy-meat!' He fell about laughing at my face. But three missing fingers were no joke.

'You chopped them right *off*?'

'I'm learning the trade, see. I got a great side of beef, hung onto it tight to stop it rolling around, raised my chopper – down it goes with a great *whack* . . . only my aim was a bit skewed.'

'How awful!'

'No it ain't – not when you're into butchery. My master, old Jarvis, he's got three whole fingers missing – and Samuel and Sidney, his older lads, they've lost one apiece. It's only to be expected. But when you've done it once, it don't half sharpen your aim for the future!'

'I don't think I should care to be a butcher's boy.'

'Yes, well, when I left the workhouse they said to me, Bertie, my boy, do you want to go into Parliament, or do you fancy a career in the city, or maybe you'd like to set yourself up as a gentleman farmer – but do you know something, Beautiful, those jobs didn't appeal to me. Butchery, that's what I thought.'

I felt myself blushing. 'You were in the work-house?' I exclaimed.

'Yes, and I ain't ashamed of it, either. Weren't my fault my ma ended up there, and I dare say it weren't her fault either, so don't you go looking down on me.'

'Oh, I'm *not*!' I glanced over to see if Mrs

Briskett and Sarah were listening, but they were chatting together. Mrs Briskett was busy setting the pieces of meat out on plates and covering them with mesh domes while Sarah started sewing the hem of a tablecloth.

'My mama was in the workhouse too,' I said.

'So you know what it's like,' said Bernie.

'Well, I was brought up in the Foundling Hospital.'

He shook his head. 'A foundling and an orphan. Well, we're a matching pair, ain't we?'

'An orphan? So your mother died?'

'Yup, when I was about ten.'

'You poor thing,' I said.

'Well, I didn't truly know her, did I? We were kept separate, see. We met up on Christmas Day, and that was a rum time, and it meant the world to all of us – but we still had to get through the three hundred and sixty-four other days.'

'So where do you live now, Bertie?'

'I live at the shop – where else? I've got me nice little bed under the counter.' He said it cheerily enough, but I imagined lying all night in the dark with meat dripping bloodily all around me. Perhaps I was more fortunate than I realized, living in the scullery.

'When's your afternoon off, then, Beautiful?' Bertie asked.

'I don't think I get one.'

'Oh, I'll make sure of that. You watch.' He sidled up to Mrs Briskett. He looked smaller than ever beside her huge bulk. 'Like them lovely steaks, Mrs B? They were supposed to be going up to Letchworth Manor, but I swapped them round because you're my favourite customer, and a lady line you appreciates quality.'

'Hark at the lad! He's got the patter, all right, even though he's such a little squirt,' said Mrs Briskett, chuckling.

'You've got an extra kidney too – did you see?'

'What are you after, lad? A slice of my steak-and-kidney pie?'

'Well, *now* you're tempting me! But I was just wondering if I could take your little maid here off your hands on Sunday, seeing as she's a bit down in the dumps.'

'No wonder – she's a careless girl, and needs to be taught a lesson. And on Sunday she'll be coming to church along with us.'

'Of course she will, but what about *after* church? Can't you spare her for an hour or two? I'll bring her back rosy-cheeked in time for supper – how about that?'

'How about you clear off out of my kitchen and stop distracting my little maid,' said Mrs Briskett – but she didn't say no.

Bertie winked at me. 'See you Sunday, then, Beautiful. I'll come calling,' he mouthed.

I shrugged. I wasn't sure I wanted to go off gallivanting with this cheeky Cockney lad, Bertie. He was clearly mocking me, calling me Beautiful. He had obviously forgotten my name.

But when he clattered over, swinging his basket, he called, 'Bye-bye, then, Mrs B. Bye-bye, Sarah Sew-a-fine-seam. And bye-bye, Miss Hetty Feather.'

Mrs Briskett and Sarah tittered.

'My, you're a dark one, Hetty, setting your cap at Jarvis's boy already!' said Mrs Briskett. 'I told you, I don't want you to have no followers. It just causes trouble – and you're not old enough anyway.'

'I don't *want* any followers,' I said, but I found I was a little cheered all the same. I still had miles of stone flags to scrub, and my cut finger was throbbing more sorely than ever, but it didn't seem such a terrible task any more. When I was done at long last, Mrs Briskett fried me a slice of yesterday's currant cake in butter, dusted it with sugar and served it to me on a plate. It tasted truly delicious.

I was set to more work straight afterwards, running up and down stairs tending the fires and fetching hot water. Then Mrs Briskett got it into her head that her saucepans weren't quite clean, and I had to boil them all for half an hour on the range, then attack the enamel pans with a rag and Monkey Brand. It nearly broke my heart when she dirtied them all again cooking Mr Buchanan's dinner.

I was so tired and my hand throbbed so badly I could barely write that night, even though Mrs Briskett gave me another stub of candle. I fancied starting a made-up story, however, if Miss Smith thought my memoirs unpublishable. I picked up my notebook and wrote:

Lady Sapphire was a very kind and liberal mistress. If the cook spilled milk in the kitchen, Lady Sapphire commanded her pet cats to come and lick it up forthwith, a task they enjoyed exceedingly. When the saucepans became just a little bit dirty, Lady Sapphire gave them all away to grateful poor folk and bought an entire fresh set because she didn't want to work her servants unnecessarily hard as they were preparing a special dinner that night. Mr Jarvis the Master Butcher was invited, together with his lady wife, and for a special treat, his loyal but occasionally cheeky apprentice boy, young Bertie. He was very honoured, and bowed and scraped to Lady Sapphire excessively . . .

I fell asleep pondering the number of Cs and Ss

in excessively. I woke up with a crick in my neck and the candle burned out, and then barely slept the rest of the night because I was so worried that I wouldn't be up at six to light the wretched kitchen range.

I was so tired I spent the next day yawning my head off, and when I sat down for my bacon breakfast, I fell fast asleep at the table. But when Sarah went to sort the post I woke up with a start, because there was not one but two letters for *me*!

I knew there would not be a letter back from Gideon. He very probably had not been given *my* letter, and at the Foundling Hospital we were only allowed to reply on Sunday afternoons. But I had a letter back from dear Mama!

My own Hetty,

I am so glad and releeved you have a good posishon, deary, and that theyre being quite kind and sweet to my own gurl. I daresay you will find the work hard, but you're a sensible quik lerner and it makes my hert swell with pride to think of my gurl out in the world, erning her own living. How I wish I culd see you and give you a grate big hug.

All love from your very very afectshonit mother.

P.S. Excuse speling, it's my week point.

116

I held Mama's letter to my chest, I rubbed it against my cheek, I ran my finger along every line, oblivious to Mrs Briskett and Sarah.

'Ah, bless the child,' said Sarah, sniffing. 'How I wish my own dear mama were here to write to me.' She wiped her eyes with the corner of her apron.

'Now don't *you* start, Sarah, you'll set me off – you know I turn to jelly at the sight of tears,' said Mrs Briskett. 'Who's your other letter from, Hetty?'

'I don't know, Mrs Briskett,' I said – although there was something faintly familiar about the firm bold print. I saw the postmark and gave a little gasp. I opened it up, and my eyes skimmed down the page to the signature at the bottom: *Your everloving Jem.*

'Oh, my Lord!'

'Well?' said Mrs Briskett.

'It's from – from my foster brother!' I said. 'Do you not remember the young man waiting outside the hospital, Mrs Briskett? I didn't recognize him at first, but it was really him! Oh, if only I had stopped for a few words! I did beg you, remember?'

'You don't consort with family and friends when you're off to start in your first position, Hetty Feather,' said Mrs Briskett. 'Now, put your letters away till later, and go and help Sarah turn out the bedrooms – and no dawdling neither, because there's the potatoes and the carrots to peel, and two pounds of peas to pod, *and* all the Bramleys for my apple pie. He's very fond of my apple pie, is the master.'

I had to tuck Jem's letter away under my apron, where it crackled unread all the long morning. I had to wait until after luncheon. Mrs Briskett found she was running short of sugar and needed cloves for her apple pie, so she sent me off to Dedman's, the grocer's.

'Just find your way back into town and it's the big shop on the corner. You can't miss it,' she said. 'Mind you hurry back though, missy. No daydreaming!'

She wound a shawl round me and watched me from the back door. I ran up the area steps and set off smartly, swinging my arms in a business-like fashion.

'You're going the wrong way, Hetty Feather! Feather*brain*, that's what you are! Go *left* for the town. Dear Lord, what shall I do with you?'

I turned on my heel and walked back the other way, feeling foolish. Mrs Briskett watched me, shaking her head. I hurried to get out of her sight. It felt so very odd to be out alone after all those years of being cooped up in the hospital. It reminded me of the time I ran away, when Queen Victoria had her Golden Jubilee. I supposed I could

run away now. Run away where though? Run away
. . . home?

I took the unread letter from under my apron,
leaned against the park railings, and read it
through.

Dear Hetty,

*Yes, it WAS me at the hospital gates. I could
not believe it when you walked straight past me.
I had pictured our meeting for so long and I had
always seen us running into each other's arms. I
was so dumbfounded I couldn't move. I just
stood there dithering until it was too late. I
wondered if you felt too grand to speak to me
now, walking along with the lady in her red town
gown. I feared you had forgotten me altogether,
though you swore you'd remember me for ever!*

*When Mother received notification from the
hospital, saying you were leaving to go into
service on 14th May, I decided I would come all
the way to London to wish you well. I so hoped we
might be able to spend a little time together. I've
longed to know how you are faring. You looked
quite the grown-up young lady, but still my little
Hetty too.*

*Do you not remember those rare times we had
together when you were little? Do you remember
our secret squirrel tree? We had so many dear*

funny little games. They were such happy times.

Please write and tell me how you are doing, and reassure me that you still keep a place in your heart for

Your affectionate foster brother,

Jem

I seemed to have been holding my breath the whole time I was reading the letter. I breathed out, my head throbbing, having to cling to the railings to stay upright.

Your *affectionate* brother Jem. My own dear Jem, the sweet boy who had once meant all the world to me. But he still hadn't mentioned Eliza, though I had specifically quizzed him in my letter. Had he not made *her* his own special darling after I'd left home? He'd filled her little head with nonsense too – *our* nonsense, all my own imaginary games.

It had felt like such a betrayal that I'd resolved never to think of Jem again. I thought he must long ago have forgotten me – and yet he had journeyed all the way from the country to see me. He must have got up before dawn, travelling on the milk train, and then somehow found his way through the busy streets of London to the hospital. He had waited there. I had walked straight past.

Oh Lordy, how could I have been so stupid? I was

the one standing dithering now, wondering what to do. I could beg on the streets until I had enough for the train fare, and then rush back home to my dear Jem . . . But what then? I still had to earn my living. My foster sisters Rosie and Big Eliza had had to go into service. If I walked out of my position with Mr Buchanan, I would never get a character reference. And what would Mama say to that?

I sighed and leaned against the park railings – and then shrieked when a very wet tongue licked the back of my hand through the bars. I whirled round, shrieking, and waved my arms in fear and horror at the huge slavering beast attempting to swallow my hand for breakfast. Was it a small bear? A black panther? A wolf?

'Help! Help!' I shrieked.

'Hey, hey, don't take fright! Tommy wouldn't hurt a flea, little miss,' an old man cried.

'Are you sure?' I said, still backing away rapidly and wiping my assaulted hand. 'What kind of an animal is it?'

The old man looked at me as if I were completely mad. ' 'Tis only a Labrador, miss.'

When I failed to look reassured he shook his head sorrowfully. 'A *dog*, miss,' he said, in the clear loud tone you'd use for a lunatic.

Oh dear, a dog! I could not believe I had reacted so ridiculously. I had seen pictures of dogs in books.

I remembered Rover in one of the elementary readers in the Infants at the hospital, but Rover had been a scrappy little creature, not a great fiend with enormous jaws. Had there not been dogs on the farm, then? I thought hard and remembered something running like the wind, barking at all the sheep. I had run too, rolling around in the grass, oblivious to his snapping jaws. What was the matter with me? How had I been fearless at four when I was so cowed now, barely able to say boo to a goose?

I reached through the park railings and very gingerly patted Tommy's big black head. He panted happily, drooling in delight. 'Good boy,' I murmured faintly.

Then I tucked Jem's letter away beside Mama's, bade the old man goodbye, and set off into town. It still felt as if I were trekking through steamy jungles, trudging over arid deserts, wading through crocodile-infested rivers as I made my way down the quiet suburban streets. I wondered if I'd ever get used to life outside the hospital. I didn't seem to have any sense of direction whatsoever, and had to ask twice before I found my way to the main shops – and then ask a third time before I got to Dedman's, the luxury grocer's.

This was such a delightful emporium that I forgot all my fear and trepidation and tiptoed around the dark interior, gazing in awe at the shining jars of jam and fruit and pickles, the sugar loaves, the great wheels of cheese, the glazed sides of bacon, the huge sacks of rice and sultanas and prunes. A little boy had run away from his nurse-maid and was kneeling in front of these sacks, delightedly scooping up great handfuls of dried fruit. I had to clench my fists to stop myself joining him. I remembered stealing just two or three sultanas when I was helping in the hospital kitchen – and the stinging punishment inflicted by Matron Stinking Bottomly when she caught me red-handed and sticky-fingered.

'How can I help you, young missy?' said a tall man with a drooping moustache and a white apron right down to his boots.

I murmured a request for cloves and sugar, and he weighed them out and handed them to me in a brown paper parcel. 'That'll be sixpence halfpenny, please.'

I stared at him. Of course, I had to pay for them – but I didn't have any money! I felt myself blushing crimson. The tall man stroked his moustache expectantly while I shifted from one foot to the other. Was I going to have to trail home and ask for the money from Mrs Briskett and then come all the way back again?

'Which account shall I charge, missy?' the man

asked.

'Oh! Well, I work for a Mr Buchanan—'

'Then it'll be Mrs Briskett's account,' he said, nodding his head as if I were a very lucky girl. 'Mrs Briskett will train you up nicely. She's an excellent woman. As indeed is Miss Sarah. She's a very fine parlourmaid. You tell her I'm looking forward to seeing her at our Sunday evening soiree.'

Yes, sir,' I said, and backed out of the shop, after one more longing glance at the dried fruit sacks.

Good Lord, was Sarah *courting*? And if so, why was it right for her to see the moustache man on a Sunday, and wrong for me to see Bertie the butcher's boy? Not that I *wanted* to go for a stroll with Bertie. I was not interested in boys.

I felt the bib of my apron so that my letters crackled inside. What about Jem? Was I 'interested' in him? I thought back yet again to those moments at the hospital gates. I wished I could step back in time and have another go at leaving the hospital.

Yes, I'm coming out the gates with Mrs Briskett in her meaty red attire, and there is this tall, good-looking young man in rustic corduroy. Our eyes meet.

'Oh my goodness, it's Jem! My dear long-lost brother Jem!' I say, so that Mrs Briskett cannot possibly object.

'My dear little Hetty, I knew you wouldn't forget

me,' Jem breathes.

'Bless you, dearies,' says Mrs Briskett. 'Here, let us repair to a tea room – we can all have a bite to eat, and you two can catch up with each other, and then . . . and then . . .'

And then indeed! As if Mrs Briskett would permit such a meeting in any case. I resolved to write a longer, more regretful letter to Jem that night – and one to Mama too, of course.

I actually managed to find my way home without having to ask for directions even once. Tommy was still careering around the park, the old man throwing sticks for him. The dog bounded over in my direction, and I couldn't help prickling with alarm all over again, but I managed to wave at him nonchalantly enough.

I reached Mr Buchanan's house feeling reasonably proud of myself, but Mrs Briskett was frowning.

'Dear goodness, girl, did you travel to Timbuktu for the cloves and sugar? I've had my pastry ready for hours!'

'Don't be cross with me, Mrs Briskett,' I said. 'Oh, isn't Dedman's a wondrous shop!'

'What's that you've got all over your dress, young lady?' Sarah asked, brushing at me. I was covered with rust from leaning against the park railings. 'Dear goodness, can't you keep clean for two minutes? You've got to wear that dress till you make yourself another one, so think on and try to keep it spotless.'

'Mr Dedman sent you a special message, Sarah,' I said softly, not sure she'd want Mrs Briskett to overhear.

Mrs Briskett snorted all the same. 'Mr *Dedman* sent her a message?' she said. 'I very much doubt it, seeing as, true to his name, he's been a dead man these past ten years.'

'Well, *someone* sent you a message. A tall man with a funny moustache. He said he thought you an excellent woman and was looking forward to seeing you at your Sunday soiree.'

Mrs Briskett snorted so loudly this time that stuff came out of her nose and she had to grab her pocket handkerchief and mop it up hastily.

'Really, Mrs B,' said Sarah, looking offended. 'I hope you're not laughing at me.'

'Perhaps you'll hear a message from a *real* dead man!' said Mrs Briskett, tapping Sarah over the knuckles with her wooden spoon.

'Do not mock things you don't understand,' said Sarah huffily, and swept from the room.

'Hoity-toity!' Mrs Briskett called after her, but she looked a little worried now. 'Dear Lord, that girl needs her head examined. I don't hold with that sort of caper. It's not right, and no one can convince me otherwise.'

'What sort of caper? What did the message mean? What's going on?' I asked, all agog.

'Ask me no questions and I'll tell you no lies,' said Mrs Briskett, and wouldn't say another word.

When I tried asking Sarah later, she shook her head at me too. 'It's private, Hetty. You wouldn't understand,' she said. 'Now button your lip and get on with your work.'

I certainly *didn't* understand. I didn't understand so many things about this strange outside world. It felt as if I'd stepped out of the hospital onto another planet.

7

I saw very little of Mr Buchanan each day, though I became all too intimate with his personal linen and his chamber pot. Mrs Briskett and Sarah still sent me up to his cluttered study to serve afternoon tea, but after our first conversation and my bold request for stamps, we did not talk further. I knocked at his door at four o'clock, and then edged my way into his room, bearing my tray of freshly brewed tea and *wondrous* cakes: Victoria sponge, orange and lemon cake, chocolate gateau, cherry and sultana slices, fruit tartlets, iced butterfly cakes – oh, the joys of Mrs Briskett's baking!

Mr Buchanan rarely looked up from his blotchy manuscript as I entered the study. When I returned half an hour later to collect his tray, most of his cakes were nibbled, but he frequently left a slab here, a slice here.

'Don't you want to finish up all your cake, sir?' I asked.

'Mm?' Mr Buchanan squinted at me through his

spectacles as if he wasn't quite sure who I was. He smacked his thin lips ruminatively, considering. 'No, not just at the moment. I am far too busy writing.'

Now, I considered myself an overly eager writer, but it never interfered with *my* appetite. How could the wretched man leave a large slice of sponge utterly untouched? This was a particularly beguiling sponge too, positively oozing raspberry jam and thick buttercream! Mrs Briskett commented on his increased appetite, however, because *somehow* his plate of cake diminished radically as I carried his tray back to the kitchen. I nodded happily, licking away the crumbs from my mouth.

I wished Mr Buchanan could somehow be winkled out of his study. He shuffled in even before breakfast, and was frequently muttering away there late at night. Sarah sighed and shook her head because she could rarely give it a little dust, let alone subject it to a proper weekly turn-out. I sighed too, because I was all too aware of the stamps in his desk drawer.

I wrote weekly to dearest Mama, and I also seemed to have embarked on a regular correspondence with Jem. (More about this later!) I badly needed stamps, and Mr Buchanan had many. I couldn't help thinking that perhaps he wouldn't miss just a couple.

I knew that stealing was wrong – a very, very bad

thing to do – but I didn't see that I had any alternative. Well, during the daytime, I thought that, and had the actual theft all worked out in my mind: I would wait until Mr Buchanan vacated his room at last – on a visit to his publishers? A meal at the chop house with an old friend? A stroll around the garden to clear his head? Even a fleeting trip to his splendid water closet? There *had* to be some opportunity when I could whisk into his room, duster in hand. Even if Sarah accompanied me, it should not be too difficult for me to slide that little desk drawer open beneath my duster, and grab a handful of precious stamps. I even practised the action, two fingers raised beneath the imaginary duster, two fingers intent on pulling the little knob of the door and lifting out the stamps.

By day I could rehearse this eagerly – but every night I dreamed I'd actually performed the deed. I did not get caught by Sarah or Mr Buchanan himself, but I felt *observed* all the same. I had attended chapel at the hospital every week for nine whole years. It had been drummed into me that God was omnipresent. I imagined a Supreme Being striding through the city on colossal legs, bending down and applying his huge holy orb to the window of Mr Buchanan's study. He'd shake his great and glorious head in horror. He'd not threaten me with Hell. No, far worse: he'd grow great angel's wings, fly straight to Mama and tell her that her only child was a common thief. Mama would shake with tears of shame – and I'd wake up with tears running down my own cheeks.

I could not do it. But I *so* needed those stamps. As soon as I had my first quarter's wages I could purchase my own and replenish them, I reasoned to myself. But that was months away. Perhaps I could simply *ask* Mr Buchanan for more stamps? But he'd been reluctant to give me more than one; he had clearly thought himself excessively generous to give me a handful. Would he not think me ungratefully greedy if I begged for more?

I could explain truthfully enough that I was devoted to Mama. I could even say that she was not very well. In one of her letters she had mentioned that she had a slight cough and had entreated me to wrap up as warmly as possible and rub goosegrease on my chest to prevent myself from catching a similar chill. I could exaggerate her illness and say I was unduly worried about her. But this might tempt the Superior Being to smite her in order to punish me. And I now had *two* correspondents. Even if Mr Buchanan was excessively understanding about my need to write regularly to Mama because she was my dear relation, he would never slot Jem into the same category, even though he was my foster brother.

I resolved all the same to *try* asking Mr Buchanan for more stamps. He could always say no. It wasn't a *crime* to ask, unlike stealing.

My hands were trembling the next day as I lugged the tea tray upstairs (containing a pot of Earl Grey with lemon slices, several portions of buttered malt bread, and a scone fresh out of the oven, with a little pot of strawberry jam and another of whipped cream – I hoped Mr Buchanan's appetite was birdlike today).

I put down the tray, took a deep breath, and knocked smartly on the door. I was a little *too* smart. I clearly made Mr Buchanan start, because he cried out. When I went into his room, I discovered he'd blotched his page with ink.

'What's the matter with you, Hetty? You banged on the door like a veritable thunderbolt. Now look at this page! I shall have to copy it all over again.' He blotted and sighed, while I endeavoured to find a resting place for his tea and cakes.

I saw over his shoulder that he was in the habit of making blots even without sharp knocks at his door. Although he had a whole sheaf of blotting paper, he did not use it effectively, because several pages were badly smudged. Even where they were totally unsullied, it would be a terrible task to figure out more than a few words because his handwriting was such a spidery scrawl.

'Goodness, sir, how do your publishers read your stories?' I asked.

'With great difficulty! They complain bitterly, and suggest I find myself a secretary to copy out my manuscript in a fair hand. I am sure it will incur too much expense, however, and I would find working with some young lady too much of a distraction,' said Mr Buchanan, wiping his spectacles, smearing them more thoroughly in the process.

My heart started thumping. 'Would you find *me* a distraction, sir?' I asked, bowing my head and hunching my shoulders, trying to make myself seem even smaller, so that he might see me as part of the study – an inkstand, say, or a volume of poetry.

Mr Buchanan blinked at me.

'*I* could transcribe your work, sir, a little at a time. I have a very clear hand, and I never ever blot. We used to get our knuckles rapped at the hospital if we blotted, and it made us extra careful.'

'But what of your duties around the house?'

'Oh, I am sure I could fit in an hour or so in the afternoons, when I would otherwise be mending. I could get up early and go to bed later to fit in any sewing. Sarah says I am very neat at darning,' I added, wanting to put myself in the best possible light.

Mr Buchanan sipped his tea and nibbled a

corner of his malt bread, contemplating. 'Give me an example of this fine hand, Hetty Feather,' he said, holding out his pen and a clean sheet of paper.

'Certainly, sir,' I said.

I had nowhere to sit, and hardly any room to rest the paper, but I dipped the pen confidently in the ink, tapping it on the edge of the bottle, making sure it was not so full that it would drip and not so empty that it might scratch. I commenced writing in a clear, careful copperplate:

Dear Mr Buchanan,

Please let Hetty Feather copy out your stories for you. She has an excellent hand, as you can see for yourself. You will not regret it, I promise you.

Yours respectfully,

Hetty Feather, maid of all work and potential excellent secretary

Mr Buchanan read it out loud, giving the sparse hair under his fez a little scratch, so that he seemed more monkey-like than ever – especially when he gave a little screech and bared all his teeth: this was laughter!

'Very well, I am convinced. If Mrs Briskett and Sarah can spare you for an hour every afternoon, then you may come and copy my work. It may help you with your own compositions, child. You will have a chance to study my grammar and learn complex vocabulary.'

'Yes, sir – and that will *almost* be reward enough in itself.'

'*Almost?*' He peered at me, chin on clasped hands.

'Well, sir, you did say that employing a secretary would incur considerable extra expense—'

He frowned at me. 'You surely aren't suggesting that I pay you an extra wage, Hetty Feather?' he enquired.

'Oh no, sir, that would be ridiculously impertinent,' I said quickly. 'But perhaps you might see fit to proffer me with a very tiny reward every now and then?'

'A *reward*?'

'Perhaps a stamp?'

'A stamp?' (There he was, boasting about his vocabulary and grammar, but all he seemed capable of was repeating *my* nouns).

'Or two? Or three or four or five?' I said, risking all. 'I write to Mama a great deal, sir, and I have already used up the stamps you so generously gave me.'

He took another morsel of malt bread. 'Mm. Well, I will give you a weekly stamp allowance, Hetty Feather, so long as you work quietly and neatly and do not neglect your household duties. Now, off you go. Take the tray with you.'

'But you've scarcely touched your tea, sir.'

'I have had sufficient, thank you.'

So I took his tray and dawdled on my way back to the kitchen, celebrating my stamp-earning success by eating his scone smothered with a jarful of jam and a jug full of cream.

Mrs Briskett and Sarah were astonished when I told them of my new duties.

'How can a little orphan like you write posh enough to please the master?' Mrs Briskett said indignantly.

'I'm *not* an orphan. I have a lovely dear mama,' I said.

'Show us this writing, then, Hetty,' said Sarah, fetching the kitchen pencil and some brown wrapping paper.

'Well, I really need ink and proper paper,' I said.

'Ah!' said Sarah, convinced I couldn't follow through.

'But I will do my best to demonstrate even so,' I said.

I wrote, in an excessively swirly and elaborate hand:

I am Hetty Feather and I am a maid of all work, and Mrs Briskett and Sarah are very kind to me and teach me my duties.

Mrs Briskett and Sarah read my message aloud, slowly, almost as if it were a struggle. Sarah said each word a beat behind Mrs Briskett.

'Can't you read properly, Sarah?' I asked, astonished.

'Of course I can read,' she said, pouting. 'It's just you write in such a fancy way. It's hard to make out the lettering.'

'But she does write it lovely,' said Mrs Briskett. 'You're a funny little slyboots, Hetty Feather. You've only been here five minutes and you're ingratiating yourself with the master something chronic.'

'Yes, what's your little game, Hetty? Why would you take on all this extra fancy writing work. Is it just to show off to the rest of us?' said Sarah.

'No, of course not,' I said fiercely, though perhaps this accounted for ten per cent of my motivation. 'I seized the opportunity so that I could ask a favour from Mr Buchanan.'

'Aha!' said Sarah. 'So we're right, Mrs B! What sort of favour, eh?'

'Stamps,' I said.

They peered at me.

'So I can write regularly to Mama.'

'Oh, my dear – oh, *now* I understand!' said Sarah. 'Would that I could write to my own mother! Isn't that touching, Mrs B?'

'Yes, I suppose it is,' said Mrs Briskett, beaming at me. 'What a dear good daughter you are, Hetty Feather. Here, sit yourself down, and try one of my scones. They're fresh out of the oven and extra light today. See, even Mr Buchanan has eaten his up, every crumb.'

So I sat and ate my second scone, glowing. I hadn't told a lie at all. I just hadn't told them that I was also writing to Jem.

My initial reply had been brief:

Dear Jem,

Of course I remember everything about my little-girlhood. I remember our special squirrel tree. I remember every single one of our special games. They meant a great deal to me. Every night at the hospital I would think of the happy times we spent.

I know little Eliza thinks of almost identical happy times. She is convinced you will be waiting for HER when she is fourteen.

Kind regards,
Your sister Hetty

There! I thought that would show him. I did not really expect to hear back from him. But within a *day* I received another reply. Luckily it was one of my tasks to collect the letters when they fluttered through the letterbox onto the hall mat. I saw several dull-looking bills and circulars to be served up to Mr Buchanan on a little silver tray like sweet-meats – but also a letter addressed to me in Jem's distinctive hand.

Dear Hetty,

I think from the tone of your letter that you are angry with me. Surely it is not because I tried so hard to be a good brother to little Eliza? I was so achingly lonely after you'd gone to the hospital. I don't think you have any idea how much I missed you. Eliza was a restless baby who cried a great deal. I had always had a knack of soothing you, so I did my best to calm her too – and as she got older I did sometimes play 'our' games with her, to amuse her and console myself. She is a sweet child and I was very fond of her – but she never meant anywhere near as much to me as you. You must know that.

Please tell me more about your new position and whether it truly suits you.

With deepest affection I am still
Your Jem

I read this letter many times. It was like a salve to a deep wound. So Jem truly preferred me to Eliza! I felt a thrill of happiness – and then a prickle of guilt. Poor little Eliza, still fantasizing about Jem marrying her one day. Jem should never have let her think that. He had not behaved admirably – but he said he had been so lonely. *Achingly* lonely. For me!

I found myself whirling round and round the rooms as I dusted, running up the stairs two at a time, singing cheerily as I scrubbed and peeled and polished.

Jem still cared about me. He was still my secret sweetheart. And maybe one day . . .

8

I went with Mrs Briskett and Sarah to the servants' church service early on Sunday afternoon. It was a chance for me to peer around and see many new people. I stared in dismay at all the other girls. I felt so plain and shabby in my grey print frock and borrowed shawl. Mrs Briskett was wearing her meat-red costume, and Sarah sported an alarmingly purple velvet dress and mantle, fringed and tassled.

I did not care for either of their outfits, but I hung my head miserably all the same. I did not even have a bonnet, and had to cover my hair with my borrowed shawl.

'Dear, dear, we'll have to fashion you a proper Sunday outfit, Hetty,' said Mrs Briskett, twitching at my dress. 'If I gave you my old Sunday best, Sarah, do you think you could cut it down so it fitted young Hetty?'

'I'll see what I can do,' said Sarah. 'There, Hetty! Say thank you to Mrs B. What a kind offer!'

'Thank you very much, both of you,' I said. I very much hoped Mrs Briskett's former Sunday best wasn't red.

They sat me between them, spreading their skirts as if they wanted to hide me. I felt like an ugly little weed between two great overblown roses. When the service started, they pulled me up for the hymns and pushed me down for the reading of the lesson, though I had been attending church services weekly for nine years and knew exactly what to do. Mrs Briskett and Sarah nodded approvingly to each other when I sang each hymn without looking at the words and muttered the correct responses to the prayers.

'Well, you might look a drab mite in your work clothes, but you *act* like a good little Christian,' Mrs Briskett whispered.

She meant it as a compliment, but I felt more self-conscious than ever. There were two girls in the pew in front who kept looking round and nudging each other and giggling, clearly amused by me. When Mrs Briskett and Sarah closed their eyes at the start of a prayer, I pulled a hideous face at the girls. They both squealed, and an older lady leaned over and tapped them hard on their fancy bonnets, much to my satisfaction.

When it came to his sermon, the vicar in St John's droned on for an unconscionable time. I yawned and fidgeted and picked the hangnails of my sore fingers. He told us how lucky we were to serve our masters and mistresses, because that way we were serving God. We might be lowly servants here on earth, but if we were humble and hard-working, we'd step up through Heaven's gate and as angels lead a grand life free of toil. I did not find this argument particularly convincing. Why was it *our* place to serve here on earth? Why couldn't we all take it in turns?

I imagined sitting in Mr Buchanan's padded wing chair in his study, reading and writing at my leisure, while he dusted and scrubbed. It was a delightful idea, and I smiled.

'Look at little Hetty taking it all in, bless her,' Mrs Briskett whispered to Sarah.

She gave me a penny from her purse to put in the collection plate. I rather badly wanted to keep the penny for myself, and wondered if I could keep it tucked in the palm of my hand. I remembered the lucky sixpence Jem had given me the day I left for the hospital. I'd kept it in my mouth, I was so determined not to relinquish it. I had eventually hidden it in the knob of my bed-stead – but someone had stolen it long ago. I wondered if Jem had given Eliza a sixpence too.

I held my hand over the plate, clenching my palm muscles to keep hold of the penny, but Mrs

Briskett gave me a little nudge, waiting to hear a clink. I let go of the coin with a sigh.

We walked home from church – and there, sitting on the area steps, was Bertie the butcher's boy.

I felt my face going the colour of Mrs Briskett's costume. I hadn't thought he would really come calling for me. I rather wished he hadn't. I had Jem now, so I didn't want any other boy in my life, thank you very much.

'What are you doing sitting here, making my steps look untidy, boy?' said Mrs Briskett.

'Ain't it obvious, Mrs B? I've been waiting to see you three lovely ladies come home from church,' said Bertie. He blinked his eyes in an exaggerated fashion. 'My, you're a dazzling sight – enough to unsettle a simple lad like me.'

'You're simple, all right,' said Sarah, swatting at him with her hymn book.

'Why weren't you in church too, you bad boy?' said Mrs Briskett.

'Is the church a place for miserable sinners, Mrs B?'

'Of course it is!'

'Ah, but you see, I'm *not* a miserable sinner. I'm a very cheerful little saint, so I don't need no churching, do I?'

'You need a good hiding, that's what you need,'

said Sarah, untying her bonnet strings. 'Don't you let our Hetty go walking with that boy, Mrs B – or he'll lead her astray.'

'I don't have any evil intentions!' said Bertie indignantly. 'I just want to show her around a little, her being brought up in that queer hospital. She needs to see a bit more of the world than your kitchen and scullery, Mrs B, excellent and immaculate though they are.'

'Listen to him!' said Mrs Briskett. 'He's got such a way with words he sets your head spinning. Well, take young Hetty off for a nice little walk, then. Just for an hour or two, mind. We have early supper now, seeing as *one* of us chooses to go out gallivanting of a Sunday evening, meddling with all sorts.'

'I'll thank you to hold your tongue and mind your own business, Mrs B,' said Sarah haughtily, and flounced indoors.

'That gullible girl,' said Mrs Briskett, sighing and sucking her teeth. 'Now, you behave yourself, young Hetty, and be back here by half past five – well, six at the latest. And you behave yourself too, boy, or I'll be after you and I'll box your ears good and proper.' She bustled through the back door, still issuing dire warnings.

Bertie rolled his eyes at me. 'Them two old birds, fuss fuss fuss! How do you stand it, Hetty?'

'They're all right. They mean well,' I said

awkwardly. I didn't like them fussing either, but I found I didn't care to hear Bertie criticizing them. In a short space of time they'd become almost like family.

'Come on, then,' said he, stepping out jauntily.

He was wearing *his* Sunday best – a brown suit, a little tight, and shiny in the seat, with such a stiff starched collar he had to hold his head up high the whole time. His unruly hair was slicked down flat, perhaps with perfume, because he smelled powerfully sweet.

Two smirking young girls from church walked past arm in arm, tossing their heads in their dainty bonnets and swishing their fine velvet skirts. They obviously knew Bertie, because they nudged each other and grinned and giggled – and then turned their noses up at me. I pulled a ferocious face again, but I didn't smooth it out quickly enough. Bertie saw and stared at me.

'Well, that's a happy face! What are you looking like that for?'

'I'm not pulling a face at you. I'm pulling a face at them,' I said, nodding over my shoulder at the girls.

'Why's that, then?' said Bertie, swaggering. 'Did you see them making those sheep's eyes at me? Don't take it to heart, Hetty. I can't help if they're a little bit sweet on me. They work in the draper's over the road from us, so we're on nodding terms, but there's nothing serious between us, I swear.'

'Don't be so full of yourself, it's very annoying. I didn't give a hoot about the way they were looking at *you*. I minded the way they looked at *me*.'

'What way was that, Hetty?' He sounded puzzled, as if he truly didn't have any idea.

'They looked down their pretty little noses because I'm small and plain and haven't got any bright fancy Sunday clothes. I just have to go out in my drab daily work dress.'

'What?' said Bertie. 'Look, I *like* you being so small. It makes me feel almost big, see. And you've got a dear little face, with the biggest blue eyes.'

'Yes, they are my best feature. Sapphire blue.'

'There you are, then. And you don't need any bright fancy clothes, not with your flaming hair. It's all the colour you need.'

'Do you really think so?' I said.

'Course I do. Now come on, step lively, we've a long way to go, and if I don't get you back by six o'clock, old Mother Briskett will chop the rest of my fingers off and serve them up in a fricassé on toast.'

I walked beside him, almost running to keep up with his brisk step.

'So do you think my blue eyes make up for my being plain?' I asked, after a minute.

Bertie burst out laughing. 'My, for a little orphan girl you act like a princess at times, wanting all the compliments,' he said.

'I'm *not* an orphan.'

'All right, all right – you're not an orphan. And you're not plain neither. You're pretty as a picture. Happy now?'

I found I *was* happy as I stepped out beside him. I peered around at all the people on the pavement: girls walking with linked arms, boys in small clusters, couples walking along sedately, with little children running ahead bowling hoops. It still seemed so extraordinary that people were free to wander where they wanted, while all the foundlings were locked up in the hospital month after month, year after year.

'What's up *now*?' said Bertie, seeing my expression change.

'Nothing. I was just thinking back—'

'No, you don't want to do that. The trick is to think *forward*, see. Come on, Hetty, step out.'

'Where are we going, then?'

'You'll see when we get there – but you'll like it, I promise.'

'Is it . . . the country?'

'What? No, don't be silly, I'm a city lad. I don't want to take you where it's all messy and muddy, and the folk are a bit backward and suck straws, and all the men lumber about in them frocks.'

'*Smocks*.'

'Well, they look ridiculous on a gent, whatever you call them. Great lummocks, they look.'

'No they don't!' I said fiercely. I remembered my foster father's smock – the warm earthy smell of it, the tickle of the stitching against my cheek when I cuddled up close. It had seemed the most manly of garments then. I wondered if Jem wore a smock nowadays.

'You know nothing about the country and country ways,' I said to Bertie. 'It's beautiful in the country.' I thought of the cottage where I'd lived for five happy years. It shimmered in my mind – the cosy thatch, the roses and hollyhocks, the open fire, the inglenook, the little bedrooms under the eaves. I had to sniff to stop myself bursting into tears.

'Hey now, don't upset yourself! I didn't mean to cause any offence. Heaven save us if we're arguing already!'

'I lived in the country when I was a little girl,' I said.

'Well, that's fine and dandy, then. You can be my little Hetty Hayseed. Just blink those sapphire-blue eyes and look happy again, eh?'

'My mother was going to call me Sapphire,' I said proudly. 'That was her secret name for me.'

151

'Really? Gawd knows what *my* mother's name for me was. Trouble, most likely – or Mr-Bawl-his-head-off,' said Bertie.

We walked past the park where I'd met Tommy, the huge hound. I looked for him hopefully, wanting to show off that I knew such a fierce animal, but he wasn't bounding around today. There was a cricket match taking place, so we peered through the railings to watch for a minute or two.

'Seems like it's the slowest game on the planet,' said Bertie. 'Still, the chaps look good in their fancy whites. Are you a sporty girl, Hetty? You look like a whippy little thing. Good at running, are you?'

'I don't know,' I said. 'The girls at the hospital didn't do sports, only the boys. I think perhaps I'd *like* to run.'

'Well, when we get out of town you'll get a chance to run, I promise.'

We went along the main shopping street.

'There's Dedman's the grocer. I've shopped there,' I said proudly.

'I'll show you my shop, shall I – though it don't look right all shut up on a Sunday, without all the meat hanging outside.' Bertie pointed out Jarvis the master butcher's, and showed me all the other shops too, telling me tales of all the folk who worked there. I yawned ostentatiously when he spoke about the draper's shop, and silly simpering Kitty and Ivy who worked there.

'You seem to know everyone, Bertie,' I said.

'That's right, I do. But they don't know *me*. They just think I'm Jarvis's boy, the cheeky lad who gives them lip. They don't even know my name, most of them.'

'You told me your name straight off.'

'Yes, because I knew you were different. I sensed it as soon as I saw you. We're children of circumstance, you and me, Hetty. We're going to have to make our own way in the world.'

'That's right,' I said, smiling at him.

'Come on, then – not too far to go now.'

The shops petered out. We went down shabby alleyways, past warehouses and a reeking fishery.

'Is *this* your favourite place?' I asked, wrinkling my nose.

'Patience, Miss Sarcastic. You'll like it, you really will,' said Bertie.

He led me onwards, down further alleyways, and then under the bridge by the railway. It was very dark.

'Bertie?' I said nervously.

'It's fine,' he said, taking my hand. 'It echoes – listen: *Hello, Hetty Feather!*'

Ten Bertie voices shouted hello from every angle. I laughed, and ten Hettys laughed too.

'*I'm not Hetty, I'm Sapphire Battersea!*' I shouted at the top of my lungs – and the darkness sang out my special name in a magnificent chorus.

Then we were out on the other side of the bridge, and it was as if we'd stepped into another world entirely. We were down by the river. I'd seen the Thames before, but only in the middle of London, slick with grease and stinking to high heaven. The river here was fresh and sparkling, and little rowing boats and canoes bobbed up and down on the waves.

We were in a long green park by the riverside, crowded with Sunday-afternoon revellers enjoying the sunshine.

'Take a little run, Hetty!' said Bertie.

I hitched up my skirt and charged ahead. I thought I was running fast, but Bertie easily overtook me. We stopped to catch our breath, both of us laughing. There was a little stand in the middle of the grass with a brass band playing, the men in stripped blazers and straw hats. Couples sat on little white chairs, and children ran about, whirling round and round to the music.

Bertie and I sat and listened too. He sang along with the music – saucy words to jolly tunes.

'Don't you know this one too, Hetty?'

'I've only ever heard hymns or harvest songs,' I said.

'I'll take you to the music hall one day,' Bertie promised. 'Fancy a boat ride now?'

'Can we really?'

'You bet we can!'

He paid for the hire of a rowing boat for half an hour. It was great fun getting into the boat, because it tipped like crazy and we wobbled about. Bertie very nearly tumbled in headfirst, clearly not quite as experienced a boatman as he was making out.

I seized the oars excitedly.

'That's my job!' said Bertie.

'Oh, let me try, please!' I begged.

It wasn't as simple as I'd thought. It proved really hard work just pulling the oars together through the water. My arms couldn't pull with equal strength, and the boat started spinning in a circle.

'You're making me dizzy,' Bertie laughed. 'Come on, let me show you.'

He took the oars and rowed us swiftly along beside the river bank. 'You just sit back and enjoy yourself,' he said.

I was a little irritated, but I sat back obediently, trailing my hand in the water. There were so many boats bobbing about us that I kept calling out, worried we'd crash, but Bertie steered us in and out and round about, and soon we were gliding along in deeper waters.

'Can't I have another go now, please, Bertie?' I begged.

He let me try again, and I started to get the hang of it at last, though every now and then my oar missed the water altogether or I 'caught a crab'.

'You're doing very well, Hetty, but it looks bad, a puny little girl rowing a strong lad like me. Let me take charge to save my blushes,' said Bertie, removing his jacket and rolling up his sleeves.

'You just want to show off those muscles,' I said, but I let him have his way.

He rowed us swiftly to a little island in the middle of the river, where he moored the boat. 'There, let's have a bit of rest here. You could have a little paddle if you wanted, Hetty.'

'I think I'll do just that! Turn your back while I take off my stockings, then.'

I kicked off my ugly boots, rolled down my itchy woollen stockings and stepped into the water. It came up to my knees, so I had to hold my dress up to stop the hem getting soaked.

'You'd better keep your back turned, Bertie,' I said, capering about.

He peeked at me, of course, but I didn't get cross. I didn't really care. It just felt so delicious to have my hot sore feet in the cold water. I remembered paddling in the stream with Jem years back, and felt a fierce pang for him now. I wished I was with *him* – and yet Bertie was fun too, far better company than I'd thought he'd be.

He smiled at me from the grassy bank, waving his arms about to ease them. He was barely an inch taller than me, but he really did have great strong muscles – which of course he flexed ostentatiously when he saw me watching.

'You're like a little water baby,' he said as I splashed about. 'Why don't you go right in swimming?'

'For two pins I would,' I said, wishing I was young enough to tumble in nearly naked like some little children further up the bank.

'You're a girl and a half, you are, Hetty. So, you like my special place, yes?'

'I like it very much,' I said, coming to sit beside him.

'And do you like *me*?' he asked, looking me straight in the eye.

'I reckon I do like you, Bertie,' I said, but when he tried to take my hand, I swatted his away. 'None of that now! No romancing!'

'Go on, Hetty, just let me put my arm round you – to keep you from falling in.'

'You're the one in danger of falling in if you don't

watch out,' I said, giving him a little poke. The sweet smell of his perfume was overpowering in the heat.

'What's up? Why are you wrinkling that little nose of yours?' he asked.

'I thought it was ladies who were meant to wear the perfume,' I said.

He wriggled, looking uncomfortable. 'Sorry. I do stink a bit, I know. I just poured Jarvis's pomade all over me because I didn't want to smell of meat, see.'

'Oh, Bertie.' I took his hand voluntarily now. 'You smell fine. Thank you for bringing me here. It's truly lovely.'

'I'd like a little house here, right on the island. Wouldn't it be grand to wake up to the sound of water lapping all around? I've often toyed with the idea of throwing in my job with old Jarvis and running off to sea,' he said dreamily.

'My father was a sailor,' I said. 'Well, so I've been told. I've never met him. He ran off before I was born.'

'My pa did likewise. I don't even know who he was. Could have been Old Nick for all I know or care. Well, lovely as it is, I'd better get you back. We'll have to hurry to get you home by six or Mrs B will have my guts for garters.'

'Do you care what she says, then?'

'Course I don't – but I want her to let you out *next* Sunday – and the Sunday after that, and all the Sundays following. I've taken a fancy to you, Hetty Feather. You're my girl now.'

I wasn't sure I should go along with this. Wasn't I *Jem*'s girl?

'You know I'm only just fourteen,' I said.

'And I'm fifteen, and so we're just the right ages for each other,' said Bertie. 'Don't worry, Hetty, I promise I won't lead you astray.'

'I'd like to see you try!' I said, jumping back into the boat.

It rocked violently, so that I had to sit down abruptly and cling to the sides.

'Whoops! You nearly went for a swim after all!' said Bertie.

He rowed us back to the boathouse and then brought us both a hokey-pokey to eat on our way home. I bit into my iced cream, and shuddered as the cold ran up my teeth and all round my gums.

'Don't bite it, girl – lick it!' said Bertie, showing me how.

I licked and licked and licked.

'What do you think of it?' he asked.

'It's heavenly!' I said, grinning all over my face.

An old couple passing by laughed at me. 'She

looks as if she's never tasted iced cream before!' said the old woman, chuckling.

'Well, she hasn't. She's a poor little orphan girl only just out of the Foundling Hospital,' said Bertie.

'Oh, bless her,' said the old man, fumbling in his waistcoat pocket. 'Here's a threepenny, dearie. Treat yourself to another.'

I was shocked speechless, staring at the silver threepenny bit in the palm of my hand.

'Well, there's a turn-up!' said Bertie.

'I'm *not* an orphan! How many times do I have to tell you?' I said.

'Go and give him his threepence back, then,' said Bertie.

'No fear! It's mine,' I said, popping it into my pocket.

'Oh well, you can buy the lollipops next week,' said Bertie.

When we got back to Mr Buchanan's home, he squeezed my hand. 'There will be a next week, won't there, Hetty?' he said.

'Yes . . . please!'

'I'll deliver you back, then,' said Bertie.

Sarah was in her purple bonnet, all ready for her mysterious assignation.

'You can take off that bonnet and have a spot of supper before you go, or you'll be coming over poorly,' said Mrs Briskett, consulting her pocket watch. 'And what time do you call this, then?' she said, frowning at us.

'I call it one minute to six, Mrs B,' said Bertie.

'I thought I told you half past five?'

'Or six at the latest, and here we are now – six just about to chime. Punctual to the finest degree!'

'Hmph!' said Mrs Briskett, but she invited Bertie to stay for our oyster patty supper.

Sarah only nibbled the edge of hers, and then got up from the table determinedly. 'I'm sorry, Mrs B, but I'm that het up I can't eat.'

Mrs Briskett tutted at her, but let her go. 'Take care now! Don't get too over-excited, you know it's not good for you,' she said.

Bertie and I exchanged glances, while Sarah blushed.

'Where are you going, Sarah?' Bertie asked. 'Are you seeing that fine policeman fellow I've seen eyeing you up and down appreciatively?'

Sarah snorted at him. 'The very idea!' she said, but she seemed too preoccupied to get properly indignant. She waved goodbye to us, tying up the drawstrings of her bag.

'Don't waste all your hard-earned money now,' said Mrs Briskett.

'Surely the gentleman is paying for you, Sarah –

or by definition he ain't a gentleman,' said Bertie.

'You mind your own business, you cocky little urchin,' said Sarah. 'I'm off now.' She looked at Mrs Briskett. 'Wish me luck, Mrs B!'

'I'll do no such thing. You're a very foolish girl, and I don't approve,' said Mrs Briskett – but as Sarah went out of the back door, she called, 'Good luck, even so!'

'Come on, Mrs B, out with it! What's Sarah's secret? We're all agog!' said Bertie.

'It's nothing to do with you, lad. My lips are sealed. Now, finish your patty and be off with you.'

'Such excellent patties too, Mrs B. Hetty's lucky to be able to learn from you,' said Bertie.

'I know you're just trying to sweet-talk me, Mr Honey-tongue. Go on – scoot!'

Bertie crammed the last of his patty in his mouth. He stood up, gave Mrs Briskett a little bow – and blew a kiss to me as he went out of the door.

'I saw that!' said Mrs Briskett. 'I'm not sure I should let you near that boy, Hetty. I've no idea what he'll get up to. No, correction: I've got plenty of ideas, and none of them good. Come along, help me clear the table. Then you can copy out a few receipts for me, seeing as you've got this famously excellent handwriting.'

I meekly did as I was told. Mrs Briskett was all of a fidget, fussing around the kitchen, starting to turn out her larder but losing heart halfway through. She kept sighing. I wondered if she were wishing she had a Sunday outing too.

'Did Mr Briskett pass away a long time ago, Mrs Briskett?' I asked.

'What? There was never any such person! I told you, it's a courtesy title.'

'Did you ever have a sweetheart, Mrs B?'

'Mrs *Briskett*! No, I've never had no time for men,' she said. 'You can't trust them. You're a case in point. It's clear some bad lad led your poor mother astray.'

'Mrs Briskett, *is* that man in the grocer's shop Sarah's sweetheart?'

Mrs Briskett rolled her eyes. 'Of course not, Hetty. That gentleman happens to be respectably married.'

'Then why is she seeing him? Where do they go?'

Mrs Briskett tapped my nose with her finger. 'Ask no questions and you'll be told no lies,' she said.

'The matrons always used to say that to me at the hospital,' I said.

'I'm not surprised. You're a terrible girl for questions, Hetty Feather.'

'How else am I to find out about things?' I said.

'There aren't many answers worth knowing,' said Mrs Briskett, sorting jars of sour pickles. Her mouth was puckered, as if she were actually suck-ing them. I wondered what it would be like to be Mrs Briskett, with no family at all, cooking tempt-ing and tasty dishes for one pernickety old gentleman who rarely cleared his plate.

'Do you *like* working here, Mrs Briskett?'

'Questions, questions! You can't seem to help it! Yes, of course I do. You can't go much higher than this – cook-housekeeper in a lovely villa. I started off as a kitchen maid when I first went into service, but the cook was a regular harridan and scared the life out of me. Then I worked for a young couple, but the missus was too flighty and didn't give me no direction. Then I worked in another home where the missus was the exact opposite, telling me what to do all day long. I used to hear her voice nag-nag-nagging even in my dreams. And *then* I came to work for the master here, and what a joy it is to have no missus whatsoever.'

'But, Mrs Briskett, wouldn't you like to *be* a missus one day?'

Mrs Briskett stared at me as if I'd suggested she become an Indian Princess or an opera singer. 'Of course not, Hetty. I hope you're not going to turn out to be one of those girls with ideas above their station.'

I went to bed that night, determined to keep all my ideas above my station. I wrote a long letter to

Mama, telling her that I'd been to church and had a jolly boat trip with a new chum. I did not specify exactly who this new chum was. I wrote to Jem too, and I described the boat trip – but I thought it best not to mention any chum at all.

9

I got into the habit of copying Mr Buchanan's writing every day. At first it was hard work deciphering all his curlicues and squiggles, but after a few days I grew used to his style and could copy quickly and easily. I could not say his work *read* quickly and easily. He used such long convoluted sentences that you lost all sense of what he was saying. He spent page after page laboriously describing every little detail. His characters rarely talked to each other, and when they did, it was with the stiff erudition of elderly clergymen, even though they were children. They were quite the most tedious children too, forever quoting the Bible to each other and pointing out morals.

I had read Miss Smith's stories with huge enjoyment, but Mr Buchanan's tales were so turgid that I yawned as I copied them.

'Did you not get enough sleep, Hetty? That was a fearsome yawn!' said Mr Buchanan sharply.

'I'm sorry, sir. I – I'm just a little tired today,' I said, pressing my lips together.

'You're making good progress with your copying. You will have the manuscript ready for the publisher by the end of the month. Now, I have to cast my mind about and find a subject for a new story . . .' He paused. I realized he was expecting me to show some interest in this project.

'You're very industrious, sir,' I said dutifully.

'I have to work hard because, alas, my stories do not sell particularly well,' he said.

'Oh goodness, sir, I wonder why,' I said – though I knew very well!

'I think they are written in too fine a literary style,' said Mr Buchanan. 'And my characters are well-brought-up young ladies and gentlemen. Perhaps I should copy your friend Miss Smith and write about street waifs. *Her* stories are immensely popular.'

'Miss Smith goes out into the London streets, sir, and interviews the children there,' I said.

'I dare say. And very admirable too. But you are surely not suggesting I do likewise?'

I tried to picture Mr Buchanan picking his way fastidiously across muddy pavements, summoning street children imperiously. They'd simply jeer at him. They might even throw stones.

'Perhaps not, sir,' I said.

'I believe that was how Miss Smith met *you*, Hetty,' said Mr Buchanan.

'Yes, sir,' I said.

'Well, child, perhaps you can tell me a few tales from the past? He was looking at me hopefully, his nose twitching.

'What, right this minute, sir?'

'Can you not remember clearly enough?'

'Oh, I can remember every single detail, sir. Besides, I wrote it all down in my memoirs.'

'Ah yes. Your memoirs. Do you still have them, Hetty?'

'Yes I do. I was hoping Miss Smith might help me to get them published – but when she read them, she said it wasn't possible because they sounded too harsh and ungrateful. It would upset the Board of Governors.'

'I see, I see. Yes, you should show immense respect and gratitude, child. If the hospital had not taken you back, you might well be in the gutter now, living a life of wretched depravity. Instead of which you are safe and warm and well fed in a good Christian home, with not a care in the world.'

I had many, many, many cares – up at dawn, scrubbing my fingers raw, emptying his horrid chamber pot, working like a dog all day long, copying his stilted stories just to earn stamps to keep in touch with my dear mama . . . My eyes filled with angry tears.

'Ah yes! I can see you are ashamed of your ingratitude, Hetty. But never mind, I dare say your childish literary efforts at least helped you to learn the lessons of application and discipline – and after so much practice you now write in a quick clear hand. Well, continue with your good work.'

I carried on copying his dire tale, my eyes crossing with boredom as little Miss Mimsie Marie and young Master Twaddle Tommy gave a penny to a starving, shivering beggar child and then went home to toast their toes in front of a roaring fire and stuff their smug little faces with buttered muffins.

When Mr Buchanan's clock chimed five, I put down my pen and picked up his tea tray, ready to return to the kitchen.

'That's a good girl, Hetty. Run along now,' said Mr Buchanan – but then, as I was going out of the door, he called me back.

'I feel you should be encouraged, child. Show me these memoirs of yours. I will see if I can help you with your literary style. Perhaps you can rewrite a few passages. It will be an invaluable lesson for you, Hetty.'

'So – so you think there might be a chance of getting my memoirs published after all?' I said, my heart beating fast.

'Now you're being ridiculous, child.' He saw my

face fall, and checked himself. 'But perhaps, if we reworked some part together, it might be possible to publish a small extract. I could perhaps write an article about foundlings for a newspaper or journal, with a paragraph from you – the first-hand account, as it were.'

I pondered. This wasn't at all what I wanted. It certainly wouldn't make my fortune so that I could free Mama from service and buy a fine home where we might live happily ever after, just the two of us. But a small extract in a newspaper was better than no publication at all . . . and perhaps some forward-thinking, truth-discerning radical publishing person might be so taken aback by the extract that they sought me out and offered me a publishing contract for the entire work.

'Well, child, stop gawping, and go and get these little memoirs. I will see if I can find time to glance at it tonight,' said Mr Buchanan.

I scuttled off downstairs with his tea tray, so excited I didn't even finish his half-eaten cherry cake and shortbread. I slammed the tray down on the kitchen table and rushed to the scullery.

'What's up with you, girl? You're not just leaving the tray there, are you, right where I want to roll out my pastry for tonight's steak-and-kidney pie? And deal with the dirty crockery! It's not going to wash itself now, is it?'

'In a minute, Mrs Briskett. I'm just running an errand for the master,' I said, taking my memoirs out of my shabby box. The red cover was faded now, and the spine broken. I had got into a fight with Sheila in the dormitory, and she had seized my precious manuscript book and thrown it the length of the room, the spiteful girl.

'What's that scrappy book, then?' asked Sarah, following me.

'My memoirs,' I said, holding it tight against my chest as if it were my own dear child.

'Your mem-what?' said Sarah. 'You're such a tiresome girl for saying fancy stuff no ordinary folk can understand.'

'It's like a journal. It contains the story of my life,' I said grandly, my chin in the air.

I hoped Sarah would be suitably impressed, but she burst out laughing – and when she told Mrs Briskett, *she* started chuckling too.

'The story of your life, young Hetty!' she said. 'You're a caution! You haven't even *had* a life yet – you're still knee-high to a grasshopper, and you've been stuck in that hospital all the time.'

'I have experienced many momentous things,' I said indignantly.

This made them splutter more.

'Oh yes? What exactly have you experienced, eh?' said Sarah. 'Met the Queen, have you? Sailed all round the world? Flown up in the sky to say how d'ye do to the Man in the Moon?'

'I *have* met the Queen, as a matter of fact – or very nearly – on the day of her Golden Jubilee,' I said haughtily. 'That was certainly a momentous day for me, in more ways than one. So you can both stop tee-hee-heeing. I am going to see the master.'

I swept out of the scullery in what I hoped was a dignified manner, but I tripped over the bucket in the corner, which somewhat spoiled the effect. Mrs Briskett and Sarah laughed so hard they had to hold each other to stay standing.

I went up the stairs clutching my memoirs, starting to have qualms. I badly wanted to see my work published. Imagine hundreds, maybe thousands, of people reading it! That thought made me thrill with pride – but I felt very shy and shivery at the thought of one person in particular perusing every line. I suddenly did not want Mr Buchanan reading my memoirs. It would be like taking off all my clothes before him while he blinked at me beadily through his spectacles.

I paused halfway up the stairs, clutching my book to my chest. I couldn't do it. I'd tell Mr Buchanan that I'd lost it somehow. I had to protect it. But then he suddenly poked his head out of the study door and peered down at me.

173

'There you are, Hetty! I was wondering where you'd got to. Bring me these memoirs, child.'

'I – I couldn't find them, sir,' I said.

'What? Nonsense – there they are, you're holding the book right there! Bring it to me immediately.'

'But – but it's a poor thing, sir – written years ago when I was a small girl. You will find it very tedious.'

'I dare say, but I want to help you, child. Hand it over.'

I wanted to fling it far down the stairs, out of harm's way, but instead I handed it over like an automaton. Mr Buchanan bobbed back inside his study, pocketing my memoirs.

I felt very queer and strange all evening, thinking of him turning the pages, reading every little detail about my life. I asked Sarah what mood the master seemed to be in when she served him supper.

'A funny mood – very vague, almost vacant. He read as he ate, picking up his cutlery without concentrating, so that he tried to cut into his pie with his fork.'

'Yes, but vague in a good way or bad? Was he frowning?'

'How can I tell, when the master has such a wrinkled forehead?'

'You're worrying that he doesn't like these

precious memoirs of yours, aren't you, Hetty?' said Mrs Briskett. 'What sort of things did you write in them, eh?'

'All sorts of things,' I said miserably.

'Well, I hope you haven't confessed to anything too dreadful, or the master will be obliged to dismiss you forthwith, and I'd have to start all over again with a new girl just as you're starting to train up nicely,' said Mrs Briskett.

I couldn't concentrate on my letter-writing when I went to bed that night. I blew out my stub of candle and lay twitching in the dark, imagining Mr Buchanan two floors up, his nose in my notebook, glasses glinting as he read his way through my life.

I tossed and turned all night, and got up long before Mrs Briskett and Sarah. When they came down, I had the fire lit, the tea piping hot in the pot, and fried eggs and bacon sizzling in the pan.

They patted me on the head and told me I was a good girl.

'A good girl who's had very momentous experiences,' Sarah couldn't resist adding.

When she came back from serving Mr Buchanan his breakfast, I fell upon her.

'What was the master doing, Sarah?'

'What? Eating his breakfast, silly.'

'Is he reading?'

'Mm? Yes, and a very bad habit it is. He gets so

absorbed he'll likely drop egg and bacon all down his front, and I shall be the poor soul who has to try to get the stains out.'

'*What* was he reading, Sarah?'

'*I* don't know. I'm not in the habit of snatching his book up so as I can see the title.'

'It was a book, then? It wasn't . . . ?'

'Your illustrious memoirs? Yes, I believe it was – and of course . . . it's coming back to me now . . . he held it up solemnly and said to me, "Sarah, this is a veritable masterpiece. I'm going to have it bound in finest leather with gold-embossed lettering." '

I was sure she was teasing me, but I couldn't help hoping that she *might* just be telling the truth.

'He really seemed to like it?' I asked tremulously.

Sarah and Mrs Briskett laughed their silly fat heads off. I tossed my own head and stomped off to clean the bedrooms. Mr Buchanan was in his study with the door closed. I longed to peep in and see for myself if my memoirs intrigued or irritated him. Perhaps he had already cast them aside on one of his cluttered tables. They would be entirely forgotten and I would lose even this extremely slim chance of publication . . .

I was in such a fever about my wretched memoirs I couldn't settle to anything. I think Sarah was a little sorry she had mocked me so, because she let me work on my Sunday dress after lunch instead of helping her sides-to-middle a pile of worn sheets. Mrs Briskett had donated her Sunday outfit of several years ago. It was emerald-green velvet, startlingly bright, but Mrs Briskett and Sarah said it set off my red hair a treat. The velvet had gone shiny at the back, worn smooth by Mrs Briskett's formidable bottom, but there was so much material that Sarah helped me cut the pieces for a frock from the unsullied front.

She fashioned me a pattern too, but she based it on my work dresses and they seemed very plain to me. I had looked very carefully at the girls in the street on Sunday. I wanted a fitted bodice and a waist.

'Then you will need stays, Hetty!' said Sarah.

I saw that she had a point, but I couldn't possibly make do with Mrs Briskett's second-best whalebone stays – indeed, you could comfortably fit a whale itself inside them. I would just have to hold my breath, suck in my stomach and stick out my meagre chest in my new dress.

I had observed a faded pair of curtains in the mending pile in Sarah's cupboard. They had dark gold tassels and trimmings. I decided on a few secret snips so that my dress could have the perfect finishing touches.

I wondered what Bertie would think of me in my new frock. I smiled as I stitched, because it was very pleasant to be liked, and it diverted me a little from fretting about Mr Buchanan – but then Mrs Briskett started preparing his afternoon tea: little cucumber sandwiches and honey cake. It was time for me to go and confront him!

I trembled so much that the cup and saucer and plate played a tune on the tray as I stumbled up the stairs. When I knocked on the study door, my hand was slippery with sweat.

'Come in,' Mr Buchanan called.

I'm not sure what I expected. My thoughts ran wildly between two options: he would either seize me, strike me, tell me I was a wicked, ungrateful girl to tell such tales of the hospital and turn me out of his house forthwith – *or* he might clasp me to his bosom and tell me I had written a compelling work of genius, not a word of which needed changing, and he would see that it was published immediately.

He did not react in either of these ways. He barely raised his head. He was scribbling in his spidery writing in a new manuscript book. He did not stop when I balanced the tray precariously on an edge of his cluttered desk. I poured his tea and handed it to him. His hand went out for it automatically, but he was still intent on his writing and he spilled half of it. He jumped as scalding tea shot up his smoking-jacket sleeve.

'Oh, take care, sir, you'll burn yourself,' I said.

'Yes, yes. I'm fine, it's fine,' he said, flapping his wet sleeve.

'Shall I fetch you a dry jacket, sir?'

'No, no, don't fuss.' He carried on writing, reaching out blindly again and stuffing a sandwich into his mouth. He could just as easily have stuffed the plate in instead, and crunched up the china with equal absent-mindedness.

'You seem very busy, sir,' I said.

'I am indeed, Hetty Feather. I have started writing my new book.'

I glanced at the page in front of him. His handwriting was even more blotched and sloped at a bizarre angle.

'Take care not to get too carried away, sir – or even I won't be able to read it,' I said. 'I'll make a start on it as soon as I've finished copying your other work.'

Mr Buchanan suddenly snapped to attention. 'That won't be necessary, Hetty. I think it's better if I make a fair copy myself – then I can alter sentences as I go, rearrange paragraphs, et cetera. It will take longer but will be far more satisfactory in the long run.'

I stared at him, appalled.

'Don't look so stricken! You can still continue with the old manuscript. You must not take this personally. You've worked hard, I grant you, and

179

you write a very legible hand, if a little childish in appearance.'

'But what about my stamps?'

'What? Oh, your postage stamps! Yes, you can have the agreed ration until you finish the manuscript.' He reached into his desk drawer, and took out the stamp box. 'In fact, I will continue to provide you with stamps whenever you ask, so long as you don't take it into your head to communicate with every child in the Foundling Hospital.' He handed me another four stamps.

'Thank you, sir. That's very generous of you. And don't worry, it's just so I can write to Mama.' I silently mouthed 'and Jem' when he started writing again, for honesty's sake.

Mr Buchanan gave me the old manuscript and a spare pen, and I started writing too, but I couldn't settle properly to my task. I kept peering around the room, looking for my memoirs. It was so difficult to detect in this mad chamber, crammed to the ceiling with books and papers and manuscripts. I craned to look in the wastepaper basket, wondering if he'd tossed my poor work in there.

'Do you have a crick in your neck, Hetty?' Mr Buchanan asked.

'Oh no, sir, I was just looking . . . I couldn't help wondering . . .' I couldn't wait any longer. 'What did you think of my memoirs, sir?'

Mr Buchanan removed his fez to scratch his head vigorously. Then he set the quaint hat back on his head at a comical angle, wrinkling his nose to hitch up his spectacles.

Tell me, you ridiculous little monkey man! I screeched inside my head, but I clamped my lips together to keep the words inside.

'Oh yes, your "memoirs",' said Mr Buchanan. He said the word as if it were ridiculous, and I felt the blood flooding my face. 'Mm, well, it was certainly a substantial effort, Hetty. I hadn't realized it would be so long, when you have led such a short life.'

'But what did you think of the content, sir?'

'It was quite . . . startling. I'm surprised at you, child. You showed shameful ingratitude to your benefactors. Some of the passages about your good matrons were quite scandalous. Miss Smith was absolutely correct. Though vividly written, the manuscript is unpublishable.'

'But it's the truth, sir.'

'Nonsense! It's the truth as you perceive it – a childish tirade by an angry, undeserving creature, utterly self-absorbed and far too passionate. I am ashamed of you, Hetty. I cannot understand how you could write this.'

'Then give me my memoirs back, sir,' I said defiantly.

'When I am less distracted by my own work, I

will glance at it again. Perhaps there might be a few simple passages we can work on. Your childhood in the country might make a pleasing pastoral piece. People like to read about simple country bumpkins.'

'They're not simple country bumpkins,' I said hotly. 'They're my family.'

'Of course, of course,' he said soothingly. 'And perhaps, when I'm not quite as busy, I'll help you to construct a written portrait that will do them justice. Now, I think you'd better run back to the kitchen, Hetty. I don't want you to copy any more today. I need a little space to continue my new story. You're distracting me.'

I peered all around.

'What is it now?'

'I'm looking for my memoirs. Can I have my book back, please?'

'I shall keep it safely here in my room, and if I have a spare moment in the next few weeks, I shall give it another glance.'

'Oh no, sir!'

'Are you arguing with me, Hetty Feather?'

'No, sir. Well, yes, sir, I suppose I am, because I want my memoirs back. They're mine, and I feel uncomfortable without them.'

'You're being ridiculous, girl. The book is safe in my room.'

'But *where*, sir? I can't see it anywhere. It's not on your desk, or on your shelves, or any of the piles of books.'

'I have it safe, I assure you.'

'Then *please* may I have it back?'

'Of course you may, in the fullness of time, when I have finished looking at it.'

'But that's not fair!' I wailed, stamping my foot in my passion. 'It's my book and I want it back *now*!'

'Hetty Feather!' Sarah came bursting in through the door, skirts flying. 'Whatever are you up to, shouting at the master! Forgive her, sir – she's just a wilful, ignorant orphan who does not yet know her place.'

'I am not an *orphan*!' I screamed as Sarah picked me up in her huge arms, heaved me over her shoulder like a coal sack, and bore me away.

10

Sarah carried me all the way back down two flights of stairs to the kitchen and then dumped me on the rag rug in front of the range. Mrs Briskett stared at us both in astonishment, up to her elbows in uncooked pastry.

'Oh my Lord, whatever's the matter, Sarah?' she gasped, wringing her doughy hands.

'Hetty Feather's taken leave of her senses! I was seeing to the fires on the first floor when I heard this rumpus upstairs. She was shrieking at the master!'

'Oh, Hetty, how could you! *Shrieking*, you say, Sarah?'

'Like a banshee! Is that not right, Hetty? Whatever possessed you?'

'He's got my memoirs and he won't give them back!'

'What? You're working yourself into a passion over a scribbling notebook? Have some sense, girl! The master will give you notice now.'

'Just as I was getting fond of you, child! How could you lose your temper like that?'

'It's the red hair – they're all the same. Stop that noise at *once*, Hetty Feather, or I'll give you such a slapping,' said Sarah, shaking me.

'But he's stolen it from me!'

'Why on earth would the master do that, you silly girl? He's got countless notebooks of his own.'

'He said he wanted to keep it a while, so he could improve certain passages,' I sobbed.

'Well, surely that's what you wanted, is it not?' said Mrs Briskett, perplexed.

'Yes, but *I* want to look after it, not him. It's *mine*.'

'I've never heard such nonsense in my life!'

I couldn't make either of them understand. My memoirs meant so much to me. I'd had so little that was truly my own at the hospital. I'd worked so hard at them. It was as if little pieces of myself were stuck to the pages of that notebook, my very blood mixed in with the ink. But though I put this into words as passionately as I could, they still seemed shocked at me – and I couldn't implore the master again because they would not let me near him.

At first they were both sure he would ring for me and dismiss me on the spot, but when he'd done nothing by the next day, they decided he *might* have forgiven me because I was young and inexperienced.

'And you can't *help* having that awful red hair, can you, dear?' said Mrs Briskett. She pulled my cap down so that it brushed my eyebrows, to hide as much hair as she could.

I was allowed to do all my usual chores, though forbidden to serve the master his afternoon tea. If Sarah thought she heard the master's step nearby while we were making his bed or scrubbing his bathtub, she would whisk me hastily out of the way.

I wrote a long tale of woe to Mama, telling her all about it. She was very tender and comforting when she replied, but in many ways seemed to take the same attitude as Mrs Briskett and Sarah.

Try to stay out of his way, Hetty dear, and when you do evenchooly bump into him stair at the flor and look as meak as posibol. In all other respecs this seems a good posishun so you must KEEP it. This leter is sent with all the love in the world from yore own dear Mama

But she added a P.S.: *You can allways surch for yore memoirs when dusting his studdy and shov it down yore apron quik.*

I *did* search, but I couldn't find my memoirs in any of the piles of books. Greatly daring, I tried the little drawer in his desk where he kept the stamps – but it was stuck fast. He had locked it! I wondered if he had crammed the book in there. It would just about fit. But there was no key in the lock, and I couldn't find one anywhere in his trinket tray.

I was fretting miserably about it the next morning, when Bertie called with his meat basket.

'Hey, Mrs Briskett, wait till you see the side of beef I've got for your Sunday lunch! If you make one of your Yorkshire puddings, it'll be a meal fit for the old Queen herself. It'll put you in such a good mood I dare say you'll let Hetty here stay out an extra hour – isn't that right?'

'Young Hetty isn't allowed out on Sunday at all, boy, let alone an extra hour. She's disgraced herself good and proper, she has,' said Mrs Briskett.

Bertie raised his eyebrows. 'Cor, Hetty, what've you *done*!'

'She's severely cheeked the master, when he's been so kind as to take an interest in her, that's what she's *done*,' said Sarah.

'Oooh, what did you say, Hetty?' asked Bertie, grinning.

'I simply asked for my property back,' I said haughtily.

'No, no, missy! There was no *asking*! When I heard, you was shrieking your head off and stamping your foot,' said Sarah.

'What a girl!' said Bertie admiringly. 'But you haven't lost your position, have you, Hetty?'

188

'She's very lucky not to,' said Mrs Briskett.

'It's only because the master's preoccupied with his work. He's always like this when he starts a new story. I once splashed red-hot soup into his lap when I was serving his supper and he barely flinched, he was so busy scribbling in his notebook,' said Sarah.

'He's no right to purloin *my* notebook,' I said.

'Here, perhaps he's pinching all your ideas, Hetty,' said Bertie.

Mrs Briskett and Sarah laughed heartily, as if he'd made the funniest joke in the world. I did not find this amusing, but at least it softened them up. Mrs Briskett relented over my Sunday-night curfew, though she issued so many conditions and commands she set my head spinning.

I had added incentive to finish sewing my Sunday dress. I sat up half Saturday night adding the finishing touches by flickering candlelight and was consequently so tired I nearly fell asleep during the sermon, my head nid-nodding while Mrs Briskett and Sarah took it in turns to give me a sharp poke.

It was wonderful, though, to parade into and out of church in my new green frock with its gold trimmings. I saw some of the younger maids giving it the eye, and I was sure they were looking envious. I could have done with a decent pair of white stockings instead of my old holey grey ones, and my stout boots were much too hobbledehoy. I looked at a girl wearing pale-grey kid boots with little heels and pearl buttons, and longed to possess a similar pair. I looked down at Mrs Briskett's feet and then at Sarah's, but *their* boots were almost as ugly and serviceable as my own, so there was no point hoping for their cast-offs; besides, their feet were twice the size of mine so I'd be shuffling around like a clown.

I remembered the clowns that I'd seen at Tanglefield's Travelling Circus. My stomach gave a little twist as I thought of Madame Adeline and her troupe of rosin-backed horses. I'd been a very little girl when I'd first seen her perform. I thought she looked like a fairy in her pink sparkly outfit, her long locks flowing, the most beautiful woman in the world. When I ran away from the hospital and found her again, I realized that she was a sad old lady beneath her wig and thick make-up. I wondered if she was still performing.

Bertie was waiting on the area steps, wearing his best brown suit, but not quite so perfumed this time. He rolled his eyes when he saw my new dress.

'My, Hetty, that's a fine outfit you're wearing!' he said.

'She made it herself, every stitch,' said Sarah.

'One of *my* old Sunday outfits, bless her. I always loved that bright green – but it looks even better on

190

young Hetty, with her red hair,' said Mrs Briskett.

They both beamed at me proudly while I fidgeted before them. I couldn't work out how to react to them at all. I was used to people who loved me (like Mama and my old foster family) or people who loathed me (like Matron Pigface Peters and Matron Stinking Bottomly). Mrs Briskett and Sarah ticked me off almost as much as the matrons – but they seemed genuinely fond of me already.

I wondered whether I should give them a hug goodbye. Perhaps they would think it outrageous. I was sure *Bertie* would welcome a hug, but I wasn't sure it would be wise.

'You look a total sweetheart in that lovely green dress, Hetty,' he said, spinning me round.

Was he saying I was *his* sweetheart? My heart started thumping inside my tight velvet bodice. I knew Jem assumed I was *his* sweetheart. His last letter to me had made it plain:

My dear Hetty,

What a pair of sillies we are. I thought you had forgotten all about your dear Jem – and you thought I had forgotten YOU, transferring my affections to little Eliza. I will always love her dearly as my young sister – but I hope that you and I will find the deeper love of true sweethearts

191

in the fullness of time.

Of course you're very young, still a child, and we are forced to live many cruel miles apart. But I am nothing if not patient, Hetty. I will work hard and save hard, biding my time. In two or three years' time I should be ready to branch out on my own, and then . . . well, we shall see!

Take care, my own sweet girl, and write often to your

Very loving Jem

I did not need to carry the letter on my person. I had read it so many times by flickering candlelight that I knew every word by heart. Yet even though I knew it so well, I didn't know what to make of it. I was thrilled, of course. It was exciting to think that I inspired such deep feelings in such a fine man. But this was the trouble. I'd known Jem the *boy*. When I thought of him, I still saw him as an earnest, fresh-faced ten-year-old, his hair tousled, his clothes torn, his boots muddy.

I could not match that Jem with the tall man in corduroy waiting outside the hospital. I remembered so many sweet things the boy Jem had said to me – but this heartfelt love letter unnerved me. Since I forced myself to stop thinking about Jem the year I was ten, he had grown shadowy, almost unreal, like a character in a storybook. Now it seemed almost as if Robin Hood or Dick Whittington were writing to me.

What would he think if he saw me walking hand in hand down the street with Bertie? I blushed and tried to wriggle my fingers free.

'Hey, keep hold, Hetty!' he said, curling his own fingers to keep mine safe.

'I – I'm not sure I should be holding your hand,' I murmured.

'And why's that? Do you suddenly think you're too grand for me in your fancy dress?'

'No, of course not! It's just . . . well, to be utterly truthful, Bertie, I think I have another sweetheart already.'

Bertie dropped my hand and stared at me. 'Well, that was quick work! You've only been out of that hospital place five minutes!'

'No, this is a long-ago sweetheart, when I lived in the country when I was little.'

'How little?'

'When I was five and Jem was ten.'

Bertie burst out laughing. 'Oh, come on, Hetty!'

'I know, it sounds so silly, but he was my dear brother and so kind to me.'

'You can't be sweethearts with your *brother*.'

'He's not a real brother by blood, he's my foster brother. His name's Jem and – and we always used to play we would get married one day.'

'Look, when I was five I wanted to marry the pretty little girl with plaits I glimpsed at church on Sundays, *and* the maid with the rosy cheeks who served us porridge at breakfast, *and* the kind old dame who sat me on her lap when she taught me my letters.'

'Yes, but he does still care for me, Bertie. He's started writing to me.'

'But can he come and see you and take you out of a Sunday?'

'No.'

'So what would you rather do – sit at home in your scullery week after week, or come out with me and have fun?'

'Oh, Bertie! I want to come out with you and have fun, of course I do – but I feel bad about Jem. He says he'll wait patiently for me, even if it's years.'

'Come off it! How old is this Jem? He must be . . . nineteen now. You're telling me a grown man of nineteen is happy to moon about, daydreaming about a little girl he's not seen for goodness knows how many years. Is he soft in the head, this Jem?'

'No!'

'Is he very plain? Very thin or very stout? Is he missing a limb or two?'

'*No!* He's strong and tall and good-looking.'

'Then don't you think he might have half the

village after him, if he's such a catch? I bet he's got a sweetheart at home.'

'Jem would always be true to me,' I said, but my voice wavered.

I remembered all Jem's sweet-talk with little Eliza, spinning her the same stories.

'Aha!' said Bertie, seeing my face. 'You're not so sure now, are you? Come on, Hetty, stop your nonsense. Don't spoil things. I'm taking you somewhere special today.'

'To the river?'

'No, that was *last* week. *This* week we're going on a little expedition. I've got an even better surprise.'

We walked down into town and then hopped on a bus for a ten-minute ride. We sat squashed up together on the top, the wind in our hair, looking over a high wall into green parklands. Then, far in the distance, I saw shimmering reds and yellows and bright blues. I heard music. I sniffed savoury smells.

'What is it? What *is* this place? Oh, it's not a circus, is it?' I asked, quivering.

'No, it's a fair. There are swings and merry-go-rounds with carved horses and—'

'I know what a fair is. I've been to one,' I said, remembering the children's fair in Hyde Park on the day of the Golden Jubilee.

'There! I thought it would be such a surprise,' said Bertie, looking very disappointed.

'Oh it is, it is – a *lovely* surprise,' I reassured him, standing up eagerly to see better. The bus lurched and I nearly toppled over.

'Careful!' said Bertie, grabbing me. He stroked the gold fringing on my bodice. 'This is very pretty. Did you really make it all yourself?'

'Yes, every stitch,' I said proudly.

I remembered my first darning lesson at the hospital when I was five: how I'd pricked myself with the needle a dozen times, and bunched the toes up together. Perhaps the hospital had taught me something useful, then?

I stared at the other girls all about me as I got off the bus. I was pleased to see that my dress looked almost as stylish as theirs – though some of their dresses hung a little differently, sticking out at the back. At first I thought that all the girls, though otherwise slender, simply had big fat bottoms – but surely they couldn't all have such protruding rears?

'Bertie, why do those girls' dresses stick out in that way?' I asked.

Bertie seemed to be the fount of all knowledge, but this time he shrugged his shoulders. 'Search me, Hetty. Ask one. *I* can't, I'll get my face slapped.'

I wasn't sure I dared – but when we were waiting in the queue to climb up inside the great red and yellow helter-skelter, we got talking to the couple in front. Bertie knew the boy, who worked in the draper's in the next town. His girl worked there too, and clearly made use of the shop's wares, because her dress was sewn all over with ruffles and ribbons, with little jet beads around her cuffs. I admired these, and she admired my gold fringing. She clapped her hands when I told her I'd whipped it off an old curtain.

I peered at the very prominent bump at the back of her dress. 'I love the way your dress hangs at the back,' I said, describing a curve with my hands.

'What? Oh, you mean my bustle!' she giggled.

'Ah! So, this bustle – is it stitched into the dress?'

She brought her head close to mine. 'It's a special pad. We sell them at our shop for five shillings,' she whispered.

Five shillings! But I didn't need to *buy* one. I could surely fashion a pad out of anything. I thought of all the cushions cluttering every chair and sofa at Mr Buchanan's. No one would notice if just one went missing . . .

Then we were inside the helter-skelter, climbing up and up the stairs in the dark. The draper's couple kept pausing above us, so that I blundered right into the girl's wretched bustle.

'What are they playing at?' I said to Bertie.

'Oh, I know exactly what they're playing at,' said Bertie. 'We could play that game too.'

'You'd better not try!' I said, and when he did indeed try to put his arms round me, I gave him a sharp poke with my elbow.

When we got to the top of the helter-skelter, I felt dizzy up so high, right above the gaudy canopies of the fair, able to see for miles across the wooded parklands. I clutched hold of Bertie in spite of myself.

'There now, Hetty, I've got you tight,' he said.

He sat down on a mat and pulled me onto his lap. Then someone gave us a shove in the back. We were suddenly whizzing round and round and round, at such a rate and with so many bumps I thought we might fly straight off the slide – but Bertie was true to his word, holding onto me tightly, his hands gripping my waist. We hurtled right down to the end of the slide and shot off onto the grass, tumbling in an undignified heap, screaming and laughing.

'That was good, eh, Hetty?' said Bertie, pulling me upright.

'Yes, it was wonderful,' I said, jumping up and down and clapping my hands.

'You're a marvellous girl, up for any kind of lark,' said Bertie. 'Right, I'm going to win you a coconut as a reward.'

We went to the coconut shy and he tried his hardest, aiming three balls at the hairy coconuts balanced on sticks. He hit one with his last throw, but he couldn't topple it.

'It's a cheat. They must be stuck on!' he said, red in the face with effort.

'Can I have a go?' I begged.

'It's a waste of time. You can't shift the beggars,' said Bertie.

'Please!'

'You're so obstinate!' he said, but he paid a penny for me to have a go too.

I tried my best. I missed completely with my first shot. I hit a coconut with my second ball – and it wobbled a little but stayed balanced on its stick.

'There, what did I say?' said Bertie.

I took aim with my last ball. I pictured Matron Pigface Peters' head on the stick and *hurled* the ball with all my strength. It struck the coconut with such force that it shot straight up – and then toppled to the ground.

'There! I did it! We've got a coconut, Bertie!' I shouted triumphantly.

Bertie didn't look too thrilled, though everyone else around laughed and clapped me.

'So what do we *do* with this nut? How do we eat it?' I asked.

'Crack it open,' said Bertie.

'How do we do that?'

'You're such a strong girl I should think you could do it with your teeth,' he snapped.

'What? Oh, Bertie, don't be cross with me. I thought you *wanted* to win a coconut. Are you cross with me for spending all your pennies?'

'I've got heaps more, silly. I'm just cross because *I* wanted to win it for you. Bit of manly pride and all that. Come over to the darts stall. I dare say you can win us a china ornament or a goldfish in a bowl.'

'Will you be even crosser if I do?' I said.

'Probably!' said Bertie, but he was smiling now.

'Seriously though, I feel so bad that I haven't any money for rides. I won't get paid for a couple of months yet.'

'I've got heaps for both of us,' said Bertie, patting his jingling pocket. 'I saved all my tips this week, *and* mowed Mr Jarvis's big garden for an extra shilling, so we're rich. So is it darts now, Hetty?'

'I think I'd sooner go on that wonderful merry-go-round,' I said.

'Excellent!'

We stood watching for a whole turn so that I could work out which horse I liked best. They were all painted different colours – black and brown and grey like real horses, with great manes and flowing tails of proper horsehair. There was one splendid white beast with a black patch on his eye, just like Madame Adeline's Pirate from that long-ago circus. I knew he was the one.

I pointed him out to Bertie, and as soon as the music slowed, he leaped onto the boards, dodging round other eager boys, and claimed the white horse as ours. He helped me up so that I could cling to the mane, while he sat at the back, holding the twisting golden pole.

The lad came for his pennies, the music started, and we were off, whirling round and round. It was almost as good as cantering about the ring on that real horse with Madame Adeline. I dug my heels into Pirate's painted flanks and threw my head back. My clumsily arranged hair lost half its pins and came tumbling down past my shoulders.

When we stumbled off the merry-go-round at last, deliciously dizzy, I tried to pin my hair back into place.

'Leave it, Hetty, it looks lovely loose like that,' said Bertie.

'It makes me look younger than ever,' I said, sticking pins in willy-nilly.

'What's the matter with looking young? You don't want to look like a wrinkled old lady, do you? You look all right to me. Better than all right.' He touched a stray lock of hair, stroking it gently. I was very glad I'd taken the trouble to lather it thoroughly with Pears soap last night, even though it meant going to bed with sopping wet hair.

'You've got lovely hair, Hetty,' said Bertie.

'It's red, though. Everyone hates red hair,' I said.

'I think it suits you. It's grand – so bright it dazzles your eyes.'

'I think my eyes are my best feature. They're sapphire-blue, do you see? My mama called me Sapphire before she had to give me away . . .' I hesitated. 'You can call me Sapphire, if you like.'

'Sapphire. Mmm. Sapphire, Sapphire, Sapphire. Do you know what? I think Hetty suits you better.' Bertie jingled the change in his pocket. 'What next, eh? We can have another go on the merry-go-round – or try the swing boats – or I could buy us a poke of fried potatoes?'

I thought hard. 'How about the darts stall? You win us something this time,' I suggested.

So we tried our luck. With his second dart Bertie scored a bull's-eye and we could choose any prize on the stand. I circled round and round, in an agony of indecision.

'Have a goldfish. It matches your hair exactly, dearie,' said the man running the stall.

'Don't you cast aspersions on my sweetheart's hair,' said Bertie.

This time I didn't contradict him.

'Why don't you pick an ornament, Hetty?' Bertie suggested.

'Good idea,' I said – but I still had to deliberate long and hard.

Eventually I chose a little black-and-white dog with floppy ears and an earnest expression. 'He's lovely, Bertie. Thank you so much,' I said. 'Well, if I've got a present, you must have my coconut.'

'No, you take it home and share it with Mrs B and Sarah. That'll please them – and that way Mrs B will let you out next Sunday without any argle-bargle, so long as you behave! What were you *doing*, shouting at your master? If I tried that trick with Jarvis he'd box my ears. Here, Hetty, this notebook of yours – do you record everything in it?'

'Things that take my fancy,' I said.

'Will you write about me in it?' Bertie asked eagerly.

'Perhaps,' I told him.

11

We were a little late getting home, and I got severely ticked off by Mrs Briskett. Sarah had already gone out for her mysterious Sunday evening engagement. I felt a little sorry for Mrs Briskett all the same, stuck indoors all afternoon and evening, so I produced my coconut.

'Here's a little present, Mrs B,' I said.

'Mrs Briskett to you! You're just trying to get round me, you bad girl,' she said, but she took it all the same.

She made a hole in it and poured out strange watery 'milk'. I didn't care for it at all, but Mrs Briskett drank it up eagerly.

'It works wonders for the complexion, coconut milk,' she said.

I stared at Mrs Briskett's big red face, wondering if she was about to sprout bristly brown whiskers like the coconut, but nothing untoward happened.

She took her rolling pin, put the coconut on the

floor, and attacked it vigorously. It smashed into small pieces, exposing the white inside. I gingerly tried the white meat.

'Ah! I like this part!' I said, crunching happily.

Mrs Briskett tucked in too.

'We'll leave some for Sarah when she comes back, won't we?'

'Of course we will,' said Mrs Briskett, setting a fair portion aside on a saucer. 'But I don't think she'll be back till late.'

'Mrs Briskett, do tell me – *are* Sarah and that strange man with the moustache . . . sweethearts?'

Mrs Briskett snorted. 'Oh, Hetty Feather, whatever will you come out with next? The very idea! And I don't know what Mrs Arthur Brown would say if she thought her hubby was stepping out with our Sarah.'

'Then why does she see him every Sunday?'

'She doesn't just see Mr Brown, she's with a lot of other like-minded folk. But they don't go to see each other. They're there to meet up with something very queer. Oh, it gives me the shivers just to think of it.'

'What is it? Tell me, Mrs Briskett! Who do they meet?'

'I couldn't possibly say,' said Mrs Briskett. 'But I don't approve. I don't approve *at all*.' She gave a genteel shudder.

I was more bewildered than ever. Was she seriously suggesting that Sarah and Mr Brown, two rigidly respectable people, were somehow behaving in a reprehensible manner? I thought back to the vicar's sermon in church. He had spoken out against the music hall, suggesting that it was not a suitable place for serious God-fearing folk – not quite a den of iniquity like a public house, but disturbing all the same. I wasn't sure what happened in this mysterious music hall. I pictured Sarah gaudily made-up and provocatively dressed, singing a saucy song as she strutted across the stage, pursued by Mr Brown, waggling his eyebrows and twirling his moustache. This fancy was so comical I couldn't help snorting with laughter.

'It's not funny, Hetty. I'm seriously worried about Sarah. It's taken hold of her and she won't listen to reason,' said Mrs Briskett.

Then perhaps Sarah went to a public house after all? Again, I had only a very hazy idea of what they were like inside. I pictured Sarah slumped on a bench, downing a tankard of gin, while Mr Brown drank straight from the bottle, dribbling all down his droopy moustache. I snorted again – and then hurried off to the scullery to avoid another scolding. I made up my tiny bed and sat with half a candle, writing letters.

I wrote several pages to Mama, telling her about

my new dress in some detail, and my plans for the pad at the back to turn myself into a fashion plate. I also told her about my trip to the fairground with Bertie – *but don't worry, Mama, he is just a friend. I know I am much too young for sweethearts, but he is fun to be with and he seems to like me.*

I reassured her that I was in perfect health. She was always asking if I was eating properly, wondering if I had even the slightest cough. The doctor at the hospital had once said I had a weak chest, so Mama still worried terribly.

I wrote to Jem too, but this letter was considerably shorter. I knew he probably wouldn't be interested in my new dress, and whether it should have a pad at the back or not. I did tell him briefly about my trip to the fair, but I did not mention Bertie as such. I said I went to the fair with a friend, and carefully did not specify the sex.

This only took a paragraph. I did not know what else to write. I kept trying to conjure up Jem's adult face – but although I could picture that tall figure in brown corduroy, his features were a blur. It seemed safer to think of the long-ago Jem, so I filled my page asking if he ever strolled past the special tree where we'd played endless games of house together? Did he still fish in the stream where I'd paddled? Did he plough with Saxon and Sam, the two Shire horses I'd once taken such delight in feeding chunks of carrot?

I was wide awake and still had some candle left. I wished I could write a letter to Gideon, but I didn't know where he was. He would have left the hospital by now and would be shut up in some far-away barracks, learning how to be a soldier. I ached for him, wishing I had some way of protecting him.

The letter to Jem had reminded me too much of the past. I thought of that little dark country cottage with all of us children tumbling around inside. Gideon had always come off worst in any free-for-all. He came last in our running races, though he had long legs like a colt. Our brother Saul could beat him, even though he was on crutches. I fingered my ribs automatically when I thought of Saul. He had had a terrible trick of poking me with the sharp end of his stick, leaving me all over bruises. Mother always insisted we be kind to Saul, but she forgot to tell *him* to be kind to *us*.

I knew it was a sin, but I had thoroughly disliked my brother Saul. Still, I had been very sad when he died of the influenza at the hospital.

I shivered. I did not want to think of the hospital any more. I might not be living the life of my dreams, publishing my memoirs and providing for dear Mama – but my new life as a servant with

Mrs Briskett and Sarah in Mr Monkey Buchanan's house was so, so, so much better than being shut up in the cold, forbidding hospital. And my Sunday afternoons with Bertie were positively delightful.

I wondered whether to start a new memoir book now that Mr Buchanan had purloined my old one. His wastepaper basket was often stuffed with crumpled discarded pages. I could straighten them out, maybe even smooth them with Sarah's flatiron. Then I could stitch them together, strike through every sentence of his spidery scribble, and start my own memoirs on the blank backs.

No, perhaps I would always be too sharply truthful for autobiography. I could attempt a work of fiction instead – a novel about a young girl with eyes as blue as sapphires – but she would be tall and shapely and have tumbling blonde curls. Perhaps she had been brought up in a strict and severe (unnamed) institution and cruelly treated by terrible matrons. She'd be sent off at the tender age of fourteen to earn her living as a maid, in spite of her intelligence and obvious potential, and feel cast down by the dreary routine of being a general servant. But then she meets her true sweetheart, a former workhouse inmate, now cheerily earning his living as ... a baker's boy ...? I blushed in the darkness of the scullery, ashamed to have let myself get so carried away. I blew out my guttering candle and tried to settle.

I heard Mrs Briskett's footsteps as she paced backwards and forwards across the scrubbed flags of the kitchen floor. Every now and then she muttered to herself and sighed. It was clear that Sarah was still not home.

Then I heard the clop of hooves outside in the road, anxious voices, and sudden footsteps. There was a knock on the back door, then Mrs Briskett's sudden exclamation:

'Oh my Lord, Sarah, whatever's happened!'

I jumped out of bed and ran into the kitchen. There was Sarah, swaying in her purple Sunday best, her eyes rolling, her mouth open, propped up by Mr Brown and a cabbie. Good heavens, was she really *drunk*?

'Sarah, Sarah, Sarah, look at the state of you!' said Mrs Briskett, seizing hold of her and pushing her onto a kitchen chair.

'She was certainly in no state to get herself home,' said Mr Brown. 'I had to take it upon myself to call a cab for her.'

'I'm so sorry, Mr Brown. Oh, Sarah, you silly girl! I knew this would happen!'

'She paid for a special materialization – and it worked, it worked tremendously. Sarah was ecstatic. There's no other word to describe it;

211

ecstatic! But then it all became too much for her, and she went into a swoon, quite overcome. She rendered herself incapable of getting out of the house, let alone coming all the way home. I had to practically carry her out of the cab – and she's not a light woman,' Mr Brown said ruefully.

'Oh dear, I do hope you haven't done yourself an injury, Mr Brown. Thank you so much for looking after our Sarah. Please allow me to pay for the cab,' said Mrs Briskett.

'No, no, I won't hear of it. What's a cab fare between friends? But I'm just giving you fair warning – on Sunday evenings Sarah really needs to be accompanied by a lady friend who can look after her, perhaps loosen her clothing if she's overcome once more. I've tried my best, but there are limits to the attention I can decently pay her. Do I make myself clear?'

'Clear as day, Mr Brown,' said Mrs Briskett. 'Thank you very much, gentlemen. I'll take over now.'

She bustled about Sarah, undoing her bonnet and the collar of her dress. Mr Brown and the cabbie wiped the sweat off their brows and made a hasty retreat.

Mrs Briskett frowned at me. 'Don't just stand there gawping, Hetty. Run for the smelling salts – in the cupboard over there.'

I rummaged in the cupboard, while Mrs Briskett plunged her hand right inside Sarah's bodice. There was a sudden snap, and Sarah breathed out and almost overflowed her Sunday dress.

'There, I've got her stays undone – that should help,' said Mrs Briskett. 'Where are those salts, Hetty?'

I thrust a packet of Saxa salt at her and she sighed irritably.

'*Smelling* salts, you stupid girl. The dark blue bottle in the corner!'

She grabbed the bottle from me, uncorked it, and waved it under Sarah's nose. Sarah's head jerked, her eyes blinked, and she let out a gasp.

'There now, Sarah, take a deep breath. Oh my Lord, you've given us such a fright!'

'Is she very drunk, Mrs Briskett?' I asked.

'Drunk?' Mrs Briskett stared at me. 'Hetty Feather, what a thing to say!'

'*Drunk!*' Sarah echoed. This accusation shocked her back to total consciousness. 'The very idea! I haven't had a drop of alcohol since Christmas, apart from a dribble of sherry in your trifle, Mrs B, and no one can count that against me.'

'Now, now, take no notice of the stupid girl. Of course we know you're not drunk. Don't go up-setting yourself further. I'll make a nice cup of tea to settle you. Come on now.'

Mrs Briskett nodded at me to put the kettle on the range, while she knelt down and unbuttoned Sarah's boots. 'There now, wiggle your tootsies.'

'You're ever so good to me, Mrs B.'

'Well, you're a dear girl, even if you get carried away by strange fancies. It's not good for you, though, getting yourself in such a state. Look at you, swooning all the way home! These sessions are getting too much for you. You'll do yourself a mischief. Plus you're spending all your wretched savings! Promise me you won't go any more.'

'Oh, I *have* to go, Mrs B! Tonight was so wonderful, a true miracle! I saw her! I felt her hands upon me! My own dear mother!' Sarah breathed, and then her eyes rolled as she swooned again.

'Her mother?' I said as Mrs Briskett wafted the smelling salts under her nose once more. The sharp stench made my own eyes water. 'But I thought her mother was dead!'

'Exactly. Dead and buried. And that's where she should stay,' said Mrs Briskett.

'You mean . . . she's a ghost?' I whispered.

'Something similar. I don't think it's right or Christian. We shouldn't meddle with ghouls and ghosts. If we get them to pop out at us, how do we know we can ever be shot of them?' Mrs Briskett looked all about her, as if an eerie spectral being were lurking in a corner of the kitchen.

'She's not a ghoul or a ghost!' Sarah murmured, mopping her forehead. 'She's a beautiful spirit. She speaks to me through Madame Berenice.'

'Is she a circus lady?' I asked, thinking of dear Madame Adeline.

Sarah looked affronted, but Mrs Briskett nodded grimly.

'She's exactly *like* a circus lady, performing her tricks while Sarah and all her silly cronies sit around in a circle, marvelling. And paying through the nose for the experience,' she said.

Sarah rose unsteadily to her feet. 'I'll thank you to keep your opinions to yourself, Mrs B. You've been very kind, but I'll not stop to hear you talk of Madame Berenice in such a manner. She's a saint of a woman. She simply wants to comfort poor grieving souls by bringing us messages from the spirit world. It beats me why you won't come too, and hear a few words from your own mother,' she said.

'I heard enough words from her when she was in this world – and few of them were kind ones,' said Mrs Briskett. 'Now sit down again, Sarah, or you'll *fall* down.'

'I'm going to my room,' Sarah said, and staggered across the kitchen.

'Oh, the obstinacy of the silly girl,' said Mrs Briskett. 'Come, Hetty, we'll have to take hold of her or she'll get halfway up those stairs and then tumble all the way down.'

So the two of us battled with the bulging bulk of poor Sarah, heaving her right up to her room at the top of the house. We were all three breathing very heavily by this time.

'There now!' Mrs Briskett panted, propelling Sarah towards her bed. 'Light her candle, Hetty, so we can see what we're doing.'

I did as I was told. In the wavering light we all saw the image of Sarah's mother on the wall.

'Oh! Oh, Mother dear!' said Sarah, sitting down heavily on her bed, weeping.

'Now, now, don't upset yourself,' said Mrs Briskett, busily unbuttoning her.

'These are tears of joy, Mrs B, tears of joy,' Sarah murmured. 'Joy that we're reunited at last.'

I found Sarah's white nightgown and put it over her head for decency while Mrs Briskett struggled with all her buttons and hooks and manoeuvred her lumpy body out of her bodice and stays. When her quivering flesh was entirely freed at last, Mrs Briskett pushed her gently back on her bed and pulled the covers up over her.

'There now. Go to sleep, Sarah, there's a good girl,' she said, tucking her up as tenderly as if she were her mother herself.

Sarah obediently closed her eyes, and we backed out of the door.

Mrs Briskett breathed a great sigh of relief. 'My Lord, it affected her badly this time!'

'*What* did? *How* did she see her mother?' I thought of the gravestones by the church. 'She didn't . . . she didn't *dig her up*?'

Mrs Briskett shook her head at me. 'Don't be ridiculous, Hetty. All right, I'll tell you – not that I know much, mind. I'll come down with you and have another cup of tea. It's fearfully late but it'll take me hours to get to sleep after this to-do.'

So we sat down together in the dark kitchen and sipped tea while Mrs Briskett explained properly.

'Sarah goes to see Madame Berenice every Sunday. This Madame calls herself a spiritualist-medium. She says she's in touch with the spirit world.'

'*Is* she?'

'Well, who's to say? Sarah clearly believes so – and Mr Brown and all the other folk who go there and give Madame Berenice half their hard-earned wages. They're all that desperate to see their long-departed loved ones. Mr Brown lost his only son to influenza years ago and wants to get in touch with him. *Mrs* Brown holds no truck with this kind of caper and neither do I. It's not decent, nor Christian, trying to meddle with the Lord's will. If

217

you're dead you're dead, and you should jolly well stay dead, not come back and start haunting people. It doesn't do any good. Look at the state of Sarah tonight. Oh, she'll be that mortified in the morning!'

'But what does this Madame Berenice *do*, Mrs B? How does she get in touch with the spirit world?'

'Don't ask me, Hetty. All Sarah will say is that they sit around in a ring in a darkened room, and then this Madame Berenice goes into a trance and starts talking in strange voices.' Mrs Briskett shivered. 'You wouldn't get me in that circle for a million pounds!'

I lay awake thinking about it long after I'd gone back to bed. It seemed a very strange idea to me – but then *everything* seemed strange to me in this crazy outside world.

I was woken by the sound of crockery in the kitchen. When I ran in, I saw Sarah bustling about, laying breakfast, neat in her dark work dress and white cap and apron.

'How do, Hetty,' she said cheerily. 'I thought I'd give Mrs B a little lie-in this morning, seeing as she was up till all hours on account of yours truly!'

She didn't sound the slightest bit embarrassed. She danced about the kitchen, treating the stone flags like a polished ballroom floor. She looked comical, of course – a great lumpy parlourmaid waltzing around with the breadboard and the teapot – but I couldn't laugh at her, not when she looked so wondrously happy. She buttered the good crust on the end of the loaf, spread it with Mrs Briskett's deluxe strawberry jam specially kept for the master's scones, and handed it to me.

'Get that down you, you skinny little ha'p'orth,' she said.

'My mama always gave me special little treats when I was at the hospital,' I said.

'Mothers are the very best, aren't they, Hetty!' said Sarah.

Mrs Briskett was in a good mood too, having had an hour's lie-in, so she decided to let me have a turn at baking, showing me how to make an apple pie. It was fresh out the oven when Bertie came with our meat delivery of mince and chops and a rib of beef.

He sniffed appreciatively at the sight of the big pie, its golden pastry oozing apples, cloves and cinnamon. 'My, that looks a sight for sore eyes, Mrs B,' he said enthusiastically. 'You're a wonderful cook, ma'am, especially in the pie department.'

'It's not *my* pie, Bertie. Young Hetty made it. She's got a very light hand with her pastry. I doubt I could do better myself.'

'*Hetty* baked it!' said Bertie, looking astonished.

'Don't act so surprised!' I said. 'Can he have a tiny taste, Mrs Briskett?'

'I don't see why not,' she said. 'In fact we'll all try a slice.'

She cut us a liberal piece each and ladled on a spoonful of cream too. 'Here, Sarah, you need some good food inside you after all that swooning last night.'

'You were swooning, Sarah?' said Bertie. 'Why's that? Do you have a pash on some fine fellow? Ooh, was it the thought of meeting up with me today? Well, I'm very flattered, Sarah, but I'm afraid I'm already taken. You'd definitely be in with a chance, but I'm that feared of Hetty here I daren't cross her.'

'Stop your cheek and try her pie, lad. It's very good,' said Sarah, munching.

He took a large bite of pie, and then pretended to choke. He clutched his throat, eyes popping, staggering around the kitchen as if poisoned.

'I'll *throw* the pie at you if you don't behave,' I sniffed.

Bertie stopped playing the fool and took another big bite. 'It's actually absolutely delicious, Hetty! Total knockout! My, you'll make someone a lovely little wife one day!'

'No I won't! I'm not going to be anyone's wife, little or otherwise,' I said, tasting my own portion of pie. It truly *was* delicious. 'I shall make my own way in life,' I declared indistinctly through a big mouthful.

'Won't you be lonely, Hetty?' said Bertie.

'Not at all. I shall set up home with my mama,' I said.

'Oh, bless the child,' said Sarah. 'Would that I could do the same.'

'Now careful, Hetty, you'll set her off again,' said Mrs Briskett. 'We don't want her swooning all over the place.'

'I am perfectly well, thank you, Mrs B,' said Sarah with dignity.

'Oh yes, it looked like it last night!'

'I was overcome because I was so happy to be reunited with my beloved mother, to feel her own hands upon me, her lips kissing my brow! I am so very glad I met Madame Berenice!'

'Oh, that spiritualist lady?' said Bertie. 'I deliver to her: fillet steak, crown of lamb, capons – even a goose, though it ain't Christmas! Seeing all them ghosties must work up a grand appetite.'

'Don't you mock what you don't understand,' said Sarah, swatting him with a tea towel. 'Madame Berenice is a true saint, working so hard to reunite us with our loved ones. Is your mother living, Bertie?'

'No, she passed on when I was just a little lad,' said Bertie.

'You're still a little lad now,' said Sarah, tucking into the rest of her pie. 'This is exceptionally good,

Hetty. I think your cooking days are numbered, Mrs B.'

'Hmph!' said Mrs Briskett. 'You watch your tongue, Sarah. Young Hetty's got a long way to go yet.'

'I'm just teasing, Mrs B,' said Sarah. She turned back to Bertie. 'So, Bertie, would you not like to hear your dear mother's voice?'

'I don't think I'd recognize it, Sarah, so it would be a waste of time. But I'm pleased you get to hear *your* mother.'

'She touched me last night! I asked for a special materialization, and she manifested herself right there in the room, before my very eyes.'

'You thought you really saw her?'

'I know I did! She touched me. She kissed me on the forehead!' said Sarah.

'Well, that's grand, Sarah, simply grand,' said Bertie. His eyes swivelled to me and his eyebrows shot up.

'Do hush now, Sarah,' Mrs Briskett begged. 'You shouldn't talk so much about such things.'

'I want to tell the world, Mrs B! I am not the slightest bit embarrassed. It's like a miracle. I'm a changed woman. Why won't you be pleased for me?'

'We're all thrilled for you, Sarah,' said Bertie. 'Do you reckon you're a changed woman too, Mrs B? If so, why don't you let Hetty and me stay out walking a little later next Sunday evening? After all, you let Sarah stay out late with her dear departed mother, as it were. It's only fair, don't you see?'

'*I'm* not a changed woman – and I'm not a stupid one either,' said Mrs Briskett. 'No one's taking any liberties, especially not you! You're to bring Hetty back at six sharp, do you hear me?'

'But it won't be long enough! I've got great plans. I want to take Hetty somewhere really special this time. She deserves to see a bit of London, Mrs B, seeing as she's been a poor little foundling girl locked up in that hospital all those years. I'm intent on showing her the sights, all them historic buildings up London way – *educating* her.'

'I know young lads' intentions – and if you don't stop this cheek, you won't take her out at all,' said Mrs Briskett, with such a note of finality that even Bertie saw there was no point in arguing.

12

I wondered happily on and off all week where Bertie would take me on Sunday. He was there waiting for me when we got home from church, but he didn't have his ready smile. His shoulders were hunched. Even his hair lay limp upon his head without benefit of pomade.

'Bertie? What's the matter?' I said as we walked away from Mrs Briskett and Sarah. 'Where are we going today?'

'I'm not sure we're going anywhere, Hetty,' he said flatly.

I looked at him. Oh goodness, didn't he like me any more? Had he found another sweetheart? I was horrified. I wanted to be Bertie's special one-and-only girl – although didn't I have another sweetheart myself? I'd only known him a few weeks, but I realized he'd become important to me. I'd thought he was keen on me. He liked me: he liked me being small, he liked me being spirited, he liked my apple pie, he even liked my red hair.

'What do you mean, we're not going anywhere?' I said, my voice cracking because my throat was so tight.

Bertie looked down at his boots. 'I haven't got any money, Hetty,' he mumbled, pulling out his empty pockets to show me. 'I had such plans. I was aiming to take you up to London today.'

'Yes, to show me the historic buildings.'

'No – to show you the Western Gardens up at Earl's Court. Folk say it's wonderful there, even better than the fair. There's a band, and it's all decked out in fairy lights, ever so pretty. I knew I'd need quite a lot of cash for two train fares and all the amusements, so I volunteered for more gardening jobs. I started a nice little sideline with my meat customers. If I saw their garden looked a tad untidy, I'd ask if they needed anyone to mow their lawn. It all seemed to be working out excellently . . .' His voice tailed away.

'But then?' I said.

'The parlourmaid from Whiteacres, a big house over in Berryland – she said her mistress was fretting. Her gardener's hurt his back and the weeds were getting on her nerves – so I says, like an idiot, "Well, I'll do your weeding, ma'am."'

'You're many things, Bertie, but you're not an idiot.'

'Wait till you hear me out, Hetty. So after work yesterday I go round to Whiteacres, and I reckoned I had a good hour before the light started to fade, so I kneel down and set to weeding. I worked real hard, pulling and pulling – and then gathers them all up neatly and puts them in a sack, leaving everything spick and span, thinking the mistress might give me an extra tip for tidiness. Then the parlourmaid comes out, looks at my nice tidy bare bed and starts shrieking her head off. It turns out I'd uprooted all her prize shrubs along with the wretched weeds. I thought everything green had to be a weed. I didn't realize they were waiting to flower later. Only now they're not. They're all dead, in the sack. And to stop her missus telling tales to Jarvis the butcher and then him giving *me* the sack, I've had to hand over all my savings towards new plants – *and* I have to pay her a shilling a week till she reckons I've paid for the lot. You're not *laughing*, are you, Hetty?'

'I'm sorry!' I said, spluttering. 'Oh, poor Bertie. You were trying so hard too. But you have to admit, it's just a little bit funny.'

'It's not funny in the slightest, because I can't take you out now, on account of the fact I ain't got no spare cash – and I won't have for weeks and weeks according to that mean old maid.'

'We can still walk out together, silly.'

'But that's all we *can* do, walk. I haven't got the cash for a rowing boat, or even a hokey-pokey – don't you understand?'

'Of course I do. But we can still walk – and talk. And *next* week I'll bake us a pie and we'll have a little picnic – how about that?'

'Oh, Hetty! I thought you'd be cross with me and want to go out walking with some other lad with a pocketful of cash who'd treat you properly,' said Bertie. 'You're a diamond girl, did you know that?'

'I'm a *sapphire* girl,' I said. 'Come on, let's go for a walk in the park. We can always pretend it's those gardens. I was always picturing when I was young.'

'When you were at the hospital?'

'No, before that. I doubt anyone could picture at the hospital – it was too dreadful. I meant when I was little, in the country. I used to have this special tree. We called it our squirrel house . . .' My voice trailed away when I saw Bertie's expression.

'You and that Jem?' he said.

'All of us children,' I said, though of course I'd meant just Jem and me. I didn't want to think of Jem. I'd had another letter from him yesterday. He had told me all about Mother and Father and the farm, and how Rosie was engaged to be married, and Nat was doing very well in the army, and he hoped he'd maybe meet up with Gideon one day. It was a letter just like Jem himself, strong and straightforward, tender and concerned. It ended: *I am thinking of the future, Hetty. Our future, together. With love from Jem.*

I had tried hard to picture Jem himself, but somehow I could only see him as a child, with a boy's voice, not as the man I knew he was. And it was impossible to picture him now, when I was walking along with Bertie, doing my best to console him.

'You're thinking of that Jem, aren't you?' said Bertie suspiciously.

'No I'm not,' I lied. 'I'm thinking of the pleasure gardens – *these* pleasure gardens,' I continued as we walked through the gates into the plain green park. 'Oh, see the fairy lights on the trees, Bertie, and little coloured lanterns – look!' I waved my hand at the ordinary plane trees, then pointed to a scrubby patch of grass. 'See, there's a rose bower for sweethearts – and little boys are walking around with trays of gingerbread and we can simply help ourselves—'

'This sounds better than the Western Gardens!'

'*Much* better. And over there' – I pointed vaguely into thin air – 'is a pleasure dome, like in "Kubla Khan".'

'What's Kubla Watsit when it's at home?'

'It's a strange poem. I'm not sure I understand it, but I love the way it's written. Nurse Winnie lent me this book of poetry once. I wish I still had it.'

'Hasn't that weird old stick Buchanan any poetry books? I don't suppose he could lend you one?' said Bertie.

'He's barely speaking to me since I got cross with him for taking my memoirs. He still has them, Bertie, but he doesn't mention them. Sarah says she'll give me what for if I bring it up again. She says it's not my place to make demands on the master. Oh, Bertie, don't you just *hate* having to know your place?'

'Well, I can picture too, Hetty. I can picture right into the future, when I'll be . . .'

'A master butcher like Mr Jarvis?'

'Definitely *not* a butcher. I live, breathe and eat meat, and it's started to turn my stomach. No, I'll live on your apple pies, Hetty – and I won't be no butcher.'

'Well, I don't think you'd better be a gardener,' I said, giggling.

He gave me a look, but then he laughed too.

'So what do you see yourself as, Bertie?'

He suddenly looked shy. 'You'll laugh at me!'

'No I won't. Well, I'll try not to. Go on, tell. It doesn't matter if it can't come true, it's only picturing. I have all manner of madcap fantasies. I see myself as a famous author, Sapphire Battersea, writing a few pages every day, living in a house even bigger than Mr Buchanan's, keeping my mama in luxury. Or – or I could be Sapphire the circus lady in pink, with spangly tights, riding my troupe of rosin-backed horses, while hundreds gasp and clap. Or perhaps I might even be Sapphire the sailor, crossing the seven seas with the wind in my hair, gulls screaming overhead, dolphins swimming along beside the ship. There! Now you can laugh at me!'

'Well, *I* picture myself on stage in a fancy toff suit, with a little straw hat to tilt at a jaunty angle.'

'An actor?'

'Not a Shakespearean actor, spouting all sorts of stuff you can't understand. No, comedy's more my line. Or maybe a music-hall turn – comical, with a saucy song, maybe even a little dance.' He did a little tap dance on the grass, his feet flashing. He landed elegantly with a 'Ta-*da*!' his arms held high.

'Bravo!' I said, and clapped him. 'You're good at it, Bertie, really good.'

'I thought I might act like a bit of a charmer with the ladies. I could call my act Flirty Bertie – and as I'm so small, it would work really well if I shared the routine with a very *tall* girl, to make it more comic like, but still touching. A pity *you're* not tall, Hetty – it would be grand to do a double act with you. Have you ever fancied treading the boards yourself?'

'I'm not sure! The vicar said that music halls were very bad places – but I think they sound like fun,' I said.

'They're *great* fun. I think you'd love them. I'll take you there some day – when I've got some cash!

Maybe it will inspire you, seeing as you're a bit of a writer. You could write a play yourself and then star in it,' said Bertie. 'I could have a part too, couldn't I?'

'You could play the leading man, definitely,' I said. 'And my brother could act in it too.'

'That Jem?' said Bertie, frowning.

'No! *Not* Jem. I'm sure he'd hate the very idea. Jem wouldn't ever be anything but a farmer, I'm sure of it. No, my brother Gideon. He was at the hospital with me, though we scarcely ever saw each other. Poor Gideon, he's not at all like other boys. He's always so timid and fearful. But one Christmas he was chosen to be the angel in our nativity tableau in chapel. There he was, right up high, arms in the air, and this look of utter radiance.' I thought of Gideon now, and shivered.

'What is it?' said Bertie.

'He's gone to be a soldier, and I fear he will very much dislike a soldier's life. He was terribly teased at the hospital. It's such a worry, having brothers. Do you have any, Bertie?'

'Not that I know of. Nor sisters either. It's easier that way. I can just look after myself.'

'Did the other boys ever pick on you when you were at the workhouse?' I asked, my voice lowered.

'Of course they did,' said Bertie cheerfully enough.

'Because you were small?'

232

'We was *all* small, seeing as we didn't get enough to eat and worked a twelve-hour day from when we were ten. But the older ones picked on the younger ones. I learned to dodge and duck, and then I built myself up a bit. I did a drill every morning, pumping myself up like a little strongman, hanging off the tops of doors to increase my arm muscles. In time I could take on even the biggest boys and get the better of them all. Hanging like this, Hetty!'

Bertie leaped right up and caught hold of the branch of a tree at the edge of the park. He hung on, swinging his legs vigorously, then pulled himself up until his chin was on the branch. He stayed wobbling there, his face purple with effort, obviously expecting applause.

'Ah, *now* you're picturing you're Bertie the monkey. Shall I offer you a banana?' I said.

He laughed and tumbled down, then capered about me, making silly chattering monkey noises.

'I shall take you to the Zoological Gardens where you belong,' I said. 'Look, they're just over here. Shall I put you in your cage?'

'I'll have a ride on Jumbo the elephant first,' said Bertie.

'I've *had* a ride on that elephant, truly!' I said proudly.

We sat down under the trees and I told him how

I'd run away on the day of the Queen's Golden Jubilee.

'But you never saw the old lady herself?' said Bertie. 'Well, we must rectify that. I spy the palace shining in the sunshine just over there. Let's join Her Majesty for afternoon tea.'

'*What* a good idea! Well, I'll very quickly fashion myself a new dress – *not* one of Mrs Briskett's cast-offs. I'll select a subtle sky-blue, with lace at the neck, and lace mittens to match, and I'll have pale-grey kid boots with little pearl buttons.'

'I'll have them kid boots and all,' said Bertie, examining the loose sole of his old brown boot. 'And a toff's suit, please, with one of them starched shirts with the high collars.'

'Yes, it will be so starched you'll feel as if you're wearing a suit of armour. This *might* get you into trouble when we're ushered into Her Majesty's drawing room. You will be expected to bow down low, but of course your starched shirt will keep you resolutely upright. There is a grave danger Her Majesty will take offence and summon her guards, and they will march you off to her dungeons.'

'Buckingham Palace doesn't *have* dungeons!'

'These are *secret* dungeons down in the sewers, and they will shut you in a rat-infested cage and you will cast yourself down in the mire and moan piteously.'

'This is a really cheery story!'

'Ssh, I'm coming to the best part. Meanwhile I am imploring the Queen to forgive you, confessing that I've over-starched your shirt, and she will laugh heartily and instruct her guards to release you immediately.'

'All cowering and covered in rat muck – even my starched shirt!'

'So the Queen commands that you be taken to her private bathroom and you luxuriate in her very own bathtub. The taps have little gold crowns and the royal crest is printed on the porcelain. Here, did you know Mr Buchanan has his own water closet and we're not ever allowed to use it – but I do secretly sometimes.'

Bertie roared with laughter. 'I bet you do, Hetty. And I use the Queen's very own personal facility while I'm washing off all the sewer slime.'

'And then a maid gives you a whole new outfit – toff gentleman's clothes with a fancy waistcoat and everything, but they all belonged to Prince Albert so they're miles too big for you. The maid has to pad you out with big cushions.'

'Oh yes, turn me into a figure of fun now.'

'Yes, but it's to a purpose! You come waddling back, clean again, but positively spherical. Her Majesty starts chortling away, because you look so comical, so you take advantage of this, see, and do a funny dance, waddling even more, and bowing low and then bouncing back again. She laughs and laughs and says you should be on the stage – and guess what, Bertie, there's a special Royal Command Performance at the theatre, and *you* are top of the bill: Great Big Bertie, the talk of all London – how about that?'

'That's just fine and dandy, Hetty. You're a grand girl for telling stories!' he said.

When we set off for home at five to six, Bertie squeezed my hand as we walked along the road. 'I thought this afternoon was going to be a disaster, but it's been the best ever, and it's all down to you, Hetty. You're a girl in a million.'

I felt myself glowing. It was so lovely to be appreciated, the centre of attention. I had always felt so *crushed* at the hospital. It had often scared me when I looked at all the hundreds of other girls in their identical brown uniforms and white caps and tippets. It was hard to hang onto the fact that I was *me*, Hetty, different from all the others.

'You're a *boy* in a million, Bertie,' I said. As no one seemed to be passing, I threw my arms around his neck and gave him a quick hug.

'Hetty!' he said, going crimson – but he looked tremendously pleased.

He delivered me back to number eight Lady's Ride on the very dot of six – but I discovered Sarah and Mrs Briskett in the midst of such a to-do I don't think they even noticed. Sarah was in her Sunday purple, bonnet on, trying to get out of the door, but Mrs Briskett was hanging onto her arm, imploring her not to go.

'You must stay home safe, Sarah. I'm *ordering* you!'

'You can't give me orders, Mrs B, and you know it. I'm free to do what I want – and I know what that is!'

'Very well then, girl, I'm not ordering, I'm imploring. Heaven help us, I'm *begging* you to stay at home,' said Mrs Briskett.

'Don't be so ridiculous, Mrs B. How could I possibly keep away! I'm going to pay for another materialization. I can't wait to see Mother again.'

'Yes, and you'll swoon again too, and Mr Brown made it plain he didn't feel it was fitting for him to look after you in such a state.'

'Then come with me, Mrs B!' said Sarah. 'If you'll only come too, you'll see why it's so important to me. It could be important to you too. You could be reunited with all *your* loved ones who have passed over.'

'As if I'd go along with such an idea! I think the dead should stay shut up in their graves, where they belong. It's not decent, stirring them up like this. It's downright blasphemous!'

'How dare you! I've never blasphemed in my life! And it's the sweetest, most holy experience, comm-

237

unicating with my own mother. I lost her when I was only fourteen, and she was all the world to me. I missed her so when I was sent away into service. I never dreamed I'd not see her sweet face again.'

I shivered, thinking about my own mama. 'I'll go with you, Sarah,' I said, taking hold of her hand.

They both looked at me, astonished, as if the table had started talking.

'Don't be so foolish, Hetty!' said Mrs Briskett.

'Why is that foolish, Mrs B? It's the most beautiful experience, going to one of Madame Berenice's seances.'

'You can't take a *child*!'

'Hetty's old enough to be sensible,' said Sarah.

'*You're* a lot older, and yet I can't make you see sense,' said Mrs Briskett. 'Oh, very well, go then, and take Hetty too, even though she'll likely scream herself senseless.'

'I won't scream, I promise,' I said. I was starting to feel very excited. I had no real idea of what happened at a seance, but it certainly sounded interesting. I was a little frightened at the thought of Sarah's mother emanating out of thin air, but I was sure she'd be paying more attention to Sarah than to me.

It would be a wonderful story to tell Bertie next time I saw him – and an extra outing seemed much more attractive than staying home in the scullery, writing dutiful letters to Mama and Jem. I *wanted* to write to Mama, but I still didn't know whether to tell her all about Bertie or not, so my letters were shorter and more stilted than usual. I knew absolutely that I shouldn't tell Jem about Bertie, so my letters to him were shorter still – though his were getting longer.

'I will go with Sarah and behave very sensibly, and if she swoons again I will take care of her and find us a cab home,' I said.

Mrs Briskett shook her head and sighed, but Sarah put her arms around me.

'There, you're a dear little girl. Come along then. My, you cut a fine figure in that dress.'

'I still don't hold with such shenanigans,' said Mrs Briskett, but she went to the money jar she kept in the larder, right at the back on the top shelf, took out half a crown, tied it up in a handkerchief, and gave it to me.

'That will cover the cab fare, just in case,' she said, tucking it up my velvet cuff.

I smiled at her gratefully and gave Sarah a little nod. 'We'll be fine,' I said grandly.

'Well, don't say I didn't warn you,' said Mrs Briskett, folding her arms. 'It's not right and fitting, meddling with the supernatural. It's just a form of witchcraft, that's what *I* say.'

'Well, we don't care what *she* says, do we, Hetty?' Sarah murmured to me and we set off.

13

We walked away from the town, along a stream, down many winding lanes. I tried to take note of the way we were going in case I had to steer Sarah back, but I soon became muddled. I was surprised when we stopped in front of a relatively modest cottage with an ordinary suburban garden. It had a little privet hedge, a patch of emerald-green lawn, and a bright flowerbed of marigolds and geraniums edged with scallop shells.

Sarah led me up the red and black tiled garden path and pulled the bell by the front door. A tall pale woman in black answered the door.

'Is she Madame Berenice, or her servant?' I whispered to Sarah.

'No, no. She is Emily. I believe she is Madame Berenice's sister. She will serve us refreshments afterwards.'

'Afterwards!' I repeated excitedly.

Emily took our shawls silently. Sarah pressed a little envelope of money into her hand and murmured something about materialization. Emily nodded, and still without speaking led us into a very dark room, the curtains shrouded with thick black velvet. I expected her to light a lamp but she went away again.

It was so very dark after the bright evening sunshine that for a moment or two I could see nothing, but I sensed we weren't alone. No one spoke, but I could hear someone breathing, someone rustling. I could smell liniment and floral scent. I gradually began to make out a small group of people sitting on chairs set around a table in a circle. There was tall thin Mr Brown from Dedman's grocery, sitting very erect; two elderly ladies, both in black – and a woman with compelling dark eyes wearing a strange feathered turban and extravagant robes. I did not need Sarah to introduce me. She was clearly Madame Berenice.

'Sit down, Sarah,' she said, in a deep voice. 'And who is the little person with you?'

'This is Hetty Feather, Madame Berenice. She is our new little maid, come to help me home if necessary,' Sarah whispered deferentially. 'I've asked for another materialization, madame. I do hope that's convenient?'

'I will do my best, but as you know, there are no guarantees. Our spirit friends are very sensitive, especially when there is a stranger in their midst.'

She was staring at me intently in the darkness, and I couldn't help squirming.

'Would you like Hetty to wait outside, madame?' Sarah asked.

'Oh no, please may I stay!' I said, determined not to miss out on anything.

'Are you a believer, Hetty Feather?' asked Madame Berenice.

I wasn't quite sure what she meant. 'I go to church every Sunday,' I said.

'Do you believe in the psychic sciences, child?'

'I – I'm not sure what they *are*,' I said.

'She's very ignorant, madame. She's a foundling, brought up at the hospital. She knows very little, but she's a good helpful girl, eager to learn,' said Sarah.

'There is no greater wonder in all nature than the communication between the spirit world and our own,' said Madame Berenice. She uttered her words with great expression, as if she were on stage. 'Have you lost a loved one, Hetty Feather?'

'I've lost my dear mama,' I said huskily.

'No, no, Hetty, your mother is still living,' said Sarah. 'Madame Berenice is asking you if any of your dear friends and family have passed away.'

'I don't think so,' I said, a little flustered.

'Can't we get on with the seance, Madame Berenice?' Mr Brown said.

'Calm yourself, sir. There must be no impatience, no restlessness, or the spirits won't come,' Madame Berenice rebuked him. 'Sit within the circle, Hetty Feather.'

I tried to find an empty chair in the darkness, and tripped over a footstool in my blunderings.

'Hetty! Sit *down*! You're keeping Madame Berenice waiting,' Sarah hissed.

'I can't help it. I can't *see*,' I whispered. 'Why can't we draw the curtains a little?'

'We need total darkness, child,' said Madame Berenice. 'Those dwelling in the spiritual sphere are shy and wary of our world. It is a harsh, crude environment, and we have to be considerate. If we are lucky enough to achieve a total materialization again—'

'Oh please, *please*!' Sarah begged.

'Then it would be like exposing a newborn baby to blinding light,' Madame Berenice continued. 'We have to be in harmony with the creation of all animal structures, as they are created in the darkness of the womb. Now, are we all ready?'

I found a spare chair at last and sat down abruptly.

'Let us join hands and see if the spirits will come to us today.'

I had to hold hands on one side with Sarah, which felt odd, and on the other side with Mr

Brown, which felt even odder. They both gripped tightly, almost crushing my fingers. I had a sudden intense tickle on my nose, but I couldn't wriggle either hand free to give it a good scratch. I was trapped in this silent circle in this musty dark room.

'Is there anybody there?' Madame Berenice asked, her voice even deeper.

I held my breath, but nobody answered.

'Is . . . there . . . anybody . . . there?' she cried, again and again, for a full five minutes.

Nothing happened. There was silence, though Madame Berenice was breathing heavily now, as if running to catch a train.

'Speak now, dear spirits,' she gasped – and then suddenly gave a little scream.

I jumped, and had to bite my lips to stop myself giggling hysterically.

'Hello, dear Father!' Madame Berenice lisped, in a strangely high-pitched baby voice.

'It is my Cedric!' Mr Brown choked, crushing my fingers.

'Yes, Father! I have come to tell you how happy I am,' the weird little voice squeaked.

'Will you ask my little lad if he's in any pain now?' Mr Brown asked.

'There is no pain in the spirit world, dear Father.'

'Oh, thank God! So could you ask if he is keeping up with his schooling? He was always such a bright little lad.'

'I know all the secrets of the spirit spheres, Father. I have no need of earthly schooling,' said Cedric.

'So what do you do all day, Cedric?' I asked eagerly.

I wanted to know if he flew around the world, manifesting himself in and out of houses at whim, or whether he hovered in the same spot in space, waiting to be summoned. But Sarah shook my arm fiercely, practically detaching it from my shoulder.

'You mustn't speak directly to the spirits, Hetty!' she hissed. 'Besides, he's not *your* loved one's spirit. Be quiet at once, and let poor Mr Brown commune properly.'

'Could you tell him how much his mother and I miss him?' Mr Brown asked, his voice hoarse with emotion.

'But I am always with you, Father. Please give my love to Mother,' Cedric squeaked, his voice so high-pitched it made Madame Berenice gasp.

'Oh, the Lord be praised,' Mr Brown said, and the rest of the circle murmured this too. His hand was hot and damp and I could feel him shaking.

I did not know what to make of all this. Mr Brown clearly thought a miracle had taken place and that his dead little boy had actually spoken to him. The voice hadn't really *sounded* like a little boy. It had sounded like a middle-aged lady *pretending* to be a child. Perhaps it was inevitable that Cedric would sound like Madame Berenice if he were using her as an earthly vehicle.

She was gasping again, almost as if she were having a seizure.

'Could you ask my Cedric if he could visit us in our own home?' Mr Brown asked desperately.

'I am . . . sorry – Cedric is . . . fading,' Madame Berenice panted. 'The spirits are jostling with each other for attention tonight. Oh, it's very wonderful, but a terrible strain. Who is this now? Pray speak clearly.'

'Is it Mother? Oh please, let it be my mother,' Sarah begged.

But it wasn't Sarah's mother this time, it was a dear friend of one of the old ladies. She spoke in a quavery voice, and told us that she had fully recovered her health now, and did not even cough. Then the other old lady spoke to *her* dear departed friend, who said that she was feeling fit and well too, and that she was reunited with her little cat now, and very happy.

It was almost like listening to real old ladies conversing in a shop queue, and it all went on for so long that I began to feel restless. Both my hands were numb now, as Sarah and Mr Brown were still clutching them fiercely, and the room was oppressively hot and dark.

Madame Berenice began her throaty gasping again.

'Is it Mother *this* time?' Sarah begged.

'I think . . . yes, I think it is,' Madame Berenice panted.

'Can you ask her if she'll come here to me again? Oh please – it meant the world to me.'

'I – am – coming – Sarah,' said another strange whispery voice from Madame Berenice's lips.

'Oh, Mother!' Sarah said, half standing in her eagerness.

'Sit still, my child. Sit very still, all of you,' Madame Berenice interrupted. Then she gave a final gasp and fell face down on the tablecloth.

'Oh my Lord!' I whispered, fearing she had died too, and gone to join all her spirit friends in person. I wondered why everyone was still sitting there, not trying to revive her. Then I saw a wisp of strange white smoke, and glimpsed a figure all in white gliding slowly across the room. I could barely breathe for shock. The white figure was moving slowly but surely in my direction. I could see her more clearly now, though her face was obscured by a white veil. Sarah shivered, making little moaning noises. The apparition glided onwards. I ducked my head as she came nearer, terrified she might speak to me, or maybe slide straight through me – but she was only concerned with Sarah.

'My little girl,' she said, in an eerie whispery voice.

'Mother!' Sarah sobbed.

She wasn't a little girl at all, she was a great lump of a woman, and yet somehow she seemed to be shrinking back to childhood again. I could picture her in a pinafore, her hair down her back, tears running down her round moon face.

'Oh, my mother!'

I found there were tears blurring my own eyes as the white figure hovered beside her. She gently touched Sarah's head with her fingertips, then bent and kissed her.

'Oh, Madame Berenice, please may she stay just a little longer?' Sarah begged.

'No, my dear, her visits must be brief. I think her psychic essence is already fading – yes, fading . . .'

'Goodbye – but not for long,' the white figure whispered.

'Let us close our eyes and give thanks to our spirit friends,' said Madame Berenice.

We all closed our eyes and murmured thank you, while Sarah sobbed convulsively. When we opened our eyes, the spirit was gone.

'Oh thank you, thank you!' said Sarah, weeping and sniffing.

She clearly needed the handkerchief that was tucked up my sleeve, so I tried wriggling my hand free.

'Do not break the circle! There is still a spirit there, clamouring to be heard,' Madame Berenice snapped.

I gripped hands again, peering around the circle in surprise. It was difficult to see properly in the dark, but it seemed as if everyone had had their visit. Sarah's mother materializing had been the star spirit turn. Was there to be some sort of encore?

'Who is there?' Madame Berenice asked. 'Oh, oh, it is a young boy!' she answered herself. 'A little stranger determined to make himself known. Who do you wish to communicate with, child?'

He whispered something indistinctly, his voice high and reedy. We all had to strain to hear him.

'Try again, try again,' Madame Berenice commanded.

The whispering was a little louder this time.

'Hetty! Hetty Feather!' the ghostly voice hissed.

'Oh, Hetty, dear!' Sarah said. 'It's a spirit come to talk to you!'

'No! No, I don't want him to,' I said.

'There is no need to be frightened, child,'

Madame Berenice tried to reassure me. 'Just relax and clear your mind. You said you did not have anyone dwelling in the spirit realm, but you were clearly wrong. I will try to connect more intensely.' She breathed heavily in and out, while my mind whirled. Who could it be?

'It's not – not a brother, is it?' I said, panicking. Oh dear Lord, was it Gideon? Had some terrible accident happened at the barracks? Had Gideon found it so unbearable he had taken his own life?'

'It *can't* be Gideon,' I whispered.

'Have you forgotten me, Hetty Feather?' said the voice, sounding reproachful.

Then there was a sudden rap beneath the table – a tap-tap-tapping, like a stick . . . or a crutch!

'Saul!' I screamed.

I had never loved Saul the way a sister should. We had always fought. I had been made to feel deeply ashamed because he had a withered leg and it was very bad to torment a crippled boy – though Saul tormented *me* for all he was worth. He had lived with Gideon in the boy's wing, but he had died of influenza.

I had been so anxious that Gideon might die, because he was so unhappy and weak and delicate. I hadn't even thought about Saul dying. Now here I was, years later, making the same mistake all over again. I had almost forgotten Saul – but he had not forgotten me! He was here now, coming to get me!

'No! No, no, no!' I screamed.

I wrenched my hands away from Sarah and Mr Brown, and ran from the room. I was down the hallway, out of the door, through the garden gate and halfway down the road before Sarah caught up with me.

'Oh, Hetty, come *here*!' she cried, and she threw her arms around me.

'No! I won't go back!'

'It's all right, I won't make you. Don't worry, dear, I know it can be overwhelming at first. But the spirits are our friends, Hetty, our dear loved ones returning to us. Oh, did you see my dear mother, as distinct as anything?'

'Yes, I am happy for you – but I don't want to see my brother Saul!'

I kept thinking I could hear the tap of his crutch, even out here in the gentle twilight. I was in such a state that we had to take a hansom cab home for my benefit.

Mrs Briskett was waiting for us in the kitchen. When she saw me shaking, she shook her head furiously. 'That's the giddy limit, Sarah! If you want to waste all your hard-earned savings and make a spectacle of yourself in that spooky place, then that's your affair, but I won't have you reducing the child to such a state. Just look at her, poor little lamb.'

Mrs Briskett sat me down and made me a cup of tea and a slice of bread and butter in an effort to calm my nerves. I was still shivering so much that my teeth clanked against the cup and I could barely swallow my bread.

The two women put me to bed with an extra coverlet and a hot-water pig. They sat on either side of me, patting my hands, until at last the shivering subsided. I drifted off to sleep – but Saul pursued me in all my dreams that night, his crutch tap-tap-tapping as he searched for me.

14

'I am sorry if I got you into trouble with Mrs B, Sarah,' I said the next day as we made Mr Buchanan's bed together.

'Oh well, it wasn't really your fault, Hetty. You were just that worked up and over-excited. It happens frequently at Madame Berenice's sessions. You're a girl who's for ever working herself into a passion, anyways – but I know you can't help that. Your temperament's fiery, just like your red hair.'

'Perhaps I can work on it, Sarah. I feel it is time I learned to stay composed.'

'That'll be the day, Hetty!' said Sarah. 'Smooth out the creases your side of that sheet now. Hurry up – we should just about have time to do the master's study while he's still having his breakfast.'

We went into Mr Buchanan's study together. He had clearly already been working on a story that morning. Papers were scattered across his desk, and several were screwed into little balls in his wastepaper basket.

'Dear, dear, he's always like this at the beginning of a story. He makes so many false starts,' said Sarah, dabbing at a fresh inkstain on his desk.

I squatted down beside the wastepaper basket, picking up the crumpled pieces of paper and smoothing them out, thinking that I could use the unwritten sides for my own stories. I had in my hands a discarded version of his first page. I started reading – and my hands shook.

My name is Emerald Greenwich. Is that not the most beautiful name in the world? My dearest mama called me Emerald because my eyes are deep emerald-green. Oh, how I miss my mama now. I know she committed a grievous moral sin when she bore me out of wedlock, but she repented abjectly, and suffered greatly when she handed me in to the fine Christian guardians at the Foundling Hospital.

I spent a few years with some simple country folk, but my true education began when I returned to that splendid institution and learned the hard but necessary lessons of obedience and humility. I am afraid I still find it a struggle to hold my tongue and remember my place, but I am learning from the kindly example of my benefactor and employer—'

'*Kindly!* He has stolen my story – all of it, blatantly! How dare he! How *dare* he!' I shrieked.

Sarah looked at me, astonished. 'Hetty? For heaven's sake, child, lower your voice! The master will hear!'

'I don't care if he does. He is a wicked hypocritical thief! I tell you, Sarah, he has stolen my story.' I was shaking so badly I could barely stand upright. I seized the wastepaper basket and shook the entire contents over his desk.

'Hetty! Have you gone mad? Dear heaven, stop it this instant. Get back to the kitchen.' Sarah tried to grab hold of me, struggling with me so that we both toppled over with a thump.

'What on *earth* is going on?' Mr Buchanan came stamping into his study, his napkin tucked into his shirt, a fork still in one hand.

'Oh, I'm sorry, sir, beg pardon, sir, the poor child is having some kind of fit. Let me carry her away until she recovers,' said Sarah, struggling to her knees.

I had had all the breath knocked out of me, but I still could not keep quiet.

'You wicked, evil, terrible thief!' I screamed

hoarsely at Mr Buchanan. 'You said my story was coarse and unacceptable and no one would ever publish it. And now I know why! *You've* taken it, *you're* writing it! You're just changing the names and putting in long words and mealy-mouthed moral comments, but it's still *my* story.'

'Cease this ridiculous insubordinate babbling at once, or I shall turn you out of my house immediately,' said Mr Buchanan.

Sarah tried to clamp her hand right over my mouth. 'Oh no, sir, take pity on her. She doesn't know what she's saying. It's as if the Devil himself has got hold of her tongue,' she said.

I prised her fingers away, refusing to be restrained. 'I do *so* know what I'm saying! You've stolen *my* memoirs, *my* life! You're a wicked thief. You think you're so saintly, but I think you're going straight to Hell with all the other devils!'

'That's it! Go and pack your bags. I will not have you in my house another minute. I am dismissing you forthwith,' said Mr Buchanan.

'No, no, please!' Sarah begged.

'Without a character reference!' added Mr Buchanan.

'But, sir, how will she get another position without one?' said Sarah.

'That's not my concern,' he said.

'No, you are just concerned with stealing a poor girl's work!' I shouted.

'Remove this terrible fishwife child from my presence,' said Mr Buchanan to Sarah.

'Not until you give me back my memoirs! I'll not have you copying any more of them. Give them back to me!' I cried. 'Give them back this instant or I'll . . . I'll fetch a policeman!'

'Hetty, Hetty, *hush*!' said Sarah, struggling with me.

'Lord save us, what's happening?' said Mrs Briskett, running into the study, her great bulk knocking over columns of books to the left and the right. 'Oh, Hetty Feather, was that you shrieking at the master?'

'I am not her master. She is no longer in my employment. Be so good as to turn her out of this house immediately. I will not be shouted at and abused by a wretched foundling child, especially when I've shown her every kindness!' He was shouting too, his fez slipping sideways as he jerked his head in emphasis.

'I won't go! Not without my memoirs! They're my property. You shall not steal them. Give them *back*!'

'I don't know what you're talking about, you evil-tongued little harpy.'

'Yes you do. You took them from me. Give them back – please, *please*! That book means the whole world to me. It's my life, mine and Mama's.' I was crying now, tears of pure rage.

Mr Buchanan was breathing heavily, sweat standing out on his wrinkled brow. 'You've clearly taken leave of your senses. I know nothing of these so-called memoirs. Now get out of my study this instant.'

'You *liar*!' I shouted.

Mrs Briskett gasped and crossed herself piously. She tried to seize hold of me, but I clung to a corner of Mr Buchanan's desk, screaming.

'If you please, sir, she means that little red note-book, scribbled all over. Are you sure you don't still have it?' said Sarah bravely.

'I am *quite* sure – and if you don't hold your tongue, you will find yourself dismissed as well,' said Mr Buchanan, puffing himself up like a little bullfrog. A button on his waistcoat burst and his watch popped out of his pocket. It dangled there on his watch chain, along with an onyx seal and a little silver key. The key to his *desk drawer*?

It was no use asking politely. This was my only chance. I darted forward and snatched at the chain, tugging so hard that it broke. I had the key in my hand before he could stop me. I slotted it straight

260

into the desk drawer – and there, inside, were two notebooks. One contained my own precious memoirs – and the other was an entirely new manuscript. I whipped open the first page.

Emerald Greenwich – the Story of a Foundling Child . . . by Chas. G. Buchanan

'There!' I said, clutching my own memoirs. 'I *knew* it! You *did* steal my memoirs! You're using them for your own story!'

'Oh, sir!' said Sarah, looking shocked.

'Now now, Sarah – be warned!' said Mrs Briskett anxiously.

'Of course I haven't stolen your ridiculous memoirs, Hetty Feather! I had no idea you called your pathetic little journal by such a grand title. "Memoirs" indeed!'

'You've copied some of it out, and put it under your name!'

'Yes, I *have* started copying out a new version. I have taken the time and trouble to try to improve your work, to show you the correct way to go about composition. I was then intending to go over it with you, carefully instructing you. Yet *this* is the way you repay me, screaming ludicrous accusations at me and attacking my person, actually breaking my

261

watch chain. Just wait till I report these events to the hospital!'

'No, *you* just wait till I report to Miss Smith on the Board of Governors that you've stolen my memoirs. Look, you've written your name by the title – that's absolute proof!'

I tried to snatch that manuscript too, but Mr Buchanan was too quick for me this time. He picked it up and beat me hard about the head with it, sending me reeling.

'Now, leave these premises immediately, Hetty Feather,' he said. 'Take her out of my sight this instant or I shall fetch a policeman myself. I shall report your behaviour and show him the broken links of my watch chain, and you will go straight to prison. It's the best place for you, you wicked, ungrateful girl.'

'Quick, Mrs B! Let's get her out!' said Sarah.

They took hold of me, each with a hand in my armpit, and hauled me out bodily, my feet scarcely brushing the floor – though I still had my memoirs clasped to my chest. They dragged me down all the stairs to the kitchen and then let me go.

'Oh, Hetty, what have you *done*! He'll never take you back now, no matter how we beg,' said Sarah, starting to cry.

'I wouldn't stay here now even if *he* begged *me*,'

I said fiercely, my head held high.

'But what will you do, you silly child? You'll never get another position as a servant without a character reference,' said Mrs Briskett, wringing her hands.

'I will – I will try my hand at something *other* than service,' I said grandly, though my heart was beating fast. 'I will make my own way in the world. Somehow.'

'But where will you sleep tonight?' Sarah asked.

'She will have to go back to the hospital,' said Mrs Briskett.

'I am not going back there, not ever. I'd sooner walk the streets,' I declared.

'Oh, Hetty, if only you weren't so headstrong!' said Sarah. 'You have no idea what life can be like for young girls cast out without a character. So many girls come to a bad end, through no real fault of their own.'

'I won't come to a bad end, I promise,' I said.

'But what will you *do*?'

I thought desperately. I remembered when I'd run away before. I'd sold flowers on the street with Sissy, and then Miss Smith had found me. Miss Smith had told us about one of her charities, set up to help destitute young girls. I supposed *I* was destitute now. The very word made me shudder.

'I shall go to London and see my friend Miss Smith. She will help me,' I said firmly. 'Don't worry, Sarah, I will be fine.'

'Of course I'll worry! You're like a little sister to me now,' said Sarah, and she gave me a hug.

'A very *bad* little sister,' said Mrs Briskett, but she came and hugged me too.

I felt like a very small slice of ham in the midst of a very large sandwich, but I was so touched by their concern and kindness that I had to fight not to cry.

I went to the scullery to pack my box – my retrieved memoirs, my books, my little fairground china dog, my letters from Mama and Jem, my writing paper and envelopes, my brushes, my spare maid's dress, my nightgown. They all fitted neatly inside. But what about my green Sunday outfit? I tried folding it this way and that, but it was heavy velvet and I could not make it small enough.

'Wait, Hetty!' said Sarah. She ran all the way upstairs and came panting back with her own leather suitcase with a strap. 'You may have this. Mother gave it to me when I first went into service.'

'But I can't take it, Sarah – not if it was a present from your mother.'

'I have no need of it now. I've nowhere to go. Mother would want you to have it, I am sure, especially now, when . . . when the two of you have met,' said Sarah shyly.

I gave her another hug, feeling dreadful that I had never quite appreciated her properly. I was surprised by Mrs Briskett too, because when I went back into the kitchen with the packed suitcase, I found she'd made me up a veritable picnic in a big paper bag.

'It's so kind of you, Mrs Briskett! It will keep me going all day long.'

'You'll also need this.' She went to the larder and took down her jar of housekeeping money. I thought she'd count me out a few shillings – but she gave me the whole jarful.

'I can't take it!'

'Of course you can. You'll likely need every penny. You'll be able to stay somewhere small but decent for a few days until this Miss Smith can find you work.'

'Oh, Mrs B!'

'Mrs Briskett to you, missy! Now, mind you write and let us know how you're getting on. We'll worry ourselves sick about you till we hear, won't we, Sarah?'

'Oh, we will, we will,' said Sarah, giving me another hug.

'You're sure you know the way to the station? You must ask for a ticket to Waterloo – that's the

London station. When you arrive there, use some of your money on a hansom cab, do you hear, Hetty? And if you get lost up in town, then look for a policeman and ask him the way. Take care now!'

'Oh don't! She looks so little. We can't let her go!' said Sarah. She stared around wildly. 'Can't we hide her somewhere, here in the house? Just for a day or two, while we sort things out for her?'

Mrs Briskett frowned, clearly wavering. But then the bell from Mr Buchanan's study started jingling fiercely.

'Oh! Oh, maybe master's changed his mind! You be ready to say you're very very sorry, Hetty,' said Sarah, straightening her cap and gown and rushing out of the kitchen to the stairs.

'I'm *not* sorry. It's the master who did something wrong, not me!' I said – but I was wavering too. Now that my temper was ebbing away I was starting to feel very, very scared. Perhaps I *would* apologize. I didn't need to mean the words. Inside my head I could scream that Mr Buchanan was a dishonest, hypocritical thief, just so long as I didn't say it out loud. Then I could stay in my position with Mrs Briskett and Sarah, where I felt so safe and cared for.

But it was no use. Sarah came back, chalk-faced and tearful. 'Oh, he won't relent!' she said. 'He asked if Hetty had gone, and when I said she was still doing her packing, he said he would have her physically thrown out on the street if she wasn't gone in the next five minutes!'

'I'd like to see him try! He's just a withered little monkey man! He couldn't lift me, for I'd scream and kick and hit him,' I declared.

'Hush, Hetty. Stop that silly talk! The master will fetch someone to do it. You might get hurt. You'd best go straight away,' said Mrs Briskett.

'He says he'll be watching from his window to make sure he's seen the back of you,' said Sarah.

'Then I'll show him my blooming back,' I said. I had one last hug with Sarah and gave Mrs Briskett a shy kiss. 'Thank you so much for looking after me,' I said.

Mrs Briskett's face started wobbling. Great tears rolled down her cheeks. 'Oh my, *now* look! You've set me off – and I can't abide crying!' she sobbed.

'Then don't cry, Mrs Briskett, please. I shall be fine. Goodbye, my dear friends.'

I took Sarah's mother's suitcase and my bag of goodies, and walked swiftly out of the kitchen, through the scullery and down the back passage. I opened the door to the area steps and climbed up onto the pavement. There was Mr Buchanan peering down at me, still looking outraged. He actually shook his monkey fist at me.

267

Well, I'd show him. I pulled the most ferocious face up at him, and made a strange gesture with my fingers – I'd seen the boys do this at the hospital. I hoped it was rude. Certainly, judging by the expression on his face, it had considerable effect. Then I sauntered down the road, my head in the air, as if I was simply out for a Sunday stroll.

Oh, my Lord – what was I going to do about Bertie? As soon as I was out of sight of the house, I slowed down and started shivering. It seemed as if I would never see Bertie again. I thought of our happy Sunday jaunts, and I had to squeeze my eyes shut to stop myself crying on the street.

Then something large and warm and boisterous bounced straight into me. It knocked the suitcase and paper bag out of my arms, and licked my face with a very big wet tongue.

'Tommy! Down, boy! *Down*, I say. I know you like the little missy, but you'll frighten her!'

It was Tommy the black Labrador, with his kindly old gentleman owner.

'Are you all right, little missy? Tommy doesn't mean any harm. He's just pleased to see you and desperate to get to his lovely park.'

'I'm fine,' I said, stroking Tommy's soft head.

'But, oh dear, he's made you drop all your belongings. Here, let me help.' The old man bent down and picked up my bag of goodies, luckily so tightly folded over by Mrs Briskett that none had spilled. He handed me the suitcase. 'Going off on a journey, are you, little missy?' he said. 'Going home to visit your mother, is that it?'

I started at him. Of course! I was sure I had more than enough money for a train trip to the coast and one night's board and lodging. I would go to see Mama!

'Yes, you're right,' I said. 'You're absolutely right. I'm going to visit Mama.'

'She'll be so pleased to see you,' he said sweetly.

I wasn't quite so sure. She'd be pretty horrified if she knew I'd broken Mr Buchanan's watch chain and stuck my tongue out at him. I wouldn't necessarily tell her the whole story. But before I set off on my journey I had to find someone else.

I said goodbye to the old man, gave Tommy another stroke, and set off for the town, stopping to wipe my face thoroughly with my handkerchief once I was out of sight.

I went past the draper's shop, pausing momentarily to glare at Ivy and Kitty behind the counter. Then I walked up to the butcher's shop. I knew it was very foolish of me, but I was a little scared to go inside. The front of the shop was hung with poultry, their yellow claws dangling purposefully, as if ready to scratch the customers' heads. The sides of the shop were draped with a furry

269

frond of hares and rabbits, their eyes staring mournfully, their little mouths dripping blood.

I wasn't used to such an alarmingly close encounter with so many dead animals. In fact, the more I stared, the more certain I was that I could never enjoy a rabbit pie or a chicken stew ever again. I ran past the poor dead creatures into the shop, to face further scenes of carnage. Great sides of beef and lamb hung from steel hooks, and a huge pig's head leered at me from the table, an apple in its mouth. Parts of its body were arranged in a grisly pattern all around it: belly and chops and kidneys, and a very long string of sausages.

The smell of meat was unpleasantly overpowering. I breathed shallowly, feeling so sorry for Bertie. I could see no sign of him, and hoped he wasn't out delivering.

I tried to avert my eyes, and joined the queue of folk waiting to give their orders. My arms ached holding my food package and the suitcase, but I didn't want to set them down on the floor. I couldn't sully Sarah's mother's suitcase with bloodstained sawdust.

I waited as seemingly half of Kingtown deliberated over their mince and mutton, while Jarvis the butcher and his two bigger lads listened and gave advice. They barely had a full set of fingers between them, but they still chopped chunks of meat with alarming speed and gusto. I found I was clenching my own fists anxiously on their behalf.

At last I was at the front of the queue, facing Mr Jarvis himself, a man as large and fat and red as his own sides of beef.

'How can I help you, little missy? Who's the cook in your household?'

'Well, it's Mrs Briskett, but I'm not—'

'Oh, Mrs Briskett! Lovely lady, but particular, and that suits me fine because I am too. So how can I help you? The meat the boy delivered yesterday was up to scratch, was it not? Is there company coming? Does she need a capon or a crown of lamb?'

'No, no, sir, it's – it's your boy I want. Bertie. Is he here? May I have a quick word with him?' I whispered.

Mr Jarvis stood stock-still. He cupped his hand to his ear in a pantomime gesture. 'Say that again!' he said. He nudged the other two lads. They stopped chopping. 'Listen to this!'

I took a deep breath. 'Please may I talk to Bertie?' I repeated.

The lads nudged each other and sniggered.

'What do you think this is, girl? A parlour where young lovers can do their courting?' Mr Jarvis bellowed, for the benefit of the entire queue behind me.

'I'm sorry, sir, of course not, sir, but it is a matter of urgency,' I said.

'A matter of *urgency*?' Mr Jarvis boomed. The whole street must be hearing him now – even Ivy and Kitty in their draper's shop. 'This *must* be young love. You want to see our Bertie *urgently*, do you?'

The lads burst out laughing. I started crying, in rage and humiliation.

'I only wanted to say goodbye,' I sobbed. 'I can't see that's so outrageous. Please tell him I came calling. My name is Hetty Feather.' I turned on my heel and tried to push past all the customers.

'Hey! Wait, missy. Don't cry now,' said Mr Jarvis, relenting. 'He's in the back, doing the offal. Go and say your goodbyes then, but be quick about it.'

He gestured for me to bob under the counter. I squeezed through and scurried out through a door at the back of the shop. I found myself standing in a bloody battlefield. Dead animals in varying states were strewn over a counter, some with their heads and hides still in place. Bertie was standing there in an apron and trousers, no shirt at all, busy disembowelling these creatures, pulling all kinds of disgusting gleaming things out of their bodies.

'Hetty!' he said, shocked. He went scarlet. 'Oh, Hetty, don't look! I don't want you to see me doing this! Why did the old man let you through?'

'I begged him. I've come to say goodbye.'

'What?' He saw the suitcase and realized I was serious. 'Why? What's happened?'

'Mr Buchanan's dismissed me.'

'He never! But what did you *do*?'

'I shouted at him because I found out he's been copying my memoirs. I broke his watch chain getting the key to his desk, and I said he was a cruel, wicked, hypocritical thief who would end up going to Hell.'

'Well, that's telling him! So he won't have given you a character.'

'No.'

'Oh, Hetty. What will you do, then?'

'I'm going to see Mama. She lives by the seaside. She might know of a position near her. Then we could see more of each other, which would be wonderful.'

'No! All right, go and see your mother, but then come back! We have to have our Sundays together. You're still my sweetheart! I'll keep my eyes and ears open on my rounds – I go all over the town, right? I'll see if anyone's wanting a likely girl. I'll recommend you. You leave it to me, Hetty.'

'Well, it's very good of you, Bertie, but—'

'No buts! See here, you're not planning to go back to the country, are you? Are you going to see that foster brother you write to?'

'I don't see how I can go back. There's no work for a girl in the village. All my foster sisters went into service.'

'Good! You're not a country girl. You belong in the city, with me.'

'Come back here now, missy, you've had long enough. And you, lad – I hope you're not slacking!' Mr Jarvis called.

'I'd better go,' I said quickly. 'I don't want to get you into trouble.'

'Do take care, Hetty. Write as soon as you can to let me know where you are. Oh Lord, I want to take you in my arms, but how can I like this?' He gestured with his slimy hands, looking at them in disgust. 'What must you think of me!'

'I think you're my sweetheart,' I said. I leaned across the loathsome carcass on the table, and swiftly kissed his flushed cheek.

Then I rushed out of the room, bobbed a grateful curtsy to Mr Jarvis, and whisked out of the shop, while everyone stared, and a few clapped and cheered.

I hurried though the town, trying to tell myself

that everything was fine. I was simply going to have a little holiday and see Mama at long last. But I couldn't help feeling very queer and shaky, even so.

I changed out of my grubby work dress and cap and apron while locked inside the ladies' waiting room at the station. I felt better and braver in my emerald best dress, and my skimpy work clothes were much lighter to carry.

The third-class rail ticket cost a great deal of money, much more than I'd reckoned. The house-keeping jar was a lot lighter when I put it back in my case. It was very unnerving reaching Waterloo and having to negotiate my way up and down the platforms to find the correct locomotive for Bignor, but I managed it successfully.

I hadn't realized that it would be such a *long* train journey to the coast. I fidgeted a great deal as I gazed out of the window. England was much larger than I'd realized. I stared until my eyes blurred, but I still hadn't glimpsed any great expanse of water.

I opened Mrs Briskett's parcel for some lunch, and then carried on nibbling on and off throughout the journey. A grim-faced lady sitting next to me sniffed in disgust and twitched her skirts away from me, acting as if I were spilling crumbs all over her. It was certainly a temptation.

A much sweeter family joined the train at Arundel: a jolly father in a straw hat and blazer, a pale mother with a babe in arms, and two girls in sailor suits, one my age, one about eight or nine. They all smiled at me, and the two sailor girls started chatting as if we were old friends, telling me they were having an early seaside holiday and it was going to be great fun.

I offered the girls a slice of Mrs Briskett's shortbread and talked to them a little. They were astonished when I said I'd never been to the seaside before.

'We go to Bignor every single year. We think it's the most splendid tip-top place ever,' said the older girl. 'We go bathing every day, and listen to the band and watch the pierrots. Oh, you will *love* it! Where will you stay? We always go to the same lodgings near the promenade. Maisie and I can see the sea from our bedroom window.'

'Where are *your* mama and papa?' asked Maisie. 'Are you travelling all on your *own*? How queer!'

'Maisie!' the mother rebuked her gently. She smiled at me. 'Are you going on a visit, perhaps?'

'Yes, to see my mama.'

'Oh, that's lovely, dear.'

'Why don't you live with your mama, then?' asked the older girl.

'Charlotte!' the mother said, shaking her head. 'You girls! Stop plaguing your new friend with your questions.'

'My mama works in Bignor,' I said.

'Your mama *works*! Why's that?'

'That's enough, girls!' said their mother, looking a little uncomfortable.

They weren't a very *grand* family. They were only travelling third class like me, and their clothes were a little shabby. I could see the telltale black line around the skirts of both girls where their hems had been let down, and although their boots were highly polished, they were cracked and down-at-heel. Even so, there was a *huge* divide between us. That little baby sleeping in the mother's arms would grow up safe within a family. She would be able to stay a child well into her teens. She would never be told it was her place to be a servant.

The baby was starting to get fretful, and wouldn't be soothed, though the mother rocked her tenderly. 'Hush now,' she said, over and over, but the baby wouldn't hush at all.

The father tried tickling her and then talking to her sternly, which made the baby cry harder. The girls chatted to each other, clearly not expecting to take their turn as nursemaid.

'Let me take her,' I offered.

'I'm afraid she's very querulous, poor lamb,' said the mother. 'I'm not sure you'll be able to quieten her. Sometimes she cries for hours. I think it's the colic.'

I was used to little babies. In my last year at the hospital I had spent many hours in the nursery, helping care for the newborn foundlings before they were despatched to foster homes in the country.

'Come to Hetty, baby,' I said, picking her up from her mother's arms.

She had a cross red face, her forehead wrinkled as if she had every care in the world. The silly little thing did not know how lucky she was. I held her upright and pressed her against me, patting her back.

'There now. Do you have a sore stomach? This will make it feel better,' I said.

I walked up and down the carriage, rocking her against me. She stopped screaming, snuffled several times, and then quietened altogether.

'Oh my! You've worked wonders!' said the papa.

'You're very good with babies, dear,' said the mother. 'There, Charlotte, there, Maisie! See how nicely she's soothed your little sister!'

I took a deep breath, aware of a sudden glorious solution to my situation. 'I would be very happy to be your nursemaid,' I said.

I meant it in all seriousness, but the family all

280

laughed merrily, as if I were joking.

'I – I would not cost very much,' I ventured further, but this made them laugh even harder.

I felt I could not pursue the point any further. I continued to walk the baby. She stayed fast asleep, even when the train drew into the station at Bignor-on-Sea at last. I carried the baby very carefully down the steps to the platform, my suitcase hanging off one arm. The father went dashing off to supervise the removal of the family's luggage from the guard's van. I waited with the rest of the family. Maisie was jumping up and down excitedly, declaring, 'I can smell the sea already!' She was so convincing that I imagined the water lapping against the brick walls of the station.

'I hope there's time for a bathe before tea!' said Charlotte. 'Will you have a bathe too? Wait till you see what it's like, Hetty! Do you have your own bathing dress? If not, you can hire one on the beach.'

'I expect I will do that,' I said.

'And you'll need a bucket and spade! Maisie and I always make sandcastles. It's absolutely ripping fun. We made such a splendid castle last year, with a proper moat, and then the sea came in and filled it up, and we made stained-glass windows out of fruit drops. Maisie had to lick them first, which was a little disgusting, but she didn't mind at all—'

'Charlotte, calm down!' said her mother, smiling at her. She reached for the baby. 'Thank you so much for looking after little Flora. I've never known her so contented.'

'It was a pleasure,' I said solemnly. My arms felt very empty when I gave her back.

'Well . . .' The mama was looking around at the crowds on the platform. 'Can you see your mama anywhere? She *will* be meeting you, won't she?'

'Oh, she doesn't know I'm coming. It's a surprise,' I said.

'Do know where to find her? Perhaps you might care to walk part of the way with us?'

'Oh, yes please!' I said.

We walked out of the station in a little procession, the papa alongside the porter, who had a huge trolley full of their luggage, then the mama and the baby, and then Charlotte and Maisie on either side of me, talking nineteen to the dozen, telling me all about the seaside.

'Where *is* it?' I asked, because we were in a perfectly ordinary street, though the light was brighter than usual and the air felt fresh and clear.

'Just down there! Oh, mama, may we run ahead just a little and show Hetty the sea?' asked Charlotte.

'Of course,' said their mama.

The girls both surged forward, skirts flying. I

ran along beside them, my case bumping awkwardly against my legs.

'Take care, girls!' she called.

I felt truly part of their family – not a nursemaid, more like a sister. I started picturing our life together. We'd have our annual jolly seaside holiday in Bignor, and then we would go back to our home in Arundel. I would go to school with Charlotte and Maisie, and help their mama with the baby when I was at home. We'd all do the cooking and the dusting and the scrubbing and the mending. I'd have my own comfortable little bed in the girls' room. I would never be stuck all alone in the scullery.

Charlotte and Maisie raced round a corner. I heard them whooping triumphantly. I followed them, and then stopped short, my heart thudding. I'd seen pictures of the sea in books, each wave carefully cross-hatched to give a life-like impression. I'd seen the Thames, which had seemed vast enough after the country stream of my childhood. But nothing had prepared me for the immensity of this sea glittering before me in the sunlight.

I had fancied it would be a dense blue like the wash of colour in my picture-book illustration, but this was a bright silvery grey, an entire sparkling world of water. I turned my head to the left and to the right, and it was still there, as far as I could see.

I dropped my suitcase and stretched my arms wide, trying to take it all in.

'Isn't it glorious?' said Charlotte.

'Yes, it is truly wonderful,' I breathed.

The sea blurred to a rainbow shimmer because I was crying now, overcome by the beauty of this vast stretch of water. I scrubbed at my eyes with my handkerchief.

'Don't be sad,' said Maisie, putting her hand in mine.

'I'm not sad, I'm happy,' I said, laughing shakily.

'You do like it here, don't you?' she asked.

'I think it's the most beautiful place in the whole world,' I said. My heart rejoiced that Mama lived here now and could see the sea every single day.

I suddenly wanted to see her so urgently that I trembled all over. I feared she would be angry and distressed when I told her that I'd lost my position, but I didn't care about her scolding me now. I just wanted to be with her.

'I must go now,' I said.

I said goodbye to Charlotte and Maisie, and they kissed me as if we were firm friends. I waved to the papa and the mama and the baby, then I picked up my suitcase and started running right along the sea front. I didn't know where Mama's road was, and the first two people I asked did not know either, but then I came across a painted notice board with a map of Bignor clearly laid out. There was even a helpful little arrow labelled YOU ARE HERE! I pictured a half-inch Hetty standing on her allotted spot, and walked her up and down the roads until, right at the edge of town, I came across Saltdean Lane. I'd written it on so many envelopes under the dear name of Ida Battersea.

I stared at the map until my eyes watered again, memorizing the way, and then I set off along the promenade. This was a fairyland town with a pier jutting out into the sea, kiosks of strange seafood, and bathing machines all along the beach. Even the streetlamps were painted a pretty pale green, and the paving stones beneath my feet were rose-pink.

I had to turn off the promenade down Victoria Avenue, and the streets immediately reverted to plain grey, but I didn't care – I was running now, so eager to see Mama that I didn't pause for breath until I reached Saltdean Lane at last. The houses weren't as large and grand as Mr Buchanan's in Lady's Ride. I liked them better – pretty villas painted cream and apricot and lilac, with bright flowers in their gardens.

I counted each house until I found number eighteen. It was cream, with white window frames and a blue door, very fresh and pretty, with pink hydrangeas in tubs on either side of the doorstep.

I was utterly delighted to see that Mama's house

was the prettiest in the whole lane. I went up the neat tiled path, shaking with excitement. I knew better now than to knock at the front door. There were no area steps, so I slipped down the side of the house and rapped lightly on the back door. I waited, my heart thumping.

Then the door opened. There was Mama! I knew she was my own dear Mama – of course I did – but she looked so different. She had always been little and slight, like me, but now she seemed somehow to have shrunk. Her dress hung loose on her, and her tiny wrists and hands stuck out of the cuffs, looking like little claws. Her dear face was so thin now that her cheekbones showed in sharp lines.

'Oh, Mama!' I said, throwing down my case and clasping her close.

'Hetty! Oh, Hetty, is it really you? You look a picture in that dress! Darling, what are you doing here?' she gasped, and then she started coughing.

She thrust me away from her quickly, putting a handkerchief to her mouth. She coughed and coughed, her faced reddening, the veins standing out on her forehead, her whole body racked.

'Oh, Mama,' I whispered.

I steered her very gently inside and sat her down on a kitchen chair, then fetched my case from the doorstep. I ran the tap at the sink, pouring Mama a glass of water, and gave it to her. She tried to drink, the glass clinking against her teeth, and gradually the terrible coughing stopped. Her eyes were watering, and little beads of sweat stood out on her forehead. I took a teacloth, held it under the cold tap, and then pressed it against her burning temples.

'You're ill, Mama, very ill. You definitely have a fever – and that cough! Why aren't you in bed? Come, let me help you. Where do you sleep?'

'No, no, I can't possibly go to bed,' Mama said weakly. 'I'm fine now. It was just a coughing fit. The surprise of seeing you!'

'But you've got so thin! Why didn't you *tell* me you were ill when you wrote?'

'I didn't want to worry you. I'm *not* ill, not really. I just have a troublesome cough, but I'm in the best place possible, breathing in this good sea air. Some days I feel really well, truly.'

'Will you stop trying to be so brave! It's *me*, Mama! You can be honest with me.'

I knew next to nothing about sickness and disease, but even so I knew that Mama was gravely ill. 'Is it – is it influenza?' I whispered.

I had suffered a bout of influenza once myself and had been very ill for days, along with many other children at the hospital. My crippled foster brother Saul had died from the disease. So had Cedric, Mr Brown's little boy.

'Oh, Mama, don't die! You can't die!' I said, bursting into tears.

'Don't, Hetty! I'm perfectly all right, I swear I am. I haven't got influenza, I promise you.'

'Have you seen a doctor?'

'Well . . .' Mama hesitated. 'There's nothing a doctor can really do for me, dear. But I go to the pharmacy and he makes me up a cough linctus. That helps considerably. But never mind *me*. What are you doing here? How did you get Mr Buchanan to give you permission to visit me?'

'Well . . .' It was my turn to be evasive now. I didn't really want to tell Mama the whole story, especially now she was so fragile. 'Mr Buchanan is – is an unusual sort of employer. He knows how much you mean to me and how badly I've been missing you. He said I could have a little holiday with you. Isn't that lovely?'

But I could never fool Mama, ill or not.

'A little holiday, my eye! Oh, Hetty, child, what's happened? You haven't lost your position already, have you? He has given you a character reference, hasn't he?' Mama started coughing again in her agitation.

'Let me make us both a pot of tea and then I'll tell you all about it,' I said.

'Oh Lord, I must take Miss Roberts *her* tea. She'll be waking from her afternoon nap any moment, and she gets agitated if I don't have it ready for her.'

'But doesn't she realize you're ill?'

'No! Well, she must hear me coughing sometimes, but she doesn't comment. I take a spoonful of linctus every time I have to talk to her, and that helps a little.'

'But doesn't she see how pale and thin you've got?'

'She's an old lady, Hetty. She has cataracts and can barely see her own hand in front of her face.'

Mama looked like an old lady herself as she shuffled around the kitchen preparing a tea tray. She let me make the pot of tea, but she cut wafer-thin slices of bread and butter and arranged them in tiny triangles on the plate, with a pot of blackberry jam.

'I gathered the blackberries myself and then made the jam,' Mama said proudly. 'You shall have a big slice in a moment, darling. Though I don't think you deserve it. You've clearly been a very bad girl. I thought you were happy working for this Mr Buchanan. You liked it that he was a writer.'

'I've never liked him. He thinks he's a great writer, but his stories are dull dull dull. And then he took my memoirs, Mama – *my* story, *our* story – and was using it to write his own story. So I confronted him.'

'Hmm! You don't "confront" your employer, Hetty.'

'*Sapphire!* Won't you call me by my true name, Mama?'

'Sapphire, Hetty, whichever name. You're still my dear, headstrong, wilful daughter, and goodness knows what I'm going to do with you!' said Mama.

A bell on the wall suddenly jangled, making us both jump. Mama started coughing again, holding her handkerchief over her face. 'She's . . . awake! Wants . . . tea!' she gasped.

'Oh, Mama, you poor thing, don't try to talk. Look, sit down. Can't I take the old girl her wretched tea? If she's half blind, maybe she won't notice it's me and not you.'

'Don't talk . . . so daft,' said Mama. She gave one last cough, clutching the handkerchief, then crumpled it up quickly and tucked it in her apron.

'Mama?'

She ignored me, took the tray, and carried it out of the kitchen, her poor stick arms taut and straining. I couldn't bear it and tried to take the tray off her, but she glared at me ferociously and I had to give way. I watched her walk slowly up the stairs, her breath rasping, shoulders hunched. Oh dear Lord, this was my lovely young mother, my Ida, who had raced up and down the steep stairs at the hospital and lugged great vats of porridge around.

When she came back, scarcely able to draw breath, I sat her down and poured her a cup of tea. I urged her to eat her own bread and jam, but she said she wasn't hungry.

'You *must* eat, Mama. Look how thin you are,' I said, taking her poor little hands in mine. They were cold, though when I felt her forehead, it was still burning.

'Mama, please. I can't bear to see you looking so frail and exhausted. You're very ill, no matter what you say. You *must* go to bed – and *I* must call a doctor.'

'I can't go to bed, Hetty dear. I have to make the supper. And we certainly can't call the doctor. He charges a fortune! There's nothing he can do for me anyway. I shall take another dose of my linctus. The only other medicine I need is you, my darling girl. Oh, Hetty, I still can't believe you're actually here!'

I stopped trying to press Mama and helped her cook supper. I made an apple pie to show off my pastry skills, and basked in Mama's praise.

'Perhaps we might get you a job as a little cook after all!' she said. 'Miss Smith might be able to set you up again.'

I kept quiet. I wasn't going back to Miss Smith. I wasn't going to be a cook. I wasn't going anywhere now. I was going to stay right here and look after Mama.

16

Mama let me stay in her room that night. I crept quietly up the stairs, my shoes in my hand, while Mama gave Miss Roberts her night-time cup of cocoa and settled her in her bed.

Mama's room was up in the attic. It made me want to weep, seeing all her modest possessions again: her little violet vase, her brush and comb, her special soap, her bundle of letters from me. She had a narrow iron bed, but I was sure there was just about room for two, especially if we wound our arms around each other. But Mama wouldn't hear of it.

She fetched fresh linen from the press, a cushion from the sofa in the drawing room, and a thick cashmere shawl belonging to Miss Roberts.

'Here, Hetty, I'll make you up a separate little bed fit for a queen,' she said.

'It's lovely, Mama, but I'd sooner sleep with you.'

'No, darling.'

'But why? I used to creep into your bed sometimes back at the hospital.'

'I don't want you too near me, in case . . . in case you catch my cough,' said Mama, and she wouldn't be swayed.

So I bedded down in my cosy nest on the floor, and Mama lay on her bed. I edged nearer in the night and put my arm up, so that I could just about reach her hand.

'You'll give yourself dreadful pins and needles,' she whispered.

'I don't care if I get pins and needles all over. I need to hold onto you. Oh, Mama, I've missed you so.'

'And I have missed you, my Hetty,' said Mama.

We clung tightly to each other's hand. I think Mama might have been crying. I know I was.

I woke very early. Mama was coughing, her hands clamped over her mouth to muffle the sounds. I got up and propped her up on my cushion as well as her pillows. It eased her chest slightly and made her cough less.

'Better now, Mama?'

'Much better, sweetheart,' she whispered. 'Now, I have been trying to work out the best way to get you a new position. I'm wondering whether I should write to Miss Smith to explain the situation, though I know my spelling leaves a lot to be desired. I don't want to let you down, Hetty.'

'You could never let me down, Mama! But I don't see that there's much point telling Miss Smith. I am sure she will take Mr Buchanan's side, I just know it. He'll tell her lies about keeping my memoirs to help improve my grammar and writing style.'

'But she must be fond of you. She's taken such an interest in you these last few years, and she's been so kind forwarding all our letters. I'm sure she might give you a character to help you find another position.'

'The only position I want is right here, Mama. I want to be with you.'

'And I want that too, darling, with all my heart, but I'm not sure how we can keep you hidden away day after day. Miss Roberts is infirm, but she still totters from room to room using her walking stick. If she were to come upon you unawares, she'd be very shocked – and then *I* would lose my position.'

'But you've said she's a kind old lady. If you told her you've been reunited with your long-lost daughter, surely she'd be happy for you and *want* us to be together? I could work for her too. I would fetch and carry and do her sewing. I could even write her letters for her.'

'Hetty, Hetty, you still don't understand the ways of the world. I am her *servant*. I'm not expected to have a daughter, especially one born out of wedlock. She would think it terribly lax and immoral to condone such a situation.'

'I think it's terribly lax and immoral of *her* to let

you wait on her hand and foot. Even if she's totally blind, she can surely *hear* how ill you are every time you cough,' I said hotly.

'Ssh! She'll hear you,' said Mama. She swung her legs out of bed and tried to get up, but the movement made her cough again. Her hand searched all round the bed as she shook and gasped, looking for her handkerchief. She found it at last and held it to her mouth, while I stood beside her helplessly, patting her poor heaving back. She was so thin that her shoulder blades were as sharp as knives.

'Please, Mama, get back into bed,' I begged, but she wouldn't listen. She stood up, still coughing, staggering over to her washstand in her old nightgown. She stood with one hand clutching the tiled top, her knuckles white. She gave one last heave. I saw the handkerchief at her lips suddenly darken with bright blood.

'Mama!' I stared in terror. She tried to hide the handkerchief, but it was too late.

'You're coughing blood!'

'Only a little, because it's such a hacking cough. Oh, Hetty, don't stare like that. See, the cough has stopped. I'm better now.'

I had a pain in my own chest, my heart beating fast. This wasn't just a troublesome cough. This was far more sinister. I knew what I had to do now. I wouldn't tell Mama because she'd argue with me and get agitated.

We both washed and dressed, and then I crept downstairs with Mama and helped her light the range and prepare breakfast.

'You're such a grand, capable girl now, Hetty. I'm so proud of you,' said Mama.

Miss Roberts stayed in bed to have her breakfast, and then fell asleep again as she read the morning newspaper. I peeped round her bedroom door to catch a glimpse of her. She was a stout little old lady who looked as if she'd been stuffed with pillows. I couldn't tell how many chins she had when she was awake, but she had at least four when lying down dozing. Her mouth was open, showing just two teeth at the top and two at the bottom, like a baby. She was wearing a large flounced nightcap, but from the curled grey wig on its stand on her dressing table I guessed she was as bald as a baby too. She was certainly as helpless as an infant. Mama had to help her wash and dress and visit the WC. It seemed so desperately unfair when Mama was the one who was so ill.

I was determined Mama was going to have the best medical treatment, no matter how costly. I tipped out the entire contents of the housekeeping jar and tied all the coins in a handkerchief in my pocket. I was careful not to chink the coins, not wanting Mama to hear.

When Miss Roberts woke for her mid-morning cup of Camp coffee, I knew Mama was going to be busy getting her up and dressed and ready for luncheon.

'May I go out for a little walk, Mama?' I asked.

'Of course you can, Hetty. It will do you good to have some air. Take care to watch where you're going, though. I don't want you to get lost,' said Mama.

As if I would ever lose my dear Mama now! I set off on my search, walking down to the sea front. I was momentarily distracted by the beach. There were children already playing on the pale sands. I had an urge to rip off my shoes and stockings and run around too. There were bathing machines lined up right along the sands, and quite a few folk bobbing up and down in the waves in maroon and navy bathing dresses, their faces red with sunburn. I'd never swum, but it looked splendid fun.

I watched for a minute, and then looked around. I saw an old gentleman laboriously pushing an elderly lady in a bathchair. They looked as if they must visit a doctor regularly.

'Excuse me, sir, madam,' I said, bobbing them a polite little curtsy. 'Might you know where there is a good doctor here in Bignor?'

'Are you poorly, little lass? You look as fit as a fiddle to me,' said the old man.

'It's my mama. She's got a very bad cough. She urgently needs a doctor,' I said.

'Then our Dr Jenkins is the man for her. I had a terrible throat this winter and he made a new man of me. He stopped me coughing in no time,' said the old man. 'Dr Jenkins, twenty-two Magnolia Square.'

'What's that you're telling her?' said the old lady, rearing up in her bath chair and squinting at me. 'She's a little maid, Henry. She'd never be able to afford Dr Jenkins.'

'Oh yes I can, ma'am,' I said, and I marched off, jingling the coins in my pocket.

I went back down the promenade to the painted map and found Magnolia Square easily enough. The houses were tall and grand, with beautiful pink flowering trees in their front gardens. I found number twenty-two – and there was a gentleman walking briskly down the steps, carrying a black bag.

I'd seen a black bag like that before, when the doctor was called to the hospital. I'd been very ill, but he had made me better.

'Oh please, sir, are you Dr Jenkins?' I asked, rushing up to him.

'I am indeed, my dear. I'm off on my rounds now.'

'Oh please, could you call at number eighteen Saltdean Lane? It's very urgent!'

'Is your mistress ill?'

'No, it's Mama – but don't worry, I have lots of money and can pay you royally.'

His mouth quivered. 'What ails your mama, child?'

'She has a very frightening cough, so much that she spits blood. She's grown very thin and tired, and has a burning fever,' I gabbled.

Dr Jenkins looked grave now. 'I will fit her in at the end of my rounds.'

'Oh thank you! Number eighteen – you won't forget? And do you think you will be able to make her better?'

'I will do what I can to help her,' he said.

'Shall I give you the money now?' I said, fumbling for my handkerchief of coins.

'No, no, wait until I've seen your mama. Number eighteen Saltdean Lane – you see, I haven't forgotten.'

I ran all the way back to Mama's house, in spite of the hidden coins jingling in my pocket. I glanced up at the windows of number eighteen and there was Miss Roberts, dressed now, peering down at me. I had to look away quickly and walk on down the road purposefully, then steal back ten minutes later. There was no sign of her now. I nipped round to the back door and tapped softly for Mama.

'There you are, dearie! My, your walk has done you good. You've got lovely pink cheeks! But we'll have to find you a sunhat. Redheads burn easily –

they've got such fine white skin.'

'Have I really got fine skin, Mama? I thought my blue eyes were my only good feature.'

'You're fine all over, Hetty – the best girl in the whole world – though you're not good, you're very, very bad, cheeking your master so terribly. But I've been thinking carefully about your predicament.'

'Mama, I told you, I'm not contacting Miss Smith. I'm not leaving you now.'

'Listen to me, Hetty! I've been thinking hard while I've been fussing round Miss Roberts. She's got several old lady friends she takes tea with from time to time. I hear them all a-moaning and a-grumbling about their own maids. They've all got to the stage where they need nurses as well as maids, but they don't want to pay a double wage. I've heard them say that Miss Roberts is a very lucky lady having me—'

'And she *is*!'

'So I was wondering—' Mama broke off to cough, her face flushing painfully. 'Perhaps we could find you a position with one of these old girls – and then we could write to Miss Smith and ask if *she* could give you a character, like she did me.'

'Oh, Mama! What would she put? *Hetty Feather has a temper to match her red hair. She shrieks like a banshee if thwarted. She attacks her employer if he confiscates her property*. These old ladies might be a bit dotty, but surely they'd not be impressed by that.'

'I agree with you! I know we can't expect Miss Smith to tell an outright lie, but she could temper her words a little. She could write something like: *Hetty Feather is a warm-hearted, willing girl who works well and will be very true and loyal if treated kindly*.'

'*You* give me a character, Mama!'

'I wish I could! There's no better daughter in the whole world,' said Mama. Then she started coughing again – so badly that she had to sit down at the kitchen table. I ran to get her linctus and poured her two great spoonfuls, but it didn't seem to have any effect. By the time the paroxysm stopped we were both in tears.

I took Mama in my arms and held her tightly. I could feel all her little sparrow bones. She was trembling, but she relaxed against me for a moment, and then feebly tried to push me away.

'Don't get too near, Hetty,' she whispered. 'I'd tear my own heart out if I infected you.'

'It's all right, Mama. Don't worry. We're going to get you well again,' I said fiercely. 'Just you wait.'

I was on tenterhooks for the rest of the morning, waiting for Dr Jenkins to come calling. But he didn't come and didn't come and didn't come.

Mama cooked Miss Roberts a mutton chop for her lunch, with a little mashed potato. We had a big plate of mash sprinkled with grated cheese – though Mama barely touched hers.

'You must eat, Mama. You've got so thin,' I said. I tried holding the fork to her lips, coaxing her like a baby.

When we'd done the washing-up together, Mama set about writing a letter to Miss Smith. I saw how long it took her to spell out the simplest words and my heart ached for her.

'You must tell me when I make mistakes, Hetty. I know I'm very ignorant,' she said, blushing.

'No you're not! You write a lovely letter,' I lied firmly.

Then at last I heard a knocking at the front door.

'I'll go!' I said, jumping up.

'No! No, Hetty, let me—' said Mama, struggling to her feet, but it made her cough again, and she had to cling to the table to stay upright.

I ran through the kitchen and out into the hallway to the front door. I flung it open, and there was Dr Jenkins, carrying his black bag.

'You came after all!' I said.

'I am a man of my word,' he said. 'Now, where is the patient?'

He looked towards the stairs, expecting to be taken up to a bedroom, but I led him down the hall-

303

way and through to the kitchen.

'Hetty!' Mama gasped. 'What are you *doing*, showing the gentleman into the kitchen! I'm so sorry, sir. I'll take you to the drawing room directly. Have you come to see Miss Roberts?'

'No, I rather think I've come to see you,' said Dr Jenkins. 'You don't look at all well, my dear.' He put a hand on Mama's forehead. 'You have a fever – and I heard you coughing when I was in the hall.'

'No, sir, not me. I am fine,' Mama insisted, looked terribly flustered.

'It's all right, Mama. Tell the gentleman all your symptoms. I've fetched him for you. He's a doctor so he'll make you better.'

'Oh, Hetty, what have you *done*?' said Mama, starting to cry.

'Mama, don't. You *need* a doctor. And don't worry about money – I'm going to pay. Look, I have lots of money hidden in my handkerchief.'

'Hush, child,' said Dr Jenkins. 'Perhaps you can make us a cup of tea while I examine your mother.'

I did as I was told. Mama continued weeping while he listened to her chest and asked her many questions. She answered in a monotone, barely polite, but the doctor treated her gently, with respect.

'I think you know my diagnosis, don't you?' he said eventually, sitting down beside Mama and sipping his tea.

Mama nodded.

'You have an advanced case of phthisis,' Dr Jenkins said quietly.

'What's that? Please, is it serious, Doctor?' I asked fearfully, hating the hissing sound of the sinister little word.

'I'm afraid it is, Hetty. Your mother is consumptive, and has been for some while. It's a wonder she has been able to keep her position,' he said.

'But I'm going to lose it now, aren't I?' Mama said, and started coughing again.

He waited until the paroxysms stopped. 'My dear, how *can* you carry on in this state? And you know and I know that I have to tell your mistress.'

'And *you* know and *I* know that she will cast me out, and I will have nowhere to go. I doubt even the workhouse will take me in this state,' said Mama.

'I am going to see if I can admit you to the local infirmary,' said Dr Jenkins. 'There is a special ward for consumptive patients.'

'And will they make Mama better there?' I asked.

'They will give her every care,' he said.

'Yes, but can they *cure* her?' I said desperately.

'I think you are going to have to be a good brave girl, Hetty, and learn one of life's saddest lessons. We often lose the people we love the most.'

17

I wouldn't believe it. I tried not to let Mama believe it either.

'You're not going to die, Mama. I won't let you! I will care for you and feed you and nurse you, and do every single thing for you so that you never have to move, and then you won't cough, and then you will get better, just you wait and see,' I declared.

But Mama just shook her head very sadly, without even enough spirit to argue with me. She was proved horribly right about Miss Roberts. Mama had cared for her so devotedly – but as soon as the doctor broke the news to her that Mama had consumption, she panicked.

'She must leave this house immediately!' she screamed, so loudly that Mama and I could hear her downstairs. 'I can't have any sickness here! She might infect me! I will have to have the whole house thoroughly cleansed and disinfected. I will have to go to the trouble of training a new maid in my ways, and I'm a sick old woman myself. Oh, *why* did she have to do this to me? How will I ever get a maid to replace Ida?'

'What a selfish, wicked woman!' I exclaimed. 'She doesn't give a thought for *you*, Mama.'

'She's simply frightened,' said Mama. 'Go to her, Hetty. Here's your chance. Tell her that *you* will care for her.'

'I'm not working for her!' I cried.

'Hetty, please, will you try? One of us has to work – and it looks as if I am finished.'

'*Don't!* All right, Mama, I will go and talk to her.'

I'd sooner have worked for Matron Stinking Bottomly than for this self-centred, wretched woman who didn't have a word of compassion for my dear sick mama – but I could not deny her anything now.

'Try to be very polite!' said Mama.

I went up the stairs and knocked on her door.

'Who's that? If it's you, Ida, you can't come in! I daren't risk the infection – and I mustn't upset myself. I am a sick woman, aren't I, Doctor?'

I swallowed hard while he murmured to her. I wanted to burst in and boot her right out of bed, but I entered her room quietly, and bobbed her a deferential curtsy.

'Ah, the little daughter,' said Dr Jenkins.

'Whose daughter? *Ida's?*'

'Yes, ma'am – and I can take over Mama's duties while she's in the infirmary,' I said meekly. 'I have been trained as a servant and can cook and clean. Please let me assist you, ma'am. I am quick to learn.'

'There now, Miss Roberts!' said Dr Jenkins. 'Here is the answer to your prayers.'

'No, no, absolutely not! Don't let that girl come near me! She might have the infection too. And I can't have a child born out of wedlock in my house. I'm sorry, but I have my Christian principles.'

'And I have *my* principles, ma'am,' I shouted, unable to help myself now. 'I am *glad* you will not take me on. You pretend to be a good woman, but you haven't got an ounce of compassion in your withered heart. You are so taken up with your own trivial concerns that you didn't even *notice* that Mama was coughing herself to death. She's cared so dutifully for you, and yet you just want to turn her out onto the streets. You talk of Christian principles! I think you're going to get a horrible surprise when you go knocking on St Peter's gate in Heaven. He'll shake his head at you and turn you away, just you wait and see!'

I stamped out of the room, down the stairs, back to Mama in the kitchen.

'I couldn't quite hear – but that didn't *sound* very polite,' Mama said weakly.

'Oh, Mama, I did try, truly, but she didn't want me,' I said.

'Then we're done for,' Mama said weakly. 'We're both homeless.'

'No, we're *not*. That Dr Jenkins seems a kind gentleman. I'm sure he'll do his best to get you into the infirmary,' I said.

'I *try* to be kind – and I'm going to take your mama directly to the infirmary in my carriage,' Dr Jenkins said, following me into the kitchen. 'Why don't you get your mother's things packed up, my dear?'

It took only a few minutes to pack Mama's possessions into a box. She had just two changes of clothes, her nightgown, her washing things, her brush and comb, her little violet vase, and a satin pouch embroidered with one word: HETTY. I found all the letters I'd ever written to her inside, tied up in neat bundles with ribbon, plus all the childish presents I'd made for her, right back to a little ill-sewn heart. I wept then to see that she'd treasured them so carefully.

I carried Mama's box and my own suitcase, and we left Miss Roberts's house with the doctor. Mama tried to go to Miss Roberts to say goodbye, but she would not let her over her bedroom threshold and screamed at her to go away. Even so, Mama insisted on going to the neighbouring cottage, asking for the mistress there and begging her to send her maid to assist Miss Roberts.

The doctor took us to the infirmary in his carriage.

'I really can't go to this infirmary,' Mama protested weakly. 'I must try to find some kind of shelter for Hetty and me. I can still work if I put my mind to it.' But she started coughing again, that harsh hacking cough she couldn't control. Then she choked, and the terrifying bright blood stained her handkerchief.

'You cannot possibly work, my dear,' said Dr Jenkins. 'All you can do is rest now.'

The carriage drew up outside a large grey building that reminded me uncomfortably of my own hospital.

'Wait here, both of you,' said the doctor, and he hurried inside.

'I'm so, so sorry, Mama,' I said tearfully. 'I thought the doctor might be able to make you better. I didn't dream that dreadful woman would throw you out. I didn't realize.'

'I know, Hetty, I know,' Mama said, resting her poor burning head on my shoulder. 'Oh, darling, what use am I to you as a mother? Perhaps I should have given you up for good when you were a baby and never tried to be near you. I've just brought you heartache and grief.'

'You've given me great love. You're the best mother in the whole world. You mustn't worry about a thing now. You're going to get better, I promise you are. I'm going to visit you every day, and buy you little treats and care for you – just the way you did for me when I was little. But I'm big now, Mama, and can look out for myself, so you mustn't worry.'

'You, *big*? You'll always be my light-as-a-feather

311

Hetty,' said Mama.

'Sapphire,' I said.

'Sapphire,' said Mama, very gently touching my eyelids with her fingertips. 'When you were born, I wrapped you in a shawl and held you in my arms. You didn't cry or sleep like most babies. You just lay there, a tiny little thing, and looked up solemnly with your big blue eyes. You didn't seem like a stranger at all – it was as if I'd known you for ever.'

We clung to each other. Then Dr Jenkins came back, accompanied by a nurse in a high white hat and a starched apron. Her uniform reminded me of the matrons at the hospital and I was scared, but she helped Mama out of the carriage gently enough.

'Come along, you poor dear. Let us get you comfortable in bed,' she said.

'There now, young woman,' said Dr Jenkins to me. 'They will take care of your mother. They have put aside a bed for her, and she can stay there until – until she needs it no longer.'

'Thank you, sir.' I fumbled for my handkerchief. 'Exactly how much do I owe you, Dr Jenkins?'

He looked down at me, hesitating.

'It's all right, I have a great deal of money here. I can pay you the full amount, I'm sure,' I said.

'You keep your money, my dear,' said Dr Jenkins. 'I think you're going to need every penny.'

'That's – that's exceptionally kind of you, sir. I

am deeply indebted to you,' I said. I was trying to sound very grown up and business-like, but he shook his head sorrowfully, and patted me on the head as if I were a little child.

I scurried after Mama and the nurse. When I caught them up at the infirmary entrance, the nurse looked shocked to see me.

'No, no, dear. You're not allowed in here,' she said.

'But I have to go with Mama!'

'I'm taking her to the fever ward. Our patients are kept in complete isolation,' said the nurse.

'But *you* can go with her!'

'Yes, but *I* am a nurse!' she said.

'Then let me be a nurse too!' I said.

'Don't be ridiculous, child!'

'Please, please, please, can I just see where Mama's bed will be, and help her into it?' I said. I dropped to my knees. 'Look, I am *begging* you. *Please.*'

'Oh, very well, you can come in for five minutes, but then you must go. If Sister catches you there, I shall get into serious trouble,' she said.

So I walked with the nurse and Mama down long corridors smelling strongly of iodoform. Then, at last, at the very end of the building, we went through a door into a long room with beds lined up on either side.

'It's just like the dormitory at the hospital,

Mama!' I said.

I peered fearfully at the folk in the beds. They were mostly lying neat and still beneath their grey blankets, as if their limbs had been as firmly tucked in as their sheets. The few sitting propped up on pillows were all wearing bright red bed jackets. Perhaps they were provided to make the patients look bright and cheerful, but the colour only emphasized their sallow faces.

'You will have this bed here. It's in the best place of all, by the window. There, you have a sea view!' said the nurse, as if this were a special seaside hotel.

The window was opened a few inches, rattling a little in the strong breeze blowing from the sea.

'Won't Mama be in a draught?' I asked anxiously.

'She will get lots of sea air, and that will be very good for her lungs,' said the nurse. 'Now, go behind that curtain and take off your clothes. I'll provide you with infirmary linen. You won't need your own nightgown. In fact you won't need any of your things here. Your daughter can take them away.'

'I'll keep my letters,' Mama said firmly.

When I'd helped her into the plain white nightgown and garish bed jacket, she clutched the satin pouch to her chest.

I helped her gently into bed, smoothing her hair and pulling the bed jacket up around her thin neck.

314

The nurse provided her with a little china spittoon and a large handkerchief.

Mama and I stared at each other. Tears spilled down our cheeks.

'Oh, Hetty,' Mama whispered.

'There now, time to rest,' said the nurse, trying to straighten Mama's clenched fists. 'Say goodbye now.'

'This isn't goodbye for ever, Mama,' I said fiercely. 'You're going to get better, do you hear me? And I'm going to find a place for us to live and we'll be together at last, you and me. That's the way it's going to be, I promise.'

'But . . . now . . . I think you will have to . . . go to Miss Smith,' Mama gasped, starting to cough.

'No, I'm going to stay here. Don't worry, Mama, I have a plan. I will find a position here, and every day I will come to the infirmary before it gets dark. If I can't creep in somehow, I will stand in the grounds and I will wave to you at your window to show you that I'm fine. And you will wave back to me. Will you do that, Mama?'

'I will, darling,' Mama said between coughs.

I wiped her brow for her, kissed her hot forehead, and then ran out of the ward. I ran down the grim corridors, out of the infirmary, down the road, right onto the sands. I laid my head on my suitcase, clutched Mama's box, and cried my heart out.

18

'Hetty? Hetty, is that you?'
I sat up, dazed, squinting in the sunlight. I didn't have any idea how long I'd been lying there on the sands. I'd cried for so long, but then I must have fallen asleep. Perhaps I was still dreaming now, because a strangely familiar child was squatting beside me, calling my name and looking at me with concern – and yet I felt sure I didn't have a friend in the world.

'Hetty, don't you remember me? I'm Maisie. We met on the train,' she said, tucking her hair behind her ears.

I stared at her. I'd only met her a day ago, and yet it seemed like months and months. I'd been travelling with such joy and optimism, so happy at the thought of seeing Mama. Yet now she was in-carcerated in the infirmary, and though I hoped otherwise, I wasn't sure she would ever walk out. I had been trying so hard to do the best thing by calling the doctor, but maybe it would have been better to do nothing. Then Mama would at least have had her position and we could have been together. Miss Roberts might never have noticed I was there.

I started crying so bitterly that Maisie looked frightened.

'Don't cry so, Hetty, please! What's the matter? Are you lost? I am lost, but I don't mind a bit. I went for a paddle in the sea and I wandered in the water a little because it was so delightful, but when I went back up the beach, I couldn't find Mama and the others. I've been walking along the sands looking and looking for them, but *I'm* not crying one bit, see. I'm trying to be a big brave girl.'

'You *are* a big brave girl,' I said, wiping my eyes. I took several deep breaths, trying hard to calm myself. 'There now, I'm not crying either, not any more. Let me gather up my things and we'll walk along the sands together and I'm sure we'll find your family soon.'

I stood up, grasped my suitcase and Mama's box, and we started trudging along the beach together. Maisie set off to the right, but I felt sure she was going the wrong way.

'No, Maisie, I think your family will be *this* way, near the pier. I think you've been walking away from them all this time.'

'I'm not always very good at knowing which way

318

to go,' Maisie admitted. 'Will you stay with me until we find them again, Hetty?'

'Of course I will.'

'Shall I carry that box for you, as you have your suitcase?'

'No, I can manage it perfectly myself,' I said. My arms were aching, but I could not bear to relinquish Mama's box.

We travelled further along the beach. I had sand in my boots now, chafing my feet uncomfortably. Maisie had the advantage, running along in bare feet, her sailor dress tucked up comfortably in her drawers.

'This is such an adventure, isn't it, Hetty?' she said, giving a little skip.

I tried to smile at her. I wished with all my heart I could be a blessed child like Maisie, when the worst thing that could happen to her was getting lost on a beach. And she wasn't even lost any more, because I suddenly spotted a familiar little family. The mama was calling anxiously, clutching the baby, the papa was striding up and down, his head turning this way and that, and the big sister was running to the sea and back, gazing wildly about her.

'See, Maisie? There's your family,' I said.

'Oh! Yes, so it is! And see how they are searching for me!' said Maisie. She started running. 'Mama!

Papa! Charlotte! Here I am! Don't worry, I'm not a bit lost now.'

I watched her run over to them, and saw how her papa picked her up and whirled her round and round, her mama gave her a big kiss, and her sister Charlotte hugged her hard.

I felt tears pricking my eyes all over again. I turned my head and started walking quickly away – but I heard the family calling my name, and then thudding footsteps across the sand. It was Charlotte. She gave me a hug too, as if I were part of the family.

'Dear Hetty! Maisie says you found her. We're so grateful. We were all going frantic. Won't you come and let Mama and Papa thank you properly?'

She took my hand in hers and led me back to the little group.

'Well done, Hetty! We were looking everywhere for our silly little girl,' said the papa. 'How can we reward you?'

'Yes, we are considerably in your debt,' said the mama. 'I was nearly going out of my mind with worry. But what about *your* mother, Hetty? Have you not found her yet, dear?'

'Oh yes, I have, but – but she is very ill, and now she is in the infirmary and – and I don't know what to do,' I said, sobbing.

'My poor child!' She gave the baby to Charlotte and put her arms round me. I laid my head on her soft muslin blouse and wept, while she patted me gently on the back.

'There, now,' she said softly.

'I'm so sorry! It's just – I don't know what to do!'

'I know what you're going to do. You're going to come back to our lodgings and have supper with us,' said Papa.

'Yes, yes, yes!' said Charlotte and Maisie.

So I walked back with them to their lodgings, a big pink-washed house in a street leading off the promenade. I was still crying, and cowered away when their landlady came to the door. I knew I must look a terrible sight in my grubby dress, my face covered in tears and my nose running.

I thought they would send me to the kitchen to beg a morsel there – but not a bit of it.

'This little girl is a friend of ours, Mrs Brooke,' the mama said firmly. 'She will be having supper with us.'

'Certainly, Mrs Greenwood,' said the landlady, though she took in my cheap maid's dress and raised an eyebrow.

'Come, girls, let us tidy ourselves before supper,' said the mama.

She led the way upstairs to their rooms. She and

her husband shared a big blue bedroom, while Flora the baby had a cot beside their bed. The girls' room was next door, a pretty pink, with two single beds with patchwork quilts, and a proper dressing table and a washstand with pink-and-white patterned china.

Mrs Brooke brought jugs of hot water for each room and we washed in turn. The girls put on fresh clean sailor dresses, while I wore my Sunday green velvet. I felt it was too hot and formal for the seaside but the girls admired it enormously, stroking the velvet and fingering the yellow fringing.

'I would give anything to wear such a grown-up dress,' said Charlotte enviously. 'And you're allowed to put your hair up too, Hetty!'

'It doesn't stay pinned up for long though,' I said, and I brushed it out loose so that it fell a long way past my shoulders.

'You look like the lovely advertisement for Edwards' "Harlene" Hair Restorer!' said Charlotte.

'Oh, let me have a turn brushing it!' Maisie begged. Her own hair was limp and straggly, and she marvelled at mine.

'I wish I had lovely long hair like yours, Hetty! It's just like a mermaid's.' She pulled my green skirts tight around my legs. 'There, now you have a mermaid's tail too!'

I could hear the baby wailing fretfully, so I decided to make myself useful and went and knocked next door.

'Excuse me, Mrs Greenwood – would you like me to take care of the baby while you get ready in peace?' I offered.

'Why, Hetty, you're such a kind girl!' she said. 'All right, dear, see if you can work your magic with little Flora all over again. I have changed her napkin so I don't know why she's crying so. Perhaps you might ask Mrs Brooke to prepare her another bottle of boiled milk?'

'Certainly,' I carried the cross little baby carefully down the stairs and found my way to the kitchen.

Mrs Brooke was cutting thin slices of bread and butter, while fat yellow slabs of smoked haddock poached pungently on the stove.

'Please may I have a bottle for the baby?' I asked.

'Certainly . . . miss,' she said. The word came out grudgingly, but she said it all the same.

I took the bottle of baby milk and fed Flora in the window seat of the sitting room. She was clearly thirsty because she attacked the bottle with great vigour, making comically loud sucking sounds. I held her close, wondering at her intent little face, her long lashes and tiny delicate ears. I especially liked her perfect little toes peeping out beneath her rucked-up petticoats.

I thought of poor dear Mama and how she'd been forced to give me away when I was even younger than little Flora, denied the chance of holding me close like this.

We had had so short a time together. She had missed my first five years altogether, she had kept a wary distance when I came back to the hospital – and then she'd been cruelly banished. I'd planned for us to be together when I was grown up. I'd thought we'd have many, many precious years ahead, enough to make up for the sad time apart, but now . . .

I started crying again. Flora stopped sucking and stared up at me, her forehead puckering. She waved her tiny starfish hands, almost as if she were trying to comfort me.

'I'm sorry, little Flora,' I whispered, sniffing. 'I'll try to concentrate on you again.'

She drained her bottle completely, her eyes closing as she took the last few mouthfuls. She gave several contented sighs, snuggled her head right into my chest, and fell fast asleep. I held her close, and wouldn't put her down even when Mrs Brooke banged a gong and the family assembled in the dining room for supper.

I ate a few morsels of fish carefully with one hand while still holding the baby. There was fruit pie for pudding. The pastry was a little pale and uninteresting compared to my own. I was in such a turmoil I could eat very little.

'There now, children! Are you quite full now?' said Mr Greenwood, consulting his pocket watch. 'Good heavens, is that the time? Off to bed with you this minute!'

'Oh, Papa, *please* mayn't we stay up a little longer! It's still sunny outside. Are you *sure* it's bedtime?' Maisie wailed, as if the world were suddenly coming to an end.

Mr Greenwood's mouth twitched under his moustache, and Charlotte burst out laughing.

'Oh, Maisie, can't you tell when Papa is joking?'

'Don't you remember, Maisie?' Mrs Greenwood said, fondly pinching her daughter's cheek. 'We always go for a little walk along the sea front after supper.'

'Oh, so we do! Oh hurray, hurray!' said Maisie.

So we all went for a walk. I insisted on carrying little Flora, who was muffled in another shawl against the sea breeze. My heart beat hard against the baby, thinking that at any moment they would say goodbye to me and send me on my way to nowhere – but they seemed to take my company for granted. I left my suitcase and Mama's box back at the boarding house so at least I had an excuse for returning with them.

We set off down the road to the sea front.

'Now, which way shall we go, my dears?' said Mr Greenwood, standing before the painted map.

'Oh, please,' I whispered, my mouth so dry I could barely make myself heard. 'Could we – oh, could we—?'

'Let's see the pierrots!' Charlotte shouted.

'No, no, let's listen to the band,' Maisie clamoured.

'We can do both – *and* take a little stroll along the pier,' said Mr Greenwood.

Mrs Greenwood was looking at me. 'Where did *you* want to go, Hetty?' she asked.

'I – I wondered if I might possibly just run along to the infirmary. Perhaps Mama will be looking out of her window. I should so like to reassure her that I am all right.'

'You're a good thoughtful girl, Hetty. We will come with you, and then perhaps your mother will see you're among friends,' she said.

'Among very *dear* friends,' I said. 'Oh please, may we?'

It was a good fifteen minutes' walk away. I knew

everyone must be longing to see all their favourite seaside entertainments but they walked cheerfully beside me. Maisie skipped in circles, while Charlotte talked nineteen to the dozen about her school, and her best friends, and her favourite teachers, and the very worst cruel teacher ever, who made even great girls of Charlotte's age stand in a corner with a dunce's cap upon their heads. I did not think this very cruel at all compared to Matron Stinking Bottomly and Matron Pigface Peters, but I simply nodded or shook my head or tutted at appropriate times.

'Where do *you* go to school, Hetty?' Charlotte asked.

'I have left school now,' I said, truthfully enough.

'Oh, you lucky thing! How I wish I could leave school too, but Papa says it's important for a girl to have a good education, worst luck!'

I still nodded from time to time, but I was no longer listening to her sweet silly prattle. Inside my head I was chanting, *Mama, Mama, Mama.*

We approached the grim grey infirmary, and I stared hopefully up at the windows, but they all seemed so dark. I could not see in it at all, or tell whether anyone was looking out.

'I have to go *closer*,' I said, and I ran into the garden, through the shrubbery, looking around frantically, wondering if I could still work out which was the right window. Then I reached it at last and looked through the glass. I could see the ward. I could see the row of beds. Oh glory – *there* was Mama, propped up on her pillows in the garish red bed jacket, her face chalk-white, her eyes shadowed with dark circles. She was staring anxiously at the window, and when she saw me, her whole face lit up.

I smiled and blew kisses and held little Flora up, making her wave her tiny fist, hoping that Mama would think I had miraculously found a new position as a nursemaid. Mama seemed astonished at the sight, and tried to swing her legs out of bed to run to the window, but this made her cough. A nurse approached her bed and pushed her back against her pillows, but she did it gently, and she wiped Mama's brow when the coughing fit subsided at last.

I sent Mama a final kiss and she weakly blew a kiss back to me. *'I love you!'* I said – and her own lips mouthed the three words with me.

Then I ran back to the Greenwoods, hugging little Flora hard. 'I saw her! She was looking out for me,' I said, tears running down my cheeks.

'I'm so glad you saw her, Hetty,' said Mrs Greenwood. 'Now, dear, Mr Greenwood and I have had a little discussion. We will be happy to look after you for the next fortnight while we are in Bignor. You can share a room with the girls. I am sure Mrs Brooke will have a spare settle bed.'

'So – so can I be your nursemaid after all?' I said, dazed.

'No, we don't want you to be a nursemaid, though it will indeed be lovely if you continue to care for Flora so splendidly. We want you to stay with us as our guest, our little friend.'

The Greenwoods were so kind to me. I couldn't
quite believe they were real. It was almost as if
I'd made them up. I felt as if I'd made *myself* up too.
I wasn't Hetty Feather any more. I wasn't even
Sapphire Battersea. I wasn't a foundling child. I
wasn't a maid. I was a little Greenwood girl now.

I helped look after baby Flora, which was no
hardship at all. I'd grown to love this funny little
baby, and although lugging her around everywhere
made my arms tired, it somehow helped the ache in
my heart. But caring for Flora was seen as a favour,
certainly not a duty. I had no duties at all – this was
the strangest part.

I didn't have to get up early and fight with the
range and prepare breakfast. We didn't have to slip
out of our soft beds until seven thirty. I woke
around six even so, because it had become such a
habit.

I lay still, thinking of Mama, lying just a few
streets away. I sent her many loving thoughts and

liked to fancy she was sending hers back to me. I felt as if we were somehow having our own private conversation through the ether.

Then Mrs Greenwood would put her head in, her hair still tumbling around her shoulders. She wore a tartan shawl over her long nightgown, and looked more like Charlotte and Maisie's big sister than their mother.

'Time to get up, girls,' she said, softly and sleepily, and she'd stoop over each tousled head and kiss their cheeks. She gave me a little pat on the shoulder at first, but after a few days I got a kiss too. We'd take turns getting washed and queuing for the water closet. It wasn't quite as grand as Mr Buchanan's, but serviceable enough, and no sign of any spiders!

Then we'd dress to go down to breakfast. I didn't have a frock suitable for the seaside. My green velvet was too warm and elaborate, and I didn't want to spoil it on the sands, yet my plain grey maid's dresses showed the whole world that I was really a servant.

'I think you had better borrow one of Charlotte's dresses,' said Mrs Greenwood. 'You don't mind, do you, Charlotte?'

'Of course I don't! It will be fun to see Hetty in one of my frocks. Come, Hetty, have a look. See which one you like the best.'

I couldn't believe she could cheerfully offer me the pick of her wardrobe. At the Foundling Hospital we had never willingly shared anything, not even a tangerine at Christmas, a sweet from a visitor, an undarned pair of stockings. We guarded such treasures fiercely for ourselves. And it wasn't as if Charlotte or Maisie had any number of fine frocks. The Greenwoods weren't rich at all. I learned that Mr Greenwood was an ordinary clerk in an Arundel insurance office, though the Greenwood female folk were as proud of him as if he were King of Arundel Castle.

I am not sure if they were a religious family or not. We did not attend church on Sunday, but perhaps this was because it wasn't part of seaside routine. I know one thing: the Greenwoods were the most truly kind and Christian-like people I had ever known.

I picked a pale primrose muslin from Charlotte's wardrobe. It was a little long and loose on me, but I thought it quite beautiful. Charlotte and Maisie clapped their hands when I shyly paraded in front of them in my new gown.

'It looks lovely on you, Hetty – much better than on me,' said Charlotte generously.

'Yes, I totally agree, and it won't matter if it's a bit long, because you can tuck your skirts up in your drawers on the beach,' said Maisie.

333

Charlotte tried to lend me a pair of her shoes as well, but they were several sizes too big, while Maisie's were too small.

They sold very cheap white sand-shoes at a stall on the promenade. I wondered about buying myself a pair, but I didn't feel I could waste any of my precious hoard of coins. I knew I'd be fending for myself again after this fortnight. I wore my hideous old boots the length of the street from the lodgings to the sea, then I whipped them off and ran around barefoot.

Mrs Greenwood saw me gazing at the sand-shoe stall every day and asked me quietly if I'd like a pair, but I shook my head resolutely. The Greenwoods were already spending a lot of money on me, though they insisted it was a mere trifle. I'm not sure if they came to an arrangement with Mrs Brooke about my bed and board. I fervently hoped it wasn't too exorbitant.

Mr Greenwood paid for me to have a daily donkey ride with Charlotte and Maisie. Oh, those dear, funny, patient donkeys! They were led about by a strange man who barked out fierce instructions to all us children: 'Sit very still! Don't feed the donkeys! Don't ever kick them. Don't tweak their ears!' But when he spoke to his five donkeys, his voice was soft and crooning, and he patted their noses gently.

They had special names: Rosie, Maudie, Sally, Jessie and Polly. I always chose to ride on Polly, because I had had a dear friend Polly at the hospital. Polly-Donkey was the smallest and sweetest, ash-grey with a dark cross on her back. She seemed to like me too, and gave me a little whinnying greeting when I patted her. Perhaps it was because I lived up to my name and was light as a feather! Charlotte and Maisie were quite slight too, but some of the children on the beach were great stout creatures and it must have been hard for the little donkeys to bear them on their backs.

Mr Greenwood paid for the use of a bathing machine too, and the hire of a ridiculous swimming costume for me with long drawers and a frilled hat. Charlotte and Maisie were a little timid when it came to climbing down the steps and immersing themselves in the sea, but I couldn't wait. The cold was a shock – and the salty taste another – but I managed to keep my head above the waves most of the time. I did not know how to swim. I splashed wildly with my arms and legs but I did not progress anywhere. However, I found that if I lay on my back and stuck out my stomach, I could float!

'Look at Hetty! She's a real mermaid now!' Maisie shouted.

Mrs Greenwood didn't take to the water at all. She sat decorously on the sands with baby Flora, but Mr Greenwood bathed with us. He looked very comical in his striped costume, but he swam with strength and dignity. He also played the fool, pretending to be a whale and spouting a great plume of water into the air, while Maisie clapped her hands and squealed.

'Aren't papas *silly*!' Charlotte said to me.

I could only smile, because I did not have one. I did not think Mr Greenwood silly at all, I thought him excessively kind and generous. On hot sunny days he bought hokey-pokey ice creams for all of us. Mine was delicious, but it reminded me terribly of Bertie. I had not written properly to him, because I could not bear to tell him that Mama was so ill. I simply sent him a postcard of the sea front with a brief message: *Dear Bertie, Wish you were here. Love Hetty*. I wrote exactly the same message on another postcard to Jem. I did not put a return address on either because I did not have one. I stuck my last two stamps on the cards and posted them.

Whenever the tide was out, Charlotte, Maisie and I made sandcastles, sharing big wooden spades. Maisie got bored of digging very quickly, but she was good at finding shells to pattern our castles. She loved to run into the sea for pail after pail of water to fill the moat around the base of each building.

While we worked, I made up a story that we were three fairy princesses, each with her own castle. We took turns telling how our castles were decorated inside. Charlotte wanted marble throughout, with a four-poster bed with velvet curtains. Maisie wanted her walls studded with pearls, and she had a pearl dressing-table set to brush her long wavy princess hair. I chose coral for my palace, shiny and strange, in myriad patterns. I had a soft seaweed-green sofa stuffed with duck's down, where I reclined in a coral-pink embroidered tea gown, writing my memoirs.

'Aren't any of you princesses going to run off with handsome princes?' said Mr Greenwood, eavesdropping on our chatter.

Charlotte and Maisie giggled coyly.

'I might just run off with Michael Fairhill,' Maisie said, grinning.

'Oh no, Maisie, that's not fair! Michael's *my* sweetheart,' said Charlotte.

'Girls, girls, don't talk that way,' said Mrs Greenwood. 'Michael is our next-door neighbours' son, Hetty. He's a dear kind boy and he's played patiently with my girls since they were babies, but he's nineteen now, so of course he's not really their sweetheart.'

'He is so, Mama,' said Maisie. 'In fact I am perfectly sure he is going to marry me when I am a little older.'

337

'No he is not. He's going to marry *me*, because I'm the eldest,' said Charlotte.

'Stop squabbling, girls! You sound ridiculously like the Ugly Sisters!' said Mr Greenwood. He looked at me. 'What about you, Cinderella? Do you have a sweetheart?'

I hesitated, blushing.

'She does, she does – look at her cheeks! She's gone scarlet! What is his name, Hetty?' said Maisie.

'Well, I have *two* sweethearts,' I said.

This made them both squeal.

'Who, who? Tell us their names!' said Charlotte.

'Well, there's Bertie . . . and there's Jem,' I said.

'And which one do you like the best?' Maisie asked.

'I'm not sure,' I said truthfully. 'I do like them both.'

'So which one will you run off with?' Maisie demanded.

'I don't think I'm going to run off with anyone. I shall stay in my coral palace, and Mama shall come and live with me, and I shall nurse her until she's completely better,' I said.

I knelt there on the sand, my head bent so they should not see the tears in my eyes. Charlotte put her arm round me even so, and Maisie nestled close and took my hand.

'Perhaps she really will be a little better today,' Charlotte said.

Every evening after supper the whole family walked with me to the infirmary. I was bolder now, but I still couldn't get into her ward. Every time I tried to sneak in through the entrance and down the long corridor, a nurse caught me and marched me back out again. However, when the nurse in charge of the ward was having her supper in a side room, I could call softly through the open window. Mama would slip out of bed and come right up to the window, her hand clamped over her mouth to stop herself coughing. She'd reach through the gap at the bottom and we'd clasp hands tight. I'd pass her the long loving letters I wrote each night. I'd bring her tiny presents too: an embroidered handkerchief, a pretty shell I'd found on the beach, a plaited lock of my hair.

Mama was so weak she'd often start crying. I was worried about her getting chilled if she stayed at the window too long, but her eyes shone whenever she saw me. She whispered feverishly that my visits meant the whole world to her. She couldn't talk to me properly for fear of coughing and alerting the nurse, so I talked to her instead, telling her again and again that I loved her. I promised she was going to get better, and then we would live together. Meanwhile she mustn't worry about me at all. I said I was very happy with my dear Greenwood family.

I didn't tell Mama they were only here for a holiday because I knew she'd fret over what would happen next. I tried to put it out of my mind myself, though I often woke with a start in the middle of the night, terrified.

During the day I somehow managed to put most of my troubles out of my mind. The evenings were especially sweet. After seeing Mama I'd feel reassured, ready for the rest of our walk. Sometimes we promenaded on the pier, though Maisie was afraid of the gaps in the planks of wood and started whimpering. She worried that they would give way, and she would fall right through into the surging sea. Mr Greenwood had to give her a piggyback to get her to venture right to the end of the pier.

I loved to go there myself. I'd clutch the railings and stare out to sea and imagine myself sailing away beyond the horizon. There was an advertising poster on a kiosk on the pier for Argosy cigarettes, with a bold woman in a white cap and navy nautical dress sailing her yacht with a triumphant look in her eyes. She wasn't a woman who knew her place. She didn't *have* a place – she was as free as the wind in her hair and the waves beneath her.

There was a machine that told fortunes on the pier. Mr Greenwood paid a penny each for us all to have a go. Charlotte and Maisie got exactly the same fortunes, printed on little pink cards:

You are fair of face
A form full of grace
Wedding bells chime
True love divine!

This made them both squeal and claim Michael Fairhill as their future husband.

'Now it's your turn, Hetty!'

My fortune card was bright sapphire-blue and it said:

You have far to go
A life of woe
But your wishes come true
Happily for you!

'Oh, Hetty, perhaps Bertie or Jem will marry you!' said Maisie. 'Then everything will end happily. Which will you choose?'

'Neither! I know what I wish for,' I said, clutching my little blue card until the edges cut into my hand.

One evening we went to see the pierrots – a little troupe of performers in white clown outfits. The next day on the sands, Charlotte and Maisie and I gave our own 'Pierrot' concert to Mr and Mrs Greenwood. I even fashioned a tiny pierrot costume for little Flora. I held her in my arms and made her bob up and down, performing her own baby song and dance.

Another evening Mr Greenwood paid for us all to sit before the big octagonal bandstand and listen to the music. I did not know any of the songs, but all the Greenwoods sang along while the band played. They were a military band in smart uniform with gleaming gold epaulettes. I hoped that Gideon might be able to join a similar band.

We also went to see Mr Clarendon's Seaside Curiosities. I had noticed a distinctive red-and-white striped tent pitched at the end of the promenade and had very much hoped it might be a circus.

'No, no, Hetty, it's not a circus, it's a freak show,' said Charlotte. 'Oh, Papa, please may we go and see the curiosities?'

'I'm not sure it's suitable for young girls,' Mrs Greenwood said quickly. 'And please don't use that word, Charlotte, it sounds unpleasant.'

'What should we call the freaks, then, Mama?' Maisie asked.

'You shouldn't call them anything. They're poor unfortunate people who cannot help the way they look,' said Mrs Greenwood.

'Now don't get upset, my dear,' said Mr Greenwood. 'I think Mr Clarendon's folk rely on trickery and make-up. I'm sure there's not a genuine freak amongst them.'

'Please, what *is* a freak?' I asked.

'Perhaps we will have to show you,' said Mr Greenwood.

'It's truly not a suitable show for children. I regret that we took Charlotte and Maisie last year. It is sad and tawdry and vulgar,' said Mrs Greenwood.

'Yes, and we *loved* it!' said Charlotte. '*Please* let us take Hetty, Mama!'

Mrs Greenwood weakened, but she wouldn't come in with us. She sat on a nearby bench with little Flora, while the girls and I eagerly approached the entrance to the tent. Mr Clarendon himself stood there, bizarrely dressed in a bright scarlet suit with a bowler hat of the same hue tipped sideways on his head. He spoke into a loudhailer, instructing passersby to roll up and see the astonishing sights inside.

'Prepare to be truly amazed,' he said as Mr Greenwood paid for all of us.

He tipped his bowler to Mr Greenwood and smiled at us girls. He gave me a particular wink which disconcerted me. I did not know if I would like Mr Clarendon's freaks or not, but I decided I did not care for him.

The tent was divided into little rooms, one leading to another. The first was a little disappointing. It consisted of a display of not-very-remarkable seaside objects: a very large preserved fish with doleful eyes; some fancy seashells; a crab with enormous claws; a display of stuffed seagulls suspended precariously on wires; and a moth-eaten stuffed seal with a woebegone expression.

Charlotte and Maisie circled these exhibits a little impatiently. 'Wait till you see the *next* room, Hetty – and the one after that!' they said, taking my hands and hurrying me along.

We moved through the flap to the next room. There was a real man sitting on a chair, wearing only his trousers, hoisted up with a pair of black braces. His entire body was covered in detailed blue pictures, as if he were a human comical paper. There were even pictures engraved up his bald head.

There was a sign above him: HENRY, THE MAN WITH ONE HUNDRED TATTOOS. I stared at him, fascinated. I squinted very carefully at each picture. I tried counting, but there were too many, and perhaps there were more lurking beneath his trousers. I would never know if there truly were one hundred. Were they *real*?

'Perhaps they are just painted on?' I whispered to Charlotte.

'Lick your finger and try to rub one off, missy!' said Henry.

I jumped, and declined his invitation – but I circled him several times, still marvelling. His arms bloomed with bouquets, his chest sported strange ladies and slithery snakes, and an eagle perched permanently right on the top of his head. Exotic wild creatures stampeded across his shoulder-blades: lions, tigers, even a great buffalo with a Red Indian warrior upon his back.

'Come this way, Hetty – there's lots more to see!' said Charlotte.

We encountered Pirate Pete, Scourge of the Seven Seas, in the next room. I studied him with great interest. He looked just like a storybook pirate, with gold earrings and a kerchief tied around his long coarse hair. He had a patch over one eye, a wooden peg leg, and a real parrot on his shoulder. Maisie tried to stroke the parrot but it pecked at her irritably.

In the next room we gazed upwards in awe at Fantastic Freda, the Female Giant. Her placard said she was seven foot high, but she was standing on a large upturned bucket, which added many inches to her height. Her girth was impressive too.

She was wearing a vast blue-and-white striped bathing dress, straining at the seams. She struck several poses, miming swimming, while a little gang of boys clapped admiringly. Some shouted rude comments, and Fantastic Freda smiled and rattled her collecting cup in a saucy fashion – but her eyes looked very sad.

'My, I'd forgotten all about Fantastic Freda,' said Mr Greenwood, blinking up at her. 'Amazing woman!' He pulled Maisie's hair. 'See what happens when you eat too many hokey-pokeys!'

Charlotte had already rounded the corner to observe Harold, the Two-Headed Marvel. I took a deep breath when I saw him. He wore a full cape with two identical heads poking out at the top. He stared at me with four eyes – but as I tiptoed nearer, I saw that only one pair of his eyes swivelled in my direction. The second pair shone like glass and did not move. The second nose was as large and smooth as its twin, but the nostrils didn't quiver. The second pair of lips were slightly open, but they didn't smile. The second head was a perfect wax model stuck through a hole in a cape and set fair and square on the shoulders. The real head was carried at an angle, leering at us in a disconcerting fashion.

Maisie laughed a little hysterically, convinced that both heads were real. She declared she loved the double-headed phenomenon best of all the curiosities, but in the middle of the night she woke up screaming.

'The man with two heads is looking at me!' she shrieked, loud enough to wake the dead.

Charlotte and I tried to comfort her, but she didn't calm down until Mrs Greenwood came running in from the next room. Maisie slept in her parents' bed that night, but woke up cheerfully enough in the morning – and that evening begged to view Mr Clarendon's Curiosities all over again!

20

Time seemed suspended during that first strange seaside week with the Greenwoods. The second week hurtled by in a flash. Suddenly it was Friday, their last day. We went to the beach as usual, but we came back early in the afternoon so that they could start packing their trunks. I helped Charlotte and Maisie collect together their underthings and stockings and fold all their dresses. I took off the pale primrose dress and put on my own grey print with a sinking heart.

I heard Flora fussing in the next room, so I went to see if I could hold her and keep her quiet while Mr and Mrs Greenwood did their packing.

'You're such a good helpful girl, Hetty,' said Mrs Greenwood. 'I don't know how we're going to manage without you.'

'You've almost become a part of our family this holiday,' said Mr Greenwood.

I bent my head over little Flora and clutched her tightly to stop myself crying. I took her back to the

349

girls' room and walked her up and down. She relaxed against me, making contented little sucking noises. I rubbed my cheek against her downy head and patted her back.

'Dear little Flora,' I whispered.

I heard Mr and Mrs Greenwood talking to each other earnestly next door, but their voices were lowered so I could not hear what they were saying. After a few minutes they came in the room together, looking solemn.

'Hetty, dear, we've been conferring together, Mr Greenwood and I,' said Mrs Greenwood.

'We were wondering ... how would you feel about coming home with us to Arundel?' said Mr Greenwood.

'Oh, Papa, what a wonderful idea!' said Maisie.

'Oh *yes*, Papa, it would be lovely to have Hetty for a sister,' said Charlotte.

I burst into tears now, still clutching Flora, but shaking uncontrollably.

'There now, Hetty, I'll take baby,' said Mrs Greenwood gently.

'Don't cry so, Hetty. Don't you *want* to be our sister?' said Charlotte.

'I – I want it more than anything,' I sobbed.

'There, then! It's settled,' said Mr Greenwood, clapping his hands. 'You will be like another daughter to us.'

'I would like that tremendously, but – but I am *already* a daughter to dear Mama. I have to stay here and see her every day at the infirmary,' I said.

'I understand, Hetty – but I think it would ease your poor mama's suffering to know that you are safe, with a good family to care for you,' said Mrs Greenwood.

'I know that's exactly what Mama would want, but even so, I *have* to stay and see her, because . . . because she might not be here much longer.' I said the words in a whisper, hardly able to bear to say them aloud.

'You poor dear child,' said Mrs Greenwood. 'But where will you stay if you won't come with us?'

'I have a little money to see me through a few days, and then I shall look for work here,' I said resolutely.

'Then we will give you a character reference. I will write it this very minute. I shall say you are the most excellent little nursemaid,' said Mr Greenwood.

'And we will give you our address,' said Mrs Greenwood. 'If you need a home when – when the time comes, then promise you will come to us.'

I promised and thanked them fervently. I was so overcome that I could scarcely eat my supper. I could not believe that they could be so good and kind and generous. There was a part of me that wanted to seize this extraordinary opportunity right away. I was aware that it was a spur-of-the-moment offer. If they reflected on matters back in their own home, they might well change their minds, albeit reluctantly.

They weren't a wealthy family and I knew they lived in a modest house. Charlotte and Maisie had described it to me in detail. I would have to share a room with the girls and it would be a terrible squash for them. What would they do with me? Would they send me to school with Charlotte or send me out to work? I wasn't a real daughter, and yet I was too close to them now to be a proper servant. I was always being told I didn't know my place. I could see that I didn't really *have* a place in the Greenwood family, though we might all wish I did.

In any case I couldn't go with them now and leave Mama. I packed my suitcase too, because I couldn't stay on at their lodgings. The Greenwoods begged Mrs Brooke to let me have a room there for a few nights, but she said she had a new family with six children and a nursemaid coming on Saturday afternoon and there wouldn't be room for even a mouse to bed down.

So on Saturday I walked with the Greenwoods to the railway station, the summoned porter pushing all their luggage. I hugged them all in turn and we said our goodbyes. Mr Greenwood was the only one of us who didn't cry – and even he seemed more moist-eyed than usual.

I waved to them until the train had chuffed its way out of the station. When the white smoke cleared, I looked around the platform hurriedly, seeking out arriving holidaymakers with small children.

There were several families travelling first class, but they all had their own nannies and nursemaids with them. I hastened to the guard's van, where they were unloading all the trunks and cases, and sought out less stylish families without travelling servants. There was one family with three little fair children who looked promising. The youngest was wailing dismally while its mother patted it ineffectually. I darted forward.

'Excuse me, ma'am. I don't want to seem forward, but I'm very good at handling babies. May I quieten the little one for you?' I asked eagerly.

The mama looked horrified and backed away from me, acting as if I were about to snatch her ewe lamb away for ever.

'I don't mean any harm, ma'am. Please let me offer my services as a nurserymaid while you are on holiday. I have an excellent character reference.'

'Will you go away at once and stop pestering my wife or I'll be forced to call a policeman,' said the father, looking fierce.

I sloped off, humiliated, and approached another family with twin boys, but they seemed equally suspicious. When I started talking to a third family, a station porter came up and seized hold of me by my collar, practically choking me.

'I don't know what you're playing at, miss, but there's no hawking or begging allowed on this station, so I must ask you to move on,' he said firmly, and dragged me outside.

I still didn't give up. I watched for families making their way to lodging houses near the promenade and offered my services to each one, but they all regarded me with suspicion. I tried again when the next London trainload arrived, with equal lack of success.

I tried another tactic, walking up and down the streets of Bignor, knocking on every likely door, begging for work.

'I will turn my hand to anything. I am an excellent nursemaid, but I am an experienced parlourmaid too, and a competent cook – I'm particularly good at pastry. Please may I work for you? I have a good character and I'll be content with the smallest of salaries. Oh please, will you take me in?'

I gabbled some version of this spiel again and again. Folk frequently shut the door in my face. One kindly cook let me sit in her kitchen and made me a cup of tea, but then even she sent me on my way. By mid afternoon I was exhausted, but I wouldn't give up. I tried the shops instead, seeing if any might be willing to take me on, but people shook their heads again and again.

When it was nearly time to see Mama, I paid a penny to use a public convenience and washed my face and brushed my hair, trying to spruce myself up a little lest I alarm her. I struggled along the road to the infirmary with my suitcase.

I went right up to the window and Mama crept out of bed. We stood together, only the pane of glass between us. I kissed her lips and laid my hand against hers. We stood motionless for a minute or two, gazing deep into each other's eyes. Then a nurse came and pulled Mama back to bed. She tapped on the window for me to be gone.

I did not go straight away. I walked round the walls of the infirmary to the main entrance and approached another nurse there.

'No children are allowed in here, dear,' she said briskly.

'I'm not a child,' I said, standing on tiptoe. 'I'm a working girl. In fact I would like to work *here*. Perhaps I could train as a nurse?'

'Nonsense! You're far too young.'

'I'm sixteen, nearly seventeen,' I lied.

'Run along now and stop wasting my time.'

'I'll do any kind of work. I could do the cleaning.

I'm very used to scrubbing floors. Or I could help in the kitchen. I practically cooked single-handed in my last household,' I gabbled. 'Or perhaps there is a children's ward. I'm very experienced with babies. I have a good character reference. Please let me show it to you.'

'Go *away*, you silly girl. Why won't you take no for an answer?'

'Because I'm desperate!' I snapped.

'Well, this is no place for young girls, working or otherwise. Come along, out you go.'

She sent me firmly on my way. I trudged along the promenade, lugging my suitcase, wondering what on earth I was going to do now. I had spent all day looking for work and had got nowhere. I was so tired I sat on my suitcase for a while, gazing about me despairingly. When I ran away from the hospital I had done a little begging. I hadn't even needed to ask for money, I had just looked mournful – but no one seemed to understand the concept of begging in Bignor. People barely gave me a second glance.

I had also sold flowers with Sissy, but there was no sign of any flower sellers along the promenade.

How else could I earn money? There seemed no way at all. At least I had enough left for a couple of nights' lodging. I decided I'd better look for a cheap room now.

I wandered back along the sea front, utterly weary,

scarcely able to put one foot in front of the other. I remembered all the happy times running along beside Charlotte and Maisie, strolling on the pier, listening to the band, marvelling at Mr Clarendon's Seaside Curiosities . . . and then it suddenly came to me.

I marched along with sudden determination until I reached the red-and-white pavilion tent. Mr Clarendon stood outside in his bizarre scarlet suit and bowler hat, talking through his megaphone.

'Roll up, roll up! Come and encounter the greatest collection of living breathing curiosities you'll ever see in a month of Sundays! Marvel at Henry, with his hundred tattoos, gasp at Fantastic Freda, the Female Giant—'

'Excuse me, sir,' I said.

'Would you like a sixpenny ticket, little miss?'

'No, I have already been in and seen all the people inside. I was wondering, sir – would you like a brand-new attraction?'

He stared at me. 'What might you have in mind, missy?'

'I could be . . . Emerald, the Amazing Pocket-Sized Mermaid, half girl, half fish,' I said.

'And how are you going to be a mermaid, missy? I don't see no tail, I see two little feet in shabby boots.'

'If I come back tomorrow as Emerald the Mermaid, will you take me on?'

He looked me up and down, his eyes narrowed. I reached up and unpinned my hair, so that it fell past my shoulders in a long red wave. His lips twitched.

'I'll have to see your costume first. I'm not making no promises. But I reckon you *could* be a draw.'

'How much would you pay me?'

'That depends on the takings, girl. We'd have to negotiate.'

'Very well. I'll be back tomorrow,' I said.

I did not like him very much. I especially did not like the way he looked me up and down. But if this was my only way of earning money so I could stay on in Bignor, then I'd have to put up with it.

Now I needed a roof over my head. I did not try any of the lodging houses near Mrs Brooke's. I deliberately walked away from the sea and picked a street of tumbledown houses on the far side of town with ROOMS TO LET signs.

I took the first one available. It was an attic room with a narrow bed and the sheets looked distressingly dirty, but I was too tired to seek anything better. The landlady was as grimy as the bedding, her hair lank, her fingernails black, her dress shiny with grease stains. But she was kind enough, and brought me up a supper tray: cold sausage, and a slice of bread and dripping, with a mug of tea. I did not like to think of her filthy fingers touching the food, but I was so hungry I ate it all the same. Though the sheets were grey, I got into bed willingly enough, and fell asleep as soon as my head touched the grubby pillow.

I was up early the next day, my money counted out and wrapped in my handkerchief. As soon as the shops were open I went to the nearest draper's. I bought a sharp pair of scissors, a tape measure, a paper of pins and needles, and a reel of green cotton. I thought some more, and selected a packet of pearl beads, another of green sequins, and some fancy green braid. I thought again, and had a couple of yards of cheap pale-pink muslin measured out, with matching pink cotton thread.

'Is that it now, missy?' said the draper's assistant, rolling her eyes.

'Yes, thank you. Please wrap them all in a paper parcel for me,' I said briskly.

I went down the street until I found a fish-monger's. I asked him for two scallop shells, then I purchased a tube of strong adhesive glue from the stationer's shop. There! I had everything I needed now.

I went back to my grimy attic room, sat cross-legged on the floor, and set about constructing my mermaid costume. I measured myself with the tape measure first, and then sketched out shapes on the pages of an old newspaper. When I was sure I had the pattern right, I laid my green velvet gown out on the grubby carpet and seized the scissors. It took me several minutes before I had the courage to make the first cut. It was my only decent dress, the costume I'd fashioned with such care. I wasn't even sure that my idea was going to work. I didn't have enough material to cut out a proper tail in one piece. I took off the redundant trimmings, pinned the newspaper pattern in place, and started snipping out the shapes to make a mermaid's tail. I had to fiddle around, cutting a patch here, a length there, and somehow try to fit all the pieces of the puzzle together to make the tail. It was a tiresome, complicated procedure. Several times I held the ruined velvet to my cheek and wept bitterly, but then I carried on with my task.

I stitched and stitched until my hands were sore and pricked, but slowly, slowly, the mermaid's tail grew. When the basic shape was stitched together at last, I stuck my legs cautiously into it. Thank goodness it fitted as snugly and smoothly as a glove. I sewed green brocade in stiffened strips to the fork at the end of the tail, and then started the tedious chore of stitching handfuls of little pearls and sequins into place to give the tail the shimmering effect of scales.

My eyes were twitching now and my hands

cramped, but I still had to make my top. The mermaids I had seen in picture books were naked, though their long hair more or less preserved their decency. I wasn't sure my hair was quite long and thick enough, and I wanted to make *certain* I preserved my decency, so I sewed myself a pink gauze bodice and carefully stuck a scallop shell at either side to cover my chest (not that I yet had anything much to cover!). I sewed more pearls around the edges, and then assembled the entire costume, brushed out my hair, and peered at myself in the spotted mirror on the wall. I wasn't sure I looked *utterly* convincing, but then again, neither had Harold the Two-Headed Marvel. I looked decorative – and I guessed that might be Mr Clarendon's primary requirement.

I packed my costume very carefully into Sarah's mother's invaluable suitcase, and set off. I walked over to the infirmary first, and peered through the window. Mama was lying back on her pillows, coughing and coughing. My heart turned over at the sight of her. She saw me and tried to get up, but I shook my head fiercely, gesturing to her to stay in bed. I mouthed *I love you* over and over again, and blew her kisses. Mama managed to stop coughing long enough to smile valiantly and blow kisses back.

I set off for Mr Clarendon's Seaside Curiosities

with renewed determination. Every step I took I whispered, *I love you, Mama, I love you, Mama, I love you, Mama*, trying to give myself courage. I still felt shy and frightened when I approached the red-and-white pavilion. Mr Clarendon was outside in his ridiculous red suit, inviting all the passersby to roll up.

I stood beside him, waiting for him to reach the end of his spiel. He eyed me up and down again.

'You still don't look like a mermaid to me,' he said, waggling his eyebrows in a way that was meant to be amusing.

'I need to change into my costume, Mr Clarendon,' I said. 'You can't expect a mermaid with a tail to walk down the street.'

'Ooh, hoity-toity!' he said, chuckling. 'Well, come this way, missy. I'll escort you to your dressing room.'

I followed him through the tent, past the fish and seagulls and sad seal, past the tattoed man, Pirate Pete and his parrot, Freda the Female Giant and Harold the Two-Headed Marvel. They did not have much of an audience as yet and were lounging around, scratching and yawning. Freda saw me and nodded down at me in a friendly fashion, waving her great hand. I waved mine back, trying hard to stay composed.

The 'dressing room' was a curtained-off cramped corner at the back of the tent.

'Come on, then, little mermaid, give us a swish of your tail,' said Mr Clarendon. He stood there rubbing his hands together.

'I cannot change in front of you, sir,' I said. 'Surely you realize it wouldn't be decent. Please go away and return in five minutes.'

'You're a fiery little snippet!' he said. 'You don't order me around. I'm the one who gives the orders. I'm the boss of this establishment.'

'Yes, sir, and I very much hope you will be *my* boss – but I would still appreciate a little privacy.'

I stood firm, and he shrugged his shoulders, sighed, and walked off, though I sensed he had not gone very far away. I hoped he wasn't peeping.

I unsnapped the suitcase, pulled off my dress, and inserted myself into the elaborate tail and pink bodice. I could not walk in my costume. I could not even stand. I lay down gingerly on the dirty tarpaulin. I let my hair down and combed it vigorously, trying to look as fetching as possible.

Then I called out: 'Roll up, roll up, come and see the new attraction at Mr Clarendon's Seaside Curiosities! Marvel at Emerald, the Amazing Pocket-Sized Mermaid.'

Mr Clarendon came bustling in, laughing – and then stopped short when he saw me. My heart started beating fast but I forced myself to lie still, lounging on the squalid flooring as if it were the sandy shore. I combed my hair, arching my back, and moved my legs so that my tail twitched.

'You little beauty!' he said, walking around me, peering at me from every angle. 'Where did you get your costume from, tiddler? Are you on the stage?'

I took this as an immense compliment, and murmured something ambiguous. If he thought I was professional, maybe he'd pay me more.

'So you'll exhibit me, then, Mr Clarendon?'

'I'll say! I think we can build you up into quite a little novelty. We can make you a suitable setting – have you lying on a pile of sand, spread a bit of seaweed around, a few shells, to get the right atmosphere. I think you'll pull the lads in even more than Freda.'

'So how much will you pay me?'

'Half a crown a week – if the takings are good. A florin if they're not.'

'What? I could get more than that as a maid!'

'Well, go and get it then, little girlie.'

'But – but I'm not sure I can live on that.'

'You'll get tips. Wink at the fellows and they'll start raining coins, you'll see. And you can have free lodging with the rest of us. You can share with Freda.'

I did not like the idea of winking at the fellows. I did not see that there would be much room for me in lodgings if I had to share with a giant. Even so, joining this strange group of sad souls seemed my only viable option now.

'I'll join your troupe, then,' I said.

'That's the ticket! You'll have every morning off. Folk don't seem to have the stomach for freaks straight after breakfast. We open at two, but you'll be here at one forty-five to change into your costume. Then we go straight through till midnight.'

'Ten hours!'

'You'll have five-minute breaks at four and nine, and a half-hour for supper at six thirty.'

'Can I go out during my supper break?'

'Well, you're not going to get far in that costume, are you?' he said, 'No, you'll take your supper here, like all the others.'

I sat up straight. 'I'm not like all the others. I'll go without supper if necessary – but I must go and see someone at that time every day. I'll make sure I'm back at seven sharp, in costume. Is that a deal, Mr Clarendon?'

'I told you, I'm the one who makes the deals, not you,' he said, but he held out his hand and we shook on it.

21

So I started my bizarre new career as Emerald, the Amazing Pocket-Sized Mermaid. I moved into the lodging house with Mr Clarendon and the rest of his Curiosities. Mr Clarendon had an entire suite of rooms all to himself on the first floor. The rest of us had to make do in small cramped bedrooms – but at least they were clean, with washed linen.

I barely said a word to the tattoed man or the pirate or two-headed Harold. They would drink together late into the night and only surface at noon, shuffling up and down the stairs in under-vests and trousers, bleary-eyed and smelling of stale beer. The tattoed man and the pirate seemed more interested in each other, but Harold leered at me with his real head, and I learned to whisk myself away from him quickly to avoid his pats and pinches.

I hated him, and disliked the other men, including Mr Clarendon – but I grew to love Freda! I had been a little frightened of her at first, because she was so very large, even when not standing on a bucket. She had been given a double bed to accommodate her vast size. I was told I had to share it with her. I was very anxious about this, scared that she might suddenly turn in the bed and squash me flat. I resolved to sleep on the floor with a blanket.

When we went upstairs together after my first very long and gruelling afternoon and evening as Emerald, Freda was kindness itself.

'You poor little baby, you must be exhausted,' she said. 'But what a little star you are! All the boys were beside themselves!'

'They crowded round you too,' I said.

'Ah, but they only want to mock me,' said Freda sadly.

'No, I heard someone say that you're a fine figure of a woman,' I said.

'Fine figure of a freak, more like,' said Freda. 'But you're a real little beauty, Emerald.'

I did not tell her my real name. I did not want anyone ever knowing that Hetty Feather – or Sapphire Battersea, indeed – was now a performing curiosity in a freak show. I pretended to Mama that I had found a respectable position as a nursery-maid. I did not write to Bertie or Jem any more. I knew what they would think of me, though I was not doing anything so very wrong, and my costume was perfectly respectable, if exotic.

'I am not the slightest bit beautiful, Freda,' I said 'I have red hair, and I am much too little and scrawny.'

'I am so tall and stout no one even notices my hair,' said Freda. She took off her flounced bathing hat and let her hair down. It was fine fair hair, but a little sparse – it barely covered her huge shoulders. She crouched down to try and look in the mirror to brush it. She knelt instead of sitting on the chair – she was probably fearful of breaking it. She was scarcely able to move, trapped in this tiny room, and I felt so sorry for her.

'Here, may I brush you hair for you?' I offered timidly. 'It is such a fine shade of yellow. It's very becoming, Freda.'

Her hairbrush was the smallest size. All her possessions were tiny and dainty: her little pot of rose face cream, her papier-mâché trinket box, her cherub candlestick. I realized that vast Freda had a tiny feminine creature imprisoned inside her. I turned round so that she could undress modestly, though I have to confess I took a tiny peek. Her body was even more extraordinary when liberated from her bathing costume. She quickly hid her huge pink bulk with her nightgown. It barely reached her knees, though it would have trailed on the ground like a bride's train on me.

I put on my own nightgown, and Freda

exclaimed at the simple lazy daisies I had embroidered on the bodice.

'They're so pretty, Emerald!'

'I will embroider some on your nightgown, Freda,' I offered.

She got into bed, trying very hard to keep to her side, but she couldn't help spreading over the mattress, taking up nearly all the room. Her poor huge feet stuck out at the end. They were sadly callused because she was forced to walk barefoot: no shoes were big enough for her.

It now seemed like an insult to lie on the floor with a blanket, so I crept into bed beside her. She was holding herself rigid, scarcely drawing breath.

'I fear you have nowhere near enough room, Emerald,' she said sadly.

'No, no, I am perfectly fine, Freda,' I said, though I was clinging to the edge.

She blew out her candle – and in the darkness we became two ordinary girls. Freda asked me what had brought me to Bignor, and I told her about Mama. I cried a little, and Freda cautiously patted my shoulder with a huge hand.

I asked Freda if she had a mama, privately wondering if she might be even more enormous than her daughter.

'I lost my dear mama when I was ten, and already a foot taller than her,' she said. 'None of my family are similarly afflicted. My father and brothers are normal height and my mother was tiny like you – but she loved me dearly and never reproached me for growing to such a size.'

'Oh, Freda! Of course she didn't! How could you help growing?'

'My father was ashamed of me. He kept me in a dark cupboard for months after Mama died, hoping it might restrict my growth.'

'How terrible!'

'And then, when I was fourteen, he sold me to a travelling fair, to be displayed as a freak of nature.' Freda sighed and the whole bed trembled. 'It was very hard at first, but now I am used to it. Mr Clarendon is kinder than most and treats me fairly enough. It is a little lonely at times, living with so many strange men – but now I have you for company, Emerald! You must not be frightened of me, even though I am so very big and queer-looking.'

'I am not the slightest bit frightened of you, Freda dear – and I am charmed to share a room with such a kind, gentle lady,' I said, and I meant every word.

As the weeks went by we grew as close as sisters. We breakfasted together while the men were still fast asleep. Freda did not care to stroll along the promenade because people would stare so and shout after her, but she liked to sit in the garden at the back of the lodgings and get a little fresh air that way. I'd sit with her and we'd chat while I sewed.

I embroidered little pink roses around the neck and cuffs and hem of Freda's large nightgown, which utterly delighted her. I was making a lot of money from tips, so I decided to make Freda a proper present. I went back to the draper's shop and bought several yards of blue silk and set about fashioning her a proper lady's costume. She had only her bathing dress and her nightgown and a shabby man's coat to keep her warm in winter. She cried with joy when she held the lengths of silk and felt their softness.

'But they are far too fine for me, Emerald. I will tear them to shreds.'

'Not if I make you a costume that fits you properly. I will sew it very carefully, with tiny strong stitches. Just be patient, Freda. You are going to have such a beautiful dress, I promise.'

I did my very best to keep my word. I had to stand on a borrowed ladder to measure Freda from her shoulders to her ankles, and we both blushed painfully when I had to stretch the tape to measure her chest and waist and hips, but once these indignities were out of the way and I could start sewing, we had an extremely companionable time together.

Freda offered to read aloud to me from the little

fairy-tale books Mama had given me. I had never let anyone else even touch them before, but I found it curiously soothing for Freda to read in her soft husky voice, holding the tiny tales reverently in her huge hands. I became agitated when she started reading the tale of Jack the Giant Killer – but Freda was fascinated, astonished to discover a story about distant relatives. She didn't mind that the giants were all treated as villains by the anonymous author. She seemed to like it that they were very fierce and tried to catch little people and feed them to their ogre children.

When she'd read her way through all the tales, I did my best to make up a few fairy stories myself featuring Fearless Freda and tiny Emerald Mermaid. She loved these stories so much that I wrote them down for her when I'd finished her costume at last.

Oh, how she loved her blue silk costume! She trembled all over when I made the final fitting, stroking her own arms, marvelling at the softness of the silk. I detached the mirror from the wall and held it up for her so that she could see herself in sections, and she gave little squeals of joy.

I could not fashion her real kid or leather boots to set off her dress because I did not have the right skills – nor indeed, tools – but I managed to make her matching blue silk gaiters that came up to her calves. I reinforced the soles with thickest cardboard, stuck on with my glue.

'I'm afraid you won't be able to walk very far in them, Freda,' I said regretfully, but she still seemed delighted.

She wore her new costume very proudly while on display at the curiosity tent. Mr Clarendon made her a new painted background of the promenade, with tiny figures all pointing and exclaiming at the very fine figure of Fantastic Freda, the Fashionable Female Giant.

He had made me a backdrop too – of blue sea and yellow sand – and he displayed me on a pile of real sand stolen from the beach. Folk marvelled at Freda, but I knew I was now the main attraction. I think it was only the very little children who believed I was a real mermaid – but all the lads and gentlemen clustered around me eagerly, and even their ladies clapped their hands and declared I was as pretty as a picture.

I simpered and smiled for all I was worth, even when some of the louder lads made extremely uncouth remarks about me, because I wanted them to stuff my housekeeping jar with tips. I kept it by my side, painted with sea anemones and decorative fish, and by the end of each evening it was crammed to the brim. Every time someone dropped another coin into the jar with a satisfying clink I thought of

Mama and how it meant I could stay close to her.

I bought her little delicacies every day, and bribed a kind ward orderly at the infirmary to take them in to her: little jars of custard cream, small bottles of fortified wine, a perfect bunch of hothouse grapes. Mama always smiled and nodded and mouthed her thanks to me when I looked at her through the window – but she seemed to be getting thinner and thinner, and even when she lay as still as a statue in bed, the coughing tore her apart.

Then, one terrible evening, she started haemorrhaging as she coughed, blood seeping through her fingers as she clutched her mouth. I heaved the heavy glass window upwards with sudden desperate strength, climbed right through, and ran to her bed. As she coughed and bled, I held her tight and stroked her, and told her that I loved her over and over again, until she was still at last. I held her poor lifeless body and would not let her go. The nurses let me stay there on the bed with Mama, knowing they could not prise me away.

I went on whispering to her, even though I knew she could no longer hear me. I told her that she was the best mother in the whole world. I went through all the tender kindnesses she'd shown me through the years at the hospital, until the ward grew dark.

Then a nurse came and whispered softly, 'We must tidy your dear mother, child.'

I helped wash her and comb her tousled hair. The nurse snipped me off a lock to keep for ever. We gave Mama a clean nightgown and folded her poor thin arms neatly over her sunken chest. I tucked the satin pouch containing my letters under her fingers so that she might read them in Heaven and remember just how much I loved her.

'We will have to make the funeral arrangements,' said the nurse. 'I expect it will have to be a pauper's funeral . . .'

'No! No, I will pay for Mama to have a proper decent funeral,' I said firmly.

I went to the undertaker's with my jar of tip money – to find it still wasn't nearly enough. Dear Freda insisted on giving me the rest. It wasn't a grand funeral. At the undertaker's they outlined various options: beautiful ornate oak caskets with golden handles, black carriages drawn by a matching pair of black horses with plumes, professional mourners in top hats and tails . . . I selected the simplest funeral possible: a plain coffin, a horse and cart to carry it to the graveyard, and no paid mourners at all – only me.

I didn't have any money left for a length of black material to make a decent funeral dress. I had to content myself with a black velvet ribbon tied round my sleeve. But I promise you no professional mourner grieved more profoundly. I murmured the responses with heartfelt concentration, I threw a posy of wild flowers down on Mama's coffin, and when the ceremony was over, I knelt by the raw earth and wept for hours.

Eventually the vicar came over to me, bent down, and rested his hand on my shoulder. 'Try not to grieve so, child. Your mother is at peace now,' he said gently.

I could not imagine Mama at peace. I saw her twitching restlessly, racked with that terrible cough. 'Mama suffered so dreadfully,' I sobbed.

'She is free of earthly pain now,' said the vicar. 'Go home now, child.'

Where *was* my home? I was only here because of Mama. I did not belong anywhere without her.

I stayed for another few weeks, working for Mr Clarendon at his curiosity tent. I went through all the motions required of me – combing my hair, making eye contact with the customers, arching my back to look my best, twitching my velvet tail, smiling all the while. Tips were plentiful, and I smiled again as I carried my full jar back to the lodgings – but I cried every night cradled in Freda's great gentle arms. I smiled until I had enough to pay Freda back for her loan, and then I told her I must leave.

'I shall miss you so, Freda. You are my dearest friend in all the world. But I cannot stay here now.

It is too miserable without Mama,' I told her.

'I understand, Emerald, but oh, I shall miss you so. I have never had a friend before,' Freda said.

'I shall be your friend even if we are apart. I shall come back to Bignor every summer, I promise – and each time I'll make you a new silk dress.'

'But where will you go, Emerald?'

I had thought about it long and hard while lying on my mound of sand performing my mermaid mime. I had various options. I could go to Miss Smith in London and beg her to help me. I knew this was the most sensible idea, but I was not sure I could bear to do this. I did not want to apologize for my behaviour at Mr Buchanan's. I did not want to grovel until she took pity on me and found me a similar position. I was especially frightened that she would make me return to the hospital while she was seeking this position for me.

I could seek out the Greenwood family in Arundel and see if their offer still held – but somehow I shrank from this too. Our fortnight together already had a strange dream-like quality, as if it hadn't really happened. Even if they welcomed me into their home, I wasn't sure it was what I wanted now. Too much had happened to me this summer. I was not sure I could be a child again with Charlotte and Maisie. I felt too old and too sad to play games any more.

I could go back to see Bertie – dear valiant Bertie, who said I was his sweetheart. But we weren't *real* sweethearts. We certainly weren't old enough to set up home together. We could picture for all we were worth on our Sunday afternoons together, but he was still stuck in that reeking butcher's shop every day, up to his elbows in gore. It would be years and years before we had saved up enough money for a little house of our own – and did I really *want* that with Bertie? I'd wanted to share a house with *Mama*. I did not want to live in any house without her.

I'd had a real home once, long ago – that dear cottage in the country. I had a mother there too. She had been fierce with me sometimes, and paddled me royally, but I knew she loved me in her own way. I felt a real longing for her warm strong arms. I had been part of that family once. Jem had written to me again and again. He had made it plain that he wanted me back. I had doubted him, but he had stayed constant in his love. He longed for me – even though he did not really *know* me any more. He only knew that fierce, funny little five-year-old who had played at his side.

I was not sure I wanted to go back now. I wanted to go *forward*.

'Oh, Mama, what shall I *do* ?' I asked the empty air. 'If only I could ask you.'

And then I knew where I had to go.

22

The train journey on Sunday seemed endless. I had bought myself a cheese roll and an apple at the station, but they were poor substitutes for Mrs Briskett's picnic. I was exhausted and very hungry and thirsty by the time I got to Waterloo Station. I stared longingly at all the food stalls, but I did not want to spend so much as another penny now. I was not sure how much my evening might cost. It might take all my money.

I negotiated my way around the station and found a train bound for Kingtown. I remembered making the journey with Mrs Briskett when I left the hospital. It seemed many years ago, and yet it was only a matter of months. I'd been so young and innocent then, so full of hope. Everything had seemed so bizarre and new and puzzling, but I'd had the thought of Mama sustaining me. She had seemed so far away then – but it was so much worse now, when she'd gone away for ever.

I shut my eyes and pressed my lips together. I

would not let myself think that. I had to believe that Mama was still here – soon I might even be talking to her . . .

It seemed so strange stepping out of Kingtown station early that evening. I thought of Bertie and longed to see him. Did he still care for me – or had he forgotten about me already? Was he out walking with some other girl today? I thought of Kitty and Ivy in the draper's shop. Had Bertie taken Kitty out in the rowing boat, along the river to our secret island? Was he strolling in the park with Ivy, picturing for all he was worth?

No, surely Kitty would squeal and fidget and capsize the boat – and dim Ivy could not conjure up any fancies worth a farthing. I tossed my head. Bertie might well find it difficult to find a girl to replace me.

But I was not here to try to find Bertie. I walked along the familiar roads until I reached Lady's Ride. I passed Mr Buchanan's splendid big house, peering up at his study window. I was ready to thumb my nose at him, but there was no sign of little Monkey Man. I looked at the area steps and wondered whether to slip in to see dear old Mrs Briskett – but it was getting late and I didn't think there was time. I was sure I would see Sarah shortly.

I walked on, trying hard to remember the way,

once anxiously tracing my steps when I took a wrong turning. At last I found myself in the little street of cottages with bright flowers in the gardens. I counted along to the right one and walked up the garden path. I saw that the blinds at the windows were closely drawn.

I took a deep breath and knocked on the door. After a few moments the same tall dark woman, Emily, opened it and gazed at me enquiringly.

'Good evening. Is Madame Berenice holding a seance tonight?'

'Yes, she is. Please come in.' Emily looked at me closely in the dimly lit hall. 'I think you have visited us before . . .'

'Yes, with Sarah.'

'Ah! You are the little girl who ran away! I believe your brother made contact from the spirit world and it frightened you a little.'

'It frightened me a great deal! I never cared for that brother.'

'But you wish to communicate with him again?'

'No! No, I'm here because – my dear mama has died and I'm desperate to make contact with her again.'

'Oh, you poor child. Well, I'm sure Madame Berenice will do her very best. Would you care to leave your remuneration on the silver plate on the hallstand? It will be five shillings to hear her voice, and ten for an actual materialization. I'm afraid there are no guarantees, though. The spirits are contrary creatures and won't always come when they are bidden.'

'I understand,' I said, counting my coins. 'There!' I let a handful of threepennies, sixpennies and shillings clatter down on the plate.

Emily's dark eyes flickered over the coins, clearly counting. 'Yes, that will be sufficient,' she said. 'Follow me.'

She led me into the darkened room. Just like last time, I could barely distinguish anything. I sensed, rather than saw, my fellow clients.

'Come and join us, child,' said the deep, thrilling voice of Madame Berenice.

I felt my way to the chairs around the table.

'Hetty! Is that you?' Sarah whispered. She reached out and took my hand. 'Oh, Hetty, how we've worried over you! How are you, dear? Did you come here specially to find me?'

'I – I came here to find . . . someone else,' I said. 'Oh, Sarah, my mama . . .' I couldn't continue, but she understood, and gripped my hand harder.

'Oh, you poor child! I am so sorry. But you have come to the right place. You will be wondrously comforted,' she said.

Emily was whispering to Madame Berenice.

'I believe you have requested a materialization,

Hetty?' said Madame Berenice. 'I'm afraid Sarah has requested one too, but there can only be one each night. There is no greater wonder in all nature, but it takes immense effort to summon up psycho-plastic matter. I cannot possibly manage two such projections in quick succession.'

'Let it be Hetty's materialization, Madame Berenice,' said Sarah. 'I have experienced this wonder many times.'

'That is very generous of you, Sarah,' said Madame Berenice.

'Thank you! Thank you so much!' I said, giving Sarah a hug.

'Now now, settle down, child. Let us all concentrate. The spirits are restless tonight, eager to communicate. We will join hands anew and see who visits us first.'

I sat between Sarah and an old lady who clung to me with her dry little mittened hand. I could dimly see the old lady on her other side, and the drooping figure of Mr Brown. There were three other women. It was going to be a very long evening. My heart pounded in my chest. Would Mama come? Would she speak to me? Would I see her dear face again?

'Is there anybody there?' Madame Berenice asked throatily. 'Yes! Yes, there is a child here, an eager young chap.' Her own voice became little and piping. 'Hello, Father dear!'

'It's my Cedric!' said Mr Brown, choking with emotion.

We sat in our circle while little Cedric chatted inconsequentially and Mr Brown shed happy tears. Then long-lost sweethearts and cherished companions took it in turns to commune. They talked of heavenly peace and shining light and cosmic harmony, but they didn't say anything specific about their spirit world. They were all very loving, but their messages seemed unbearably tedious as time ticked slowly by in the dark, stifling room. They enquired genteelly about someone's cough or bad back. One of the old ladies in the spirit world explained to her friend in the room exactly how to make a beneficial peppermint tisane.

I fidgeted desperately, willing her to *hurry up*. My mama might be waiting to get a word in while we were being solemnly instructed to add a teaspoon of sugar to each pint of peppermint.

I managed to curb my impatience when it was Sarah's turn at last, and her mama spoke to her softly and warmly, as if big lumpy Sarah were a small girl again. I could scarcely breathe now. It was *my* turn! Would *my* mama cross over from her new home in the spirit world to talk to me?

'Is there anybody there – a new spirit, anxious to reassure her little daughter?' Madame Berenice asked.

There was no answer.

'Is there anybody there?' Madame Berenice repeated.

We waited, again in vain.

I gave a little sob, and Sarah's hand tightened over mine.

'Won't you come, Mama?' I whispered in the dark.

'Hush, child. The spirits can only communicate through me,' said Madame Berenice. 'We must all stay holding hands, shut our eyes, and pray for a materialization. I sense a presence – but the spirits are shy, especially when asked to materialize.'

We held hands, we shut our eyes, we waited. Then I was aware of a slight rustle of material. I opened my eyes. An indistinct figure, all in misty white, was standing near us, very slowly moving towards me. Her face was obscured by a long white veil.

'Is it *you*, Mama?' I asked. 'Oh, Madame Berenice, is it really my mama?'

'It is your own dear mother, Hetty,' a strange, eerie voice whispered.

'You sound so – so different, Mama. Are you all right? Are you still coughing?'

'There are no ailments in the spirit world, my dear. I am in perfect health now. I am very happy. You must not grieve for me, Hetty.'

She glided nearer. She walked with slow strange grace, her skirts rustling.

Mama had always walked with quick darting steps.

She bent down before me. She was tall and stately.

Mama was scarcely taller than me.

She bent nearer and I smelled her rose cologne.

Mama never used cologne in her life – she simply smelled of her own sweet warm flesh.

She kissed me on the forehead with smooth cool lips.

Mama's lips were chapped and rough because she licked them anxiously – and she never kissed my brow. She kissed my cheeks and lips, and sometimes the tip of my nose when she was being playful.

'Mama?' I said.

'My dear little child.'

I wasn't her dear little child at all. She wasn't my mama. I started trembling. I knew who she was – Emily, the tall woman who had let me in and taken my money. Madame Berenice's sister – and accomplice. I wanted to rip her white floating veil from her head, switch on the light, and expose her to all the people sitting there so stupidly, paying their money week after week for a fraudulent trick. But somehow I held myself rigid. I bit my lips in an effort not to fly into a temper.

All these people sitting with me in the dark believed utterly. My dear friend Sarah lived for these moments with her 'mother'. She had given up her chance of a materialization tonight for my sake. I could not take away the most precious consolation of her hard life.

So I held my tongue while the ghastly false Mama kissed me again and circled the table, and the others cried out and marvelled. She told me to be a good brave girl, and she promised to watch over me and visit me often on Sunday evenings. Then Madame Berenice told us to close our eyes again and give thanks for this marvellous materialization from the spirit world.

I kept my eyes open and watched the white woman steal silently out of the door. I waited while Madame Berenice murmured some spirit mumbo-jumbo, taking short rapid breaths as if she'd been running. Then she called out for light. Emily returned, bearing a lamp. She was dressed all in black now. She had obviously thrust her ghostly white garments into some cupboard. It seemed quite clear to me that she was the apparition pretending to be Mama. She had the same stance, the same walk, even the same smell – but all the others were totally oblivious to this. They marvelled at the success of the evening and crowded around me joyfully.

Sarah gave me a warm hug. 'I'm so very happy for you, Hetty,' she said.

The others patted me fondly and congratulated me.

'Say thank you nicely to Madame, Hetty,' said Sarah. 'She has worked so hard on your behalf.'

I stared at Madame Berenice. She was worse than Mr Clarendon. At least he only charged a few pennies per person, and he didn't just prey on the bereaved. I bent forward and whispered into her turbaned ear, so that only she could hear me: 'You're a wicked old fraud. I want my ten shillings back!'

She looked at me with narrowed eyes, her rouged lips set in a strained smile. She did not acknowledge me in any way – but at the door on the way out, Emily took me a little roughly by the shoulder and thrust a ten-shilling note at me.

'Take it and never come back,' she hissed.

Then Sarah caught me up, still so innocently happy for me. I had to keep up the pretence, though inside my heart was breaking. I so wished I'd been convinced by the clumsy materialization, but I was too close to dear Mama to be fooled by a charlatan.

Sarah burbled on and on about *her* dear mother. I listened sadly, trying my best to make encouraging responses.

'But you must tell me all about you now, Hetty

dear. How have you been keeping? Have you got a new position? Come back and have a cup of tea with Mrs B and me and tell us everything!'

Sarah was so persuasive, linking her arm in mine, smiling at me fondly as if I were her long-lost sister, that I took her up on her offer. I had nowhere else to go, after all.

It seemed very strange approaching Mr Buchanan's house and going down the area steps. Sarah looked anxiously up at the dimly lit study window, but Mr Buchanan was safely at his desk out of sight. Sarah put her finger to her lips even so, and I tiptoed down the steps as if I were her silent shadow.

The kitchen smelled warmly and wonderfully of savoury pie. The table was all set for supper. Mrs Briskett was busy cutting the pie into slices. She paused dramatically when she caught sight of me, and then rushed towards me, mercifully dropping the knife before embracing me, hugging me hard against her upholstered chest.

But there was another person in the kitchen – a pretty little fair girl with big blue eyes, almost as blue as my own.

'Who are you?' I asked, taken aback.

She smiled sweetly at me. 'I am Rose-May. I know exactly who *you* are. You're naughty Hetty Feather! I've heard such tales about you!'

'Rose-May's our new little maid,' said Mrs Briskett, and she gave her a fond pat on her curly head. 'She's shaping up nicely now.'

'Mrs Briskett and I have been making rabbit pie,' said Rose-May. 'Won't you try a slice, Hetty?'

I looked at the steaming pie, the pastry crust crisply golden, risen high, a fancy edging pricked all the way around. 'Did you do the pastry?' I asked Rose-May.

She nodded proudly, flexing her fingers. 'Mrs Briskett says I have a really light touch,' she declared.

'Well, isn't that just fine and dandy,' I said. I looked at Sarah, who was taking off her bonnet, still flushed with excitement after her encounter with her mama. 'Why did you not accompany Sarah to Madame Berenice's?' I asked prissy little Rose-May. 'Did she not ask you? *I* used to go with her to make sure she didn't have a swooning fit.'

'I care about Sarah, of course, but I couldn't possibly go with her to that meeting. I am a Baptist, and we don't hold with spirit meetings and such-like,' said Rose-May.

'Rose-May's very devout,' said Sarah, sounding a little in awe of her.

'Mr Buchanan sent me to the Baptist Society to find a new maid of all work. He wanted to find a good meek girl who wouldn't cause any trouble,' said Mrs Briskett. 'He didn't want to risk another foundling! But tell me, Hetty, what are you doing here? Did you meet up with our Sarah by chance?'

'Hush now, Mrs B, poor Hetty's been through a great deal. Her mother passed over this summer.'

'Oh, dear child, I'm so sorry,' said Mrs Briskett.

'But Hetty has been reunited with her dear mother this evening. Isn't that wonderful?' said Sarah, still flushed and glowing with the excitement of it all.

'I'm not so sure *wonderful* is the word I'd use,' said Mrs Briskett. 'Look at the state of the poor girl. White as a sheet, and skinnier than ever.' She steered me gently to the table and sat me down on the bench. 'Eat some pie, child,' she commanded.

'Poor Hetty!' said Rose-May. She bent her head, clasped her hands, and said piously, 'For what we are about to receive, may we be truly grateful. Amen.'

I *was* truly grateful to be offered a slice of pie, and I suppose it tasted delicious, but I found it hard to eat. I chewed long and hard on the rabbit meat, but I couldn't seem to make it go down.

'Don't you like rabbit pie, Hetty?' said Mrs Briskett. 'Young Bertie brought us such a nice fat rabbit, ready skinned.'

'He said he'd make me a little fur tippet out of all his rabbit skins,' Rose-May said, giggling. 'Like Baby Bunting.'

I stared at her sweet simpering little face. I wanted to push it straight into the wretched pie. My stomach heaved.

'Excuse me,' I gasped, my hand over my mouth.

I ran out of the kitchen, making for the horrible privy out in the back yard. I heard Sarah asking if I was all right, and Rose-May wondering if she should run after me, and Mrs Briskett saying, 'Poor little thing, she really *is* an orphan now.'

I got to the privy just in time, for I was violently sick. Then I stood outside in the dark, staring up at the crescent moon, tears running down my face. I could not bear to go back into the kitchen. I didn't belong there any more. I did not belong with anyone. I wasn't special to anyone at all, only Mama – and now I had lost her for ever. I was an orphan.

You are NOT an orphan!

It was Mama's voice, clear and distinct, as if she were standing right beside me in the moonlight.

'Oh, Mama, is it really *you*?'

Of course it's me, you silly girl. Don't you know your own Mama?

'But – but *how* is it you? Did Madame Berenice conjure you up after all?'

That dreadful turbaned charlatan! As if I'd ever lower myself to speak through HER! Now listen to me, girl. You are NOT an orphan. You still have one parent alive.

'You mean . . .?'

Why don't you try to find your father?

'But – but you said he doesn't even know I exist.'

Then perhaps it's time to tell him!

'But, Mama—'

No buts.

'I'm not sure I *want* a father. I want *you*. I want to feel your arms around me! Can't you materialize somehow?'

We don't need materializations, darling. YOUR arms are around ME – because I am in your heart.

I crossed my hands over my chest. I felt my heart beating wildly, blood throbbing through my body, so that I tingled all over. I stood there, still crying, though I was happy now. I wasn't alone any more.

'Thank you, Mama,' I whispered into the dark.

I'll always be with you, Hetty.

'I'm not Hetty any more, Mama, I am Sapphire Battersea – and I'm going to find my father.'

Will **HETTY** ever find her father?

☆

Will she see **BERTIE** again?

☆

Will she meet **JEM** at last?

☆

Will she find **GIDEON**?

☆

Will she ever meet up with any
of the other **FOUNDLINGS**?

☆

Will she encounter **MR TANGLEFIELD'S
TRAVELLING CIRCUS** once more?

**All will be revealed in the third and final
volume of the *Hetty Feather* trilogy!**

Turn over for an exclusive extract from the fantastic new story about Hetty Feather,

EMERALD STAR!

'What are you doing here, child? This is no place for a little lass like you. Come on, tell me your name.'

I drew myself up as tall as I could, standing on tiptoe in my clumpy boots.

'I'm not a child,' I said haughtily, though I knew I was so small and slight I did not look anywhere near fourteen. 'My name is . . .' But then I hesitated foolishly.

My name is Hetty Feather, but I had never felt it was my *real* name. It was a comical name chosen at random when Mama handed me to the matron at the Foundling Hospital

1

when I was only a few days old. I had been christened Hetty Feather in the hospital chapel and people had been calling me that name in irritation and anger ever since. I was not a placid child and found it hard to stick to the rigid rules and regulations of the hospital. My hot temper and wild spirit made me stand out from all the other foundlings as clearly as my bright red hair.

I was plain, the smallest and slightest in my year, and cursed with my carrot hair – but I did have bright blue eyes, my one good feature. I fancied my mama might have called me Sapphire if she'd been able to keep me. When at last I found her, I discovered she really *had* wondered about naming me her little Sapphire.

I tried to call myself Sapphire Battersea when I left the hospital to go into service, proudly adopting Mama's distinctive surname. But they laughed at me in my new position and said Sapphire wasn't a servant's name.

I did not *want* to be a servant. When I was dismissed in disgrace, I ran away to Mama, only to discover the dreadful truth – that she was dying of consumption. I had to earn my living all that sad summer by the sea when I visited her daily. I could not find any respectable work at all so I chose a disreputable job instead. I fashioned my beautiful green velvet Sunday best dress into a mermaid costume and joined Mr Clarendon's Seaside Curiosities as a star attraction. I was Emerald the Amazing Pocket-Sized Mermaid. My new dear friend, Freda the Female Giant, called me Emerald every day.

'*Are you deaf or simple? What is your name?*' the innkeeper repeated.

I did not want to call myself Hetty Feather. I did not care for the name – and the governors at the Foundling Hospital might well be trying to track me down. I longed to say that my name was Sapphire Battersea, but I had to be wary in this new strange village. This was where my dear mother had been brought up. Folk might recognize the name and run to tell my father. I wanted to seek him out myself and break my news gently.

The innkeeper tossed his head and turned to walk away.

'I am Emerald,' I blurted out.

The old men leaning on the sticky bar sniggered into their foaming pints.

'Emerald?' the innkeeper repeated. 'What sort of a name is that?'

'A fine distinctive name,' I said.

'What about a surname then?'

'I am Emerald . . . Star,' I announced, giving birth to my new self right that moment.

'Emerald Star!' said the innkeeper.

This time the old men laughed openly.

'She's cracked in the head!' he said to them, and they guffawed and drank and spat contemptuously in the sawdust at their feet.

'I'll thank you not to mock,' I said. 'Emerald Star is my stage name. I am very well known in the south. In fact people pay to come and see me.'

'What do you do then, Emerald Star?' the innkeeper asked, an unpleasant tone to his voice.

'I perform upon the stage,' I said.

I wasn't exactly lying. When I exhibited myself as Emerald the Amazing Pocket-Sized Mermaid, it was upon a sturdy plinth, so that people did not have to bend down to see me reclining there, twitching my green velvet tail on a little pile of sand.

The word 'stage' made the men's heads rock. They set down their pints and stared at me as if I were about to perform then and there. Some looked smugly disapproving.

'So she's one of they actresses,' said one, and tutted with his two teeth.

'Are you a turn at the music hall then, lass?' asked another with interest. 'I go regular on a Saturday night over at Brackenly. I've seen them all – Simon Spangles, little Dolly

Daydream, Georgie and his Talking Doll, the Romulus Brothers, Lily Lark . . . Great acts, all of them. But I've never seen you.'

'I'm not a travelling player. I perform on the *London* stage,' I insisted, telling a terrible lie.

'You don't look like one of them theatricals, all painted faces and high-pitched voices,' said the innkeeper.

'More's the pity,' said one of the old men. 'What sort of a costume's *that*?' He pointed to my drab grey dress. 'You're nothing but a little maid, spinning us all fairy stories. I don't believe a word of it.'

'Believe what you want. I don't care at all. My business is not with you.' I turned to the innkeeper. 'My business is with *you*, sir.'

'She wants her pint of porter!' said the old man, chuckling.

'I simply want a bite to eat and a room for the night,' I said. 'I have adequate funds.' I patted my full pocket. 'And you advertise both on the sign outside.'

6

It was the only sign I'd seen. I'd tramped the length and breadth of this bleak little Yorkshire village searching for rooms. It was a seaside of sorts, but it did not seem to have hotels and hostelries. Beautiful Bignor on the south coast had these aplenty, and every second house had lodgings. It had bathing machines along the beach, and pierrots and hokey-pokey men and all manner of amusements. This bleak village of Monksby had a small harbour and a stinking fish market and a few streets of mean dwellings. Now it was past ten o'clock, the only place with any light and life was this Fisherman's Inn.

I was desperately tired. I had been travelling all day, cooped up in the third-class railway carriage, my heart beating wildly at the thought of finding my father. I was not sure quite how I would manage this. I did not even know his last name. Mama had simply called him Bobbie. I had not liked to ask her all the hundreds of questions humming in my head

7

because she found it so painful talking about her past.

'Give the child a room, Tobias, and stop persecuting the poor little thing,' said the woman behind the bar. She was big and tough, with a great crooked nose like a picture of a witch in a storybook. She looked very frightening – but she was nodding at me kindly. 'Look at her – she's swaying on her feet with tiredness, and all you men can do is turn her into a little guy. You come with me, dear.'

'Thank you, ma'am,' I said meekly.

'Who are you to issue invitations, Lizzie? Do you own this inn?' said Tobias.

'No, but I own a human heart, and this girl needs food and drink and a bed for the night,' she said, and beckoned me behind the bar.

I ducked under the wooden top and Lizzie led me through a door into a gloomy kitchen at the back.

'You're shivering, child. I'd light a fire but old Tobias won't admit summer's over

now. Here, put this on.' She took her own
grey woollen shawl and wrapped it tight
around my shoulders. I had proudly held
my own when Tobias and the old men were
baiting me, but Lizzie's simple little act of
kindness made the tears start trickling down
my face.

'There now,' she said, giving me a pat. She
sat me at the table and bustled around the
kitchen. She took a saucepan from the sink
and tried to scrape it out. 'He had a fish stew
for his supper but he's cleared the pot. I'll have
to scratch around for something cold for you.'

She found a loaf in a crock and cut me two
thick slices of bread and a generous chunk of
cheese. They were both a little stale but I ate
them gratefully enough. Instead of a cup of
tea she fetched me a pint of ale from the bar.

'There now, this will warm you up,' she said.

I did not care for the taste at all, but I
drank a few sips obediently. When Lizzie saw
I was leaving most of it, she downed it herself,

and wiped the froth off her lips appreciatively.

'Now, I'll show you the privy. I'm afraid it's not very nice – you know what men are like, and you sound like a London lass, used to fancy ways,' she said, lighting a candle and leading me by the hand.

The privy was unspeakably disgusting. Perhaps it was as well I couldn't see it properly in the dark. Still, I had no choice but to use it and then wash my hands thoroughly at the outside pump. Lizzie led me back inside and up the stairs. I was shivering now, and so tired I could barely carry my small suitcase.

'Let me give you a hand with that,' said Lizzie, taking it from me. 'Is this all your worldly belongings? You haven't run away, have you?'

'Not exactly. I – I am running *to* someone,' I said.

'Not a sweetheart, I hope?' said Lizzie. 'Never trust a man – a shilling's your best friend.'

'No, he's family, not a sweetheart,' I whispered.

'That's better. Though how come you're looking for family round here? You don't come from these parts, do you?'

'I think my mother did,' I said. I looked hard at Lizzie, trying to gauge her age. The lines on her face were set hard and deep and she looked many years older than my dear little mama – though in the last few desperate months of her life *she* had aged visibly too.

'She was called Ida,' I said, clutching hold of Lizzie, suddenly desperate, and deciding I could trust her. 'Ida Battersea.'

I willed Lizzie's face to soften, to say, *Oh my goodness, Ida Battersea! She was my dear friend.*

But she shook her head. 'Can't say I've ever heard of her, dear. Anyway, let's find you a room. Tobias has three or four guest rooms up here, though they're seldom in use. We'll find you the best one, eh?'

11

The rooms all looked the same to me – bare and basic, with a stripped narrow bed and striped ticking mattress, a washstand and a cupboard, and a rag rug on the cold lino. There were stern moral pictures on all the walls. Lizzie held the candle up to a representation of a woman in the gutter guzzling from a bottle and clutching a crying baby, while an uncouth man carrying a pint pot beat his poor dog in the background. It was clearly preaching against the demon drink – a strange choice for rooms in a public house.

'It's not exactly cosy up here, is it?' said Lizzie. 'Still, I promise you it's clean. I have a sweep and scrub every week or so, for Matty's sake. She was Tobias's wife and my dear friend – and now I try to keep the place decent for her. I trot up to the churchyard every Sunday, and when all the folk have gone away, their ears still ringing with the sermon, I go and sit by Matty and we have a little chat just like we did when she was alive.' She shot me a look, as if daring me to laugh. 'I know it sounds daft like.'

'It doesn't sound daft at all, it sounds lovely,' I said. 'I talk to Mama in my head and she talks back to me. Well, perhaps it's only my fancy, but it seems as if she does. She told me to come here, Lizzie.'

'Well, that's extraordinary, because this is a harsh, hard village without much comfort even for those born and bred here. Still, maybe she has her reasons. Now, I'll get you clean linen from the press and settle you down for the night.'

We made up the bed together, Lizzie nodding with approval when she saw me tucking the sheets in with precision. Years of hospital training had stood me in good stead in some ways.

'I'll come in early tomorrow and make sure you get a proper breakfast,' said Lizzie. 'Goodnight . . . Emerald?' She gave a little snort. 'Though that's never your real name!'

'It is now,' I said.

Lizzie left me with the candle. She insisted on leaving her shawl with me too, and I certainly needed it. It was only early autumn but the north wind straight off the sea rattled the windows and I had only the thinnest of blankets. I wound the shawl tightly around me and laid out all my precious possessions on the bed: my little books of fairy tales, Mama's brush and comb and violet vase, a fairground dog, and the fat manuscript in which I'd recounted all my adventures so far. I turned the page, and put the date, *Friday September 29th 1891*, at the top of the page.

My name is Emerald Star, I wrote, in my best hospital-taught copperplate. *I am here in Monksby!!!* But in spite of the three exclamation marks I could not feel excited. Doubt made my heart thump, my stomach churn, and had me fidgeting from one side to the other in that narrow bed long after I had blown out the candle. Had Mama *really*

said Monksby? Was it perhaps Monksford . . .
Monkslawn . . . Monkton?

When we curled up together during those
sweet stolen nights at the hospital, we had
whispered the stories of our missing years.
I had told Mama about the cottage in the
country that had been my home till I was five. I
had told her about my dear foster brother Jem,
though I found it painful talking about him
then, because I thought he had forgotten me.

Mama wasn't so interested in any of
my foster siblings but she asked endless
questions about my foster mother Peg. I tried
to give a truthful picture of that warm, work-
worn woman but it was difficult remembering
details. I just had an impression of her strong
arms cuddling me close or giving me a royal
paddling when I had been disobedient or
overly fanciful. She frequently said I was
more trouble than all her other children put
together, but I knew she loved me dearly all
the same. Mama could not see it that way

when I told her tales of Peg. She sucked in her breath when I said I'd been paddled and became very agitated.

'How could any woman hit a tiny child, especially one as small and sensitive as you, Hetty,' she said fiercely, holding me close and rocking me as if the paddling had only just occurred. Poor Peg could do no right in her eyes. She asked what she'd given me to eat and poured scorn on my slices of bread and dripping.

'What sort of nourishment is there in chunks of bread and pig fat?' she said. 'No wonder you were such a little scrap of a girl with no flesh on your bones. And she was getting paid for your keep too! Didn't she ever give you any meat?'

'We had rabbit stew,' I said, licking my lips at the memory, but this didn't impress Mama either.

'Didn't she ever give you a decent plate of roast beef, or a proper chop or cutlet?'

This was unfair, because she knew they were simple country people and couldn't afford such splendid meals. Mama was totally unreasonable where I was concerned. She felt Peg had been a pretty poor mother to me – and frequently wept because she had lost the chance of mothering me herself for ten long years.

At first I had asked her many questions about her own past, but right from the start I could see she found it troubling to talk about.

She told me my father was called Bobbie and had bright red hair just like me and she'd loved him with all her heart – but he had left her to go to sea. I didn't know if he had left her because she was going to have his child, or whether he'd never known about me. It seemed cruel to question her because her voice always shook and her blue eyes filled with tears.

'He was a fine man, your father. All the girls in the village were after him, but he picked *me*,' Mama said proudly.

I wasn't so sure a truly fine man would get a young girl into trouble and then abandon her. Perhaps I wouldn't like this father at all if I ever found him – but I was sure Mama wanted us to meet.

'Go and find your father now!' she'd said to me, her dear voice clear in my head even though she had been dead for weeks.

I had no address – I didn't even have his last name – but I knew he'd grown up in the same village as Mama. She'd said it was called Monksby – or some such name. I hadn't quizzed her because her tears spilled again when she talked of it. I knew her mother and father had turned her out when they discovered she was having a baby – they could not stand the shame. I cried too at the thought of poor Mama, destitute and sick, making the long journey to London to leave me at the Foundling Hospital.

I fancied I heard her crying now, curled up beside me in the cold bed.

'I'm here, Mama,' I said, reaching out across the bare sheet and clasping thin air. 'You mustn't cry. I will be all right. I will find my father and I will love him almost as much as I love you, and we will live happily ever after – as happily as I can ever be without you.'

I squeezed tight, imagining the pressure of Mama's thin fingers squeezing back, and I fell asleep, our hands still clasped.

Have you read Hetty Feather's first amazing story?

Victorian orphan Hetty is left as a baby at the Foundling Hospital – will she ever find a true home?

*Can Ella's love bring
Mum back?*

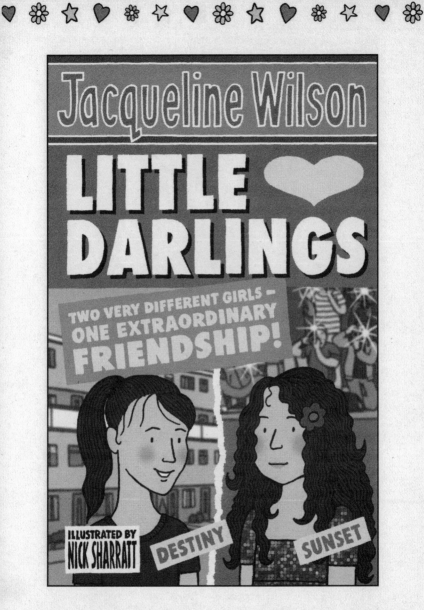

A red carpet fairytale featuring Destiny and Sunset – two very different girls, one extraordinary bond.

Sometimes Lily wishes she really was
home alone . . .

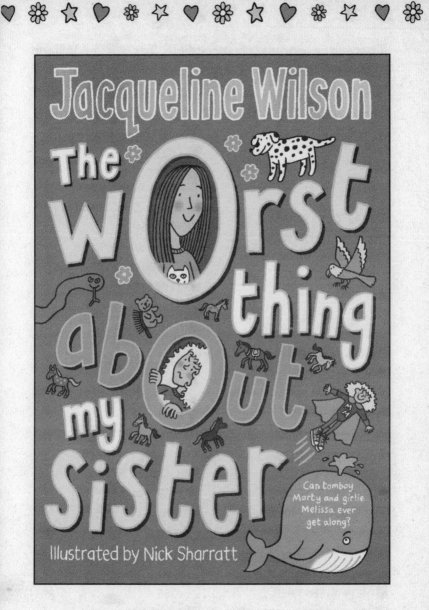

Jacqueline Wilson

The wOrst thing abOut my sister

Illustrated by Nick Sharratt

Can tomboy Marty and girlie Melissa ever get along?

*Can tomboy Marty and girlie Melissa
ever get along?*

♥ ❀ ☆ ♥ ❀ ☆ ♥ ❀ ☆ ♥ ❀ ☆ ♥ ❀

There are oodles of incredible Jacqueline Wilson books to enjoy! Tick off the ones you have read, so you know which ones to look for next!

☐ THE DINOSAUR'S PACKED LUNCH

☐ THE MONSTER STORY-TELLER

☐ THE CAT MUMMY

☐ LIZZIE ZIPMOUTH

☐ SLEEPOVERS

☐ BAD GIRLS

☐ THE BED AND BREAKFAST STAR

☐ BEST FRIENDS

☐ BIG DAY OUT

☐ BURIED ALIVE!

☐ CANDYFLOSS

☐ CLEAN BREAK

☐ CLIFFHANGER

☐ COOKIE

☐ THE DARE GAME

☐ THE DIAMOND GIRLS

☐ DOUBLE ACT

☐ EMERALD STAR

☐ GLUBBSLYME

☐ HETTY FEATHER

☐ THE ILLUSTRATED MUM

☐ JACKY DAYDREAM

☐ LILY ALONE

☐ LITTLE DARLINGS

☐ LOLA ROSE

☐ THE LONGEST WHALE SONG

☐ THE LOTTIE PROJECT

☐ MIDNIGHT

☐ THE MUM-MINDER

☐ SAPPHIRE BATTERSEA

☐ SECRETS

☐ STARRING TRACY BEAKER

☐ THE STORY OF TRACY BEAKER

☐ THE SUITCASE KID

☐ VICKY ANGEL

☐ THE WORRY WEBSITE

☐ THE WORST THING ABOUT MY SISTER

FOR OLDER READERS:

☐ DUSTBIN BABY

☐ GIRLS IN LOVE

☐ GIRLS IN TEARS

☐ GIRLS OUT LATE

☐ GIRLS UNDER PRESSURE

☐ KISS

☐ LOVE LESSONS

☐ MY SECRET DIARY

☐ MY SISTER JODIE

♥ ❀ ☆ ♥ ❀ ☆ ♥ ❀ ☆ ♥ ❀ ☆ ♥ ❀